T0302432

ASHES

ALSO BY

Laurie Halse Anderson

Chains

Forge

Fever 1793

Independent Dames:
What You Never Knew About the Women and Girls of the American Revolution

Thank You, Sarah:
The Woman Who Saved Thanksgiving

Laurie Halse Anderson

ASHES

THE SEEDS OF AMERICA TRILOGY

A Caitlyn Dlouhy Book

atheneum

ATHENEUM BOOKS FOR YOUNG READERS

NEW YORK • LONDON • TORONTO • SYDNEY • NEW DELHI

We hold these truths to be self-evident, that all men are created equal, that they are endowed by their Creator with certain unalienable Rights, that among these are Life, Liberty and the pursuit of Happiness.

—Declaration of Independence

This book is dedicated to the fulfillment of that promise.

If you purchased this book without a cover, you should be aware that this book is stolen property. It was reported as "unsold and destroyed" to the publisher, and neither the author nor the publisher has received any payment for this "stripped book."

atheneum

ATHENEUM BOOKS FOR YOUNG READERS
An imprint of Simon & Schuster Children's Publishing Division
1230 Avenue of the Americas, New York, New York 10020

This book is a work of fiction. Any references to historical events, real people, or real places are used fictitiously. Other names, characters, places, and events are products of the author's imagination, and any resemblance to actual events or places or persons, living or dead, is entirely coincidental.

Text copyright © 2016 by Laurie Halse Anderson
Cover illustrations copyright © 2016 by Christopher Silas Neal
Map on p. v by Leo Hartas
All rights reserved, including the right of reproduction in whole or in part in any form.
ATHENEUM BOOKS FOR YOUNG READERS is a registered trademark of Simon & Schuster, Inc. Atheneum logo is a trademark of Simon & Schuster, Inc.
The Simon & Schuster Speakers Bureau can bring authors to your live event.
For more information or to book an event, contact the Simon & Schuster Speakers Bureau at 1-866-248-3049 or visit our website at www.simonspeakers.com.
Also available in an Atheneum Books for Young Readers hardcover edition
Book design by Debra Sfetsios-Conover
The text for this book was set in Regula.
Manufactured in the United States of America
0421 OFF
First Atheneum Books for Young Readers paperback edition August 2017
8 10 9 7
CIP data for the hardcover is available from the Library of Congress.
ISBN 978-1-4169-6146-8 (hc)
ISBN 978-1-4169-6147-5 (pbk)
ISBN 978-1-4424-4508-6 (eBook)

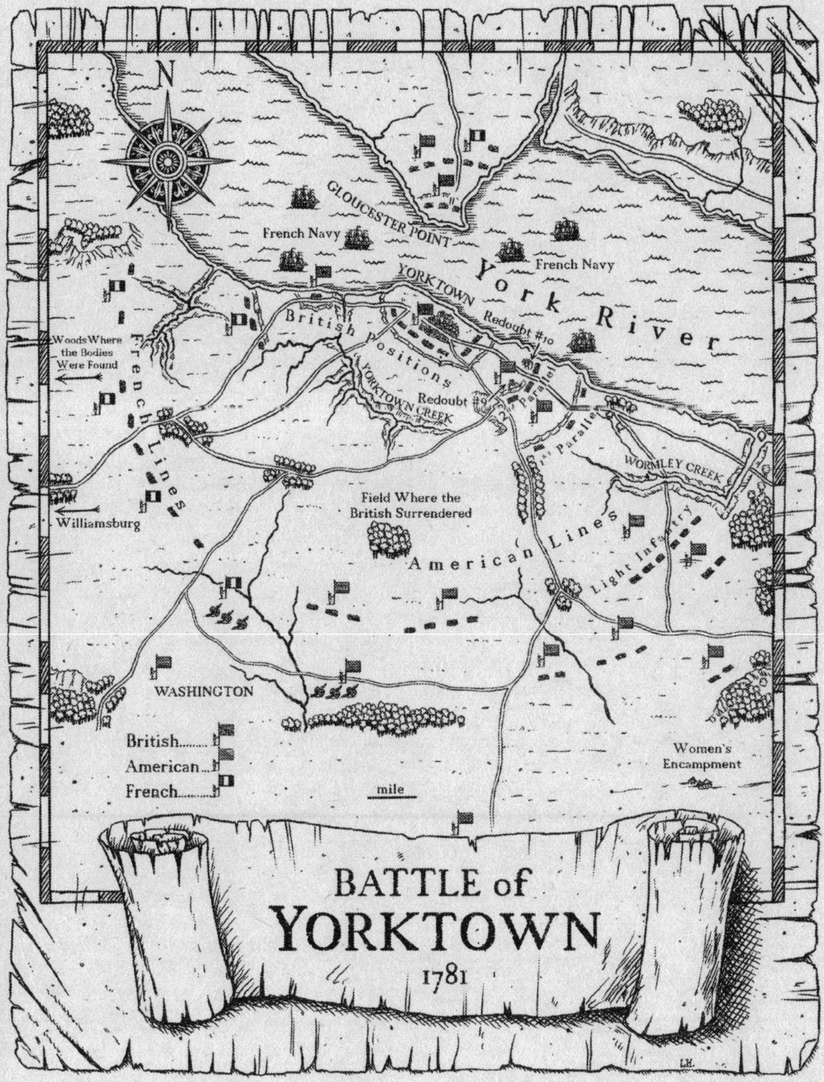

N
GLOUCESTER POINT
French Navy
French Navy
York River
YORKTOWN
Redoubt #10
British Positions
YORKTOWN CREEK
Redoubt #9
2nd Parallel
1st Parallel
WORMLEY CREEK
Woods Where the Bodies Were Found
French Lines
Williamsburg
Field Where the British Surrendered
American Lines
Light Infantry
WASHINGTON
British
American
French
mile
Women's Encampment
BATTLE of YORKTOWN
1781

ASHES

CHAPTER 1

Monday, June 25, 1781

IN SHORT, MONARCHY AND SUCCESSION HAVE LAID . . .
THE WORLD IN BLOOD AND ASHES. 'TIS A FORM OF
GOVERNMENT WHICH THE WORD OF GOD BEARS
TESTIMONY AGAINST, AND BLOOD WILL ATTEND IT.
–THOMAS PAINE, *COMMON SENSE*

"VEXATION, BOTHER, AND BLAST," I muttered, trying to blink away the sweat that stung my eyes.

Curzon dug his elbow sharply into my side, scowling, then tapped his finger on his lips. He wanted me to be silent as the grave, even though the British patrol we were hiding from was much too far away to hear us.

"A little closer," I whispered low, "maybe I could read it then."

"Any closer and you'll be gutted by bayonets." He turned his head so his lips touched my ear. "Patience."

That foul word again. "Pox on your patience."

I shifted my gaze to the lobsterbacks gathered at the edge of the woods. If they weren't a patrol, then they were a foraging party sent to plunder farms. Whatever their purpose, they looked about to expire of the heat. The cool shade of the enormous live oak had so delighted them that they'd quickly stripped off their sweat-soaked coats and waistcoats and hung them from branches to dry. Two had even removed their shirts and rinsed them in the stream, showing a shock of white skin paler than any ghost would ever dream of being. 'Twas a frightful sight, but their desire to cool themselves had allowed Curzon and me to crawl safely to a hollow that was sheltered by tall ferns and overhanging magnolia and bayberry branches.

We'd had several encounters with patrolling soldiers in the previous weeks. Our course of action had always been to retreat slow and careful, and then circle wide to avoid them. This time we could not. A milestone stood at the crossroads a few paces from their fire. Hidden under their collection of bloodred coats and dingy haversacks was the carving of letters and numbers that showed travelers the direction and distance to Charleston, South Carolina.

After walking more than a thousand miles, after months spent laboring first in Lancaster, then Baltimore, then Richmond, and at whatever mountain farm would have us . . . After having been cheated, lied to, near captured twice . . . After months lost in worry, waiting to see if Curzon would recover from the wounds inflicted by a falling hemlock, then another half a year wasted as I fought an intermittent fever that gripped my lungs so tight I could barely walk . . . After dodging two armies, wild packs of banditti, and armed Loyalists deep in liquor . . . After sleepless nights haunted by ghosts and endless days of empty bellies . . . After all that, I was close to finding my baby sister, Ruth.

The thought of it made my heart pound.

All I needed was the information on that milestone.

We stayed hidden under the ferns in the hollow so long that the sun swung from the east to the west, and the damp ground soaked through both my skirt and the shift under it. The smell of the rabbits roasting over the British cook fire pained me. We'd eaten our last meal–a small, hideous fish boiled with bitter greens plucked from the edges of the swamp–more than a day and night previous. We were out of salt and hadn't tasted bread nor porridge for weeks.

A mosquito bit my neck. I pinched it dead between my fingertips. In our years of journeying I'd grown accustomed to being bone tired, starving, and filthy, but I could not abide the bloodsucking demons.

"I'm going to move a wee bit closer," I said.

Thunder rumbled in the distance. "Too dangerous," Curzon said.

I killed another mosquito. "Not knowing where we are is the real danger. What if they decide to camp here for the night?"

A broad-shouldered, pink-faced soldier placed his damp coat at the end of a long stick, which he held above the fire in an attempt to dry it. Not a moment later the stick broke, the coat fell onto the rabbits roasting on the spit, and the whole lot tumbled into the flames. The soldiers roared with laughter, save the one who owned the coat. He snatched it out and stomped on the smoldering cloth, cursing vile and loud, while his companions rescued their supper.

"They're barely keeping watch." I pointed to a fallen tree trunk halfway between our position and the road. 'Twas alarmingly close, true, but several young pines sheltered it from view, the tips of their branches touching the ground like a drapery. "If I hide behind that log, I'll hear every word they say."

"The sun has fried your wits." Curzon used his sleeve to wipe away the sweat trickling down my cheek, the scarred one. The unexpected kindness of his gesture startled me.

As we lay silent, my tired mind drifted into the past, to the day I'd first met Curzon back in '76. I'd been a terrified maid of twelve, still in shock from the circumstances that had landed Ruth and me in New York. He'd been a cheerful lad, two years older than me and foolish enough to be eager for war.

Thunder rumbled again and a cool breeze stirred the moss that hung from the branches above.

I snuck a look at Curzon. He now stood a head taller than me and had the forged-steel strength of a man. He was still capable of mischief on occasion, but his smile was rare. He'd long ago traded the red hat he affected for a dark blue cap that did not draw attention. Likewise, the piratical earring he used to wear was now hidden in the lining of his filthy jacket.

There was no way of figgering what he saw when he looked at me, for he'd grown skilled at hiding the truth from his eyes. Time and hard travel had much changed us both.

Our friendship lay in ashes, another victim of the unending War of Independence. Months earlier we'd argued terribly, as fierce as two armies, when he declared that he needed to enlist again with the Patriots. We'd called each other ugly names and exchanged cruel words that cut deep. By the end of the battle he'd agreed to stay with me only until we found Ruth, but the damage was done.

The thunder rumbled again, dragging me from my remembering.

"I'll backtrack," Curzon whispered, "circle around and come down the road from the north, act as if I'm fleeing a rebel master. I'll ask for their protection."

I snorted. "So they can drag you to Charleston and put you to work with a shovel?"

"I'll invent a tale of some Continentals I saw up the road. That will shift them away from here."

"Blast your eyes!" I muttered. "You just want to play soldier."

"Play? I'll gather information and . . ." Curzon broke off speaking. His gaze shifted left, tracking a group of swallows as they flew betwixt the trees. Something shuffled in the distance behind us.

"Did you hear that?"

"A squirrel," I said. "Nothing more."

He rolled onto his back and lifted his head so he could better study the heavily wooded forest behind us. Our recent time lost in the swampy wilderness had revealed Curzon to be mortally afraid of alligators. In truth, I suspected half of his excuses for dawdling in the last few days were due to his unnatural fixation on the beasts.

'Twas not charitable to prey on his fears, but I knew my plan was the wiser one. I gave a start, as if I'd heard something else. "Over there!"

"What?" He tensed. "Where?"

"I heard something."

"You said 'twas a squirrel."

"Nay, this was a different sound, low and slithersome. As if a heavy tail was dragging through the brush."

"A tail-slither sound?"

"A long and heavy tail." I feigned deep concern. "Reminded me of that big fellow, the one we saw with the fawn in his jaws."

He swallowed hard and squinted, trying to see the alligator that did not exist.

"Or it could be nothing," I added. "The wind, mayhaps. I can go back and scout for it, if you'd like."

"'Tis likely nothing." He swallowed hard. "But I'll go."

"You swear you won't circle round to meet the soldiers on the road?" I asked.

He nodded curtly. "I swear. But don't move from this spot."

I waited until he'd slipped out of sight, then rose up on my elbows to study the soldier standing guard, musket resting on his crossed arms. When he turned away to say something to his companions, I crawled forward one pace, keeping low to the ground. I'd become rather clever at moving without attracting notice. Months of dirt had erased the colors of my clothes, so I blended into the landscape. My few belongings fit in a small haversack, and my hatchet was secured to the leather belt I'd fashioned from reins taken off the skeleton of a horse. I was as skilled at moving without being seen or heard as an army scout.

After another check of the guard I crept forward two more paces. Just then he stepped onto the road. I pressed myself against the dirt as he gave a quick glance north and south, then returned to the comfort of the shade.

I studied the ground ahead, eyes keen to spot poison ivy, which I never wanted to touch again. I crept ahead a third time, only to be stopped by another noise in the woods behind me, this time off to the left. I slowly turned my face in that direction. Shadows danced as the strange moss that hung from the trees swayed like tattered laundry in the breeze.

A branch snapped.

I flinched. Curzon was too wily to make any such noise this close to danger. The Carolina woods were filled with treacherous creatures: bear, wolf, and panther. Was one stalking me for its next meal?

I forced the thought aside and trained all of my senses on the enemy ahead. The minutes ripened slow and fat, caught in the sweltering heat. When the guard put down his musket and knelt to fiddle with his boot, I crawled four full paces, moving silent and steady, until I ducked under the low branches of the pines and reached the advantage of the log. I breathed slow as bits of the soldiers' conversation drifted over me: "bloody rebels," "consarned heat," and "affliction of my great toe on both feet." Grumbling complaints were the common language of all armies.

The sound of a sharp *cr-rack*, like a branch trod upon by a heavy boot, echoed through the woods. The guard stood up, alert now, staring in my direction. He said something over his shoulder that I could not hear, and one of his companions got to his feet and joined him, musket at the ready. The two men raised their guns, aimed at the log, just above my head.

That's when the rattlesnake appeared.

CHAPTER II

Monday, June 25, 1781

I ATE PART OF A FRIED RATTLE SNAKE TODAY, WHICH WOULD HAVE TASTED VERY WELL HAD IT NOT BEEN SNAKE.
–JOURNAL OF COLONEL HENRY DEARBORN
OF THE CONTINENTAL ARMY

I DID NOT BREATHE.

Near as long as I was tall and thick as my arm, the yellow-eyed snake stared at me; tail rattling, tongue flickering like flame. I could not move. There were other noises, other dangers that needed my attention–shouts, thunder, footsteps–but I couldn't look away from those terrifying eyes.

A rattlesnake's bite meant death, or at the very least, the need for amputation before the poison made its way to your heart. The worst place to be bitten was the face, for there was not much point in the amputation of a head. The only saving grace of a rattlesnake was that the creature gave fair warning. The vigorous shaking of the rattle on the end of the tail alerted the victim not to come closer, the way a port city might send a cannonball over the bow of a pirate ship straying too close to shore. It announced that a further advance would be met with swift and fatal punishment. The only thing worse than the rattling of the snake's tail was the moment the tail fell silent, for then the creature would strike.

The snake afore me slowed the shaking of its tail but did not stop. The dull sunlight reflected off the dark brown scales, ornamented with diamond-shaped patterns in black and white. If I could move fast enough, there was a small chance I could leap up and away from its reach, but if I did that, the soldiers would seize me in an instant. The snake measured the panic in my face.

"I saw something, I tell you!" one soldier insisted. "Moving between the trees."

"Blasted moss flapping in the wind," replied another. "Quit acting like a wee bairn afeard of haints and ghosties!"

Two black butterflies, their wings dotted with splashes of sky blue and pumpkin orange, fluttered by. They paused for a moment on the log, their wings opening and closing like bellows, then twirled away. As they departed, the snake lowered its head to the ground and slid under the log. It did not cease rattling its tail until it disappeared from sight.

Before I could move away, the sharp report of rifle fire cut through the air. I peered over the log.

The guard lay on the ground, clutching his bloody shoulder and screaming. The British were hollering above the cries of their friend, arguing about where the shots had come from as they scrambled for their muskets and cartridge boxes.

Heavy boots thudded from the forest behind me, then militiamen in long hunting shirts and dark breeches ran past, skirting both sides of the hollow where I lay. They took up their positions behind the broad trunks of old oaks and ancient pines and knelt to load their weapons. Most carried muskets, but a few possessed the deadly rifles of the mountains.

This was warfare in the Carolinas: fierce battles betwixt Patriot militia groups and the redcoats, who fought alongside local Loyalists. Everyone was fighting for freedom, but few could agree on the meaning of the word.

"Prepare!" screamed a redcoat.

The militia roared in defiance, "Huzzah!"

"Ready!" The British snapped their muskets up to their shoulders and pulled back the hammers that held their striking flints.

"Now!" screamed a long-haired man clad in buckskin.

The militia stepped out from their trees and fired. The British fired at the exact same moment. The explosion of so many guns sounded like a fierce volley of lightning bolts.

The British soldiers dragged the wounded guard off the road and quickly formed a half circle to protect him, while preparing for the next volley. The air filled with shouts, screams, men from both sides being ordered to load, aim, and "FIRE!" The woods to both sides of me exploded for a second time. Bullets flew across the road, some headed east, some west, shredding leaves and thudding into tree trunks. Another voice cried out in pain. The screams of the injured guard were weakening. More footsteps ran past me. How many militia were there? How long before one of them found me? Was Curzon captured? Killed?

My nose twitched with the metal tang of gunpowder. I didn't dare move but couldn't stay. A stray bullet spun over my head like an angry hornet. Mayhaps I could back away from the scene, slow-like—

A hand suddenly covered my mouth, and another gripped my wrist and pinned it to the ground. Curzon threw himself to the dirt next to me.

"Don't move!" he warned.

I pushed away his hand, but for once, was not inclined to argue. "Did they see you?"

He shook his head. "They only have eyes for the redcoats."

"How many?" I whispered.

"Not sure."

The noise of the skirmish changed in tone. The shouting quieted. Two guns fired, one right after another, but it sounded as if they were farther away. The wounded guard had stopped screaming.

We looked at each other, gave a nod, and silently counted to one hundred, as was our custom in unsure circumstances such as this. By the end of the count the woods had fallen silent. The gritty fog of gunpowder smoke drifted away. We crawled until we could peek around the opposite ends of the log. In the distance the militiamen were chasing the British patrol south down on the road. The guard's body lay still by the fire. I did not have enough of a view to see if there were any more wounded lying about, or worse, any militia waiting to shoot at stragglers.

Curzon's view must have been blocked too, for he gave his end of the log a small push.

The rattlesnake did not take kindly to having its hidey-hole disturbed.

It coiled in tight loops and raised its head, hissing fiercely, its stiff tail shaking a dire warning. The head bobbed side to side, fangs displayed, its eyes level with Curzon's. He became still as a statue carved from rock.

The tang of gunpowder, the buzz of bullets, the threat of a deadly snake; these awaken all of the senses at once with a powerful ferocity. I could hear the retreating boot steps of the men, smell the blood stench of the dead soldier, see the pattern the snake wove in the air as it prepared to kill. I tasted fear.

My left hand, out of the snake's sight, felt for the

hatchet in my belt. I fumbled with the leather tie that kept it secured, then slowly pulled it free. I shifted closer to Curzon. The snake noticed. It turned its head to me and shook its rattles faster.

I gripped the hatchet.

Curzon scratched at the fallen pine needles with his fingers, diverting the snake's attention and giving me the advantage.

The snake opened its jaws.

With all the fury I could muster, I brought the hatchet down onto the serpent, cleaving its head from its body with one blow. I pulled the blade free from the dirt and chopped again and again until at last Curzon grabbed my arm, and I stopped, panting.

"You've killed it three times over," he said.

I spat on the remains. "Snakes vex me."

CHAPTER III

Monday, June 25, 1781

I WAS BORN IN THE PROVINCE OF SOUTH CAROLINA, 28 MILES FROM CHARLES-TOWN. MY FATHER WAS STOLEN AWAY FROM AFRICA WHEN HE WAS YOUNG.
—MEMOIRS OF BOSTON KING, WHO FLED SLAVERY TO JOIN THE BRITISH ARMY

"I WAS GOING TO KILL IT, YOU KNOW." Curzon prodded a bit of chopped snake belly with the toe of his boot. "I was going to smash it with a rock."

I shrugged. I should have been giddy with delight about my victory over the creature and the fact that our enemies had chased each other away from this place. We had again cheated death and soldiers. But instead of being joyful, I felt weary and strangely out of sorts.

"You seemed determined to do the killing," Curzon continued, crouching to admire the sharp fangs of the snake. "So I let you."

"You let me?" I absently reached to pick up a bit of the snake's body.

Curzon stayed my hand. "What are you doing?"

"It's dead." I stared at him. "We should cook it later, once we find a safe spot."

"It will rot in this heat before we can cook it, Isabel. We'd both be sickened."

He was right, of course. It was a commonsensical notion, the kind of thing a child would know. Why had I not thought of it?

He studied me close. "Are you feeling addled?"

I gave my head a small shake, trying to clear the clouds from my brainpan. "Nay, just hungry."

"I'll see if the fire spared us any rabbit," he said. "You investigate that stone and figger our course. Sooner we're gone from here, the better."

We crossed the road, keeping eyes and ears open for the approach of any man or beast. Curzon approached the smoldering cook fire and the body of the dead soldier. I made for the milestone that had been our reason for coming to this place.

We'd spied on any number of Carolina plantations in the weeks previous, careful to stay out of sight, but close enough to watch how the work was done. Occasionally, when the circumstances were secure, we visited the cabins of the enslaved people at night, befriended a few folks, and learned of the news of that place and the other plantations nearby.

We were not the only ones making our way across the state by moonlight. The upheavals of the war had given many stolen people the chance to liberate themselves. Some were searching for kin, like us. Others were seeking a safe spot of ground they could call their own, a place where they could be the master of their own body and soul, and live without fear. All of us who wandered thus owned only the clothes on our backs. We relied on our wits to keep us fed. We traded information like coin. We shared stories about where clean water could be found, which places promised rest, and which held certain peril.

That was how we'd made our way to this godforsaken spot. The last woman we'd spoken to afore we became lost in the swamp had told me to seek out this very same milestone. The sea green flecks of moss growing at its base showed that it had long stood there. More moss grew in the letter *C*–for "Charleston"–that was deeply carved into its face, as well as the number *12* and the arrow that pointed south, indicating that Charleston lay only twelve miles in that direction.

Charleston had been our goal for years because the Locktons owned a fine house there, in addition to the rice plantation called Riverbend and the New York mansion where they'd held my sister and me in slavery. I'd convinced myself that Ruth had been sent to the Charleston house to work in the kitchen. Even though she'd been a sickly child, she was raised to do the heavy work of the scullery and larder.

But Charleston was under rule of the King's army, as were New York and Savannah. Weeks earlier we'd learned that anyone in Charleston who was not white skinned was required to carry a British army certification proving the whos and whys and hows of their being. I'd easily forged our free papers the winter we lived above the printer's shop in Baltimore (in a fit of hopefulness I'd even composed one for Ruth as well). But I had no notion of what a British army certification would resemble. Without the proper papers, we'd be snatched up soon as we set foot in Charleston. The scar on my cheek made me unfortunate-easy to identify, and I'd be in bondage again.

Ruth, I reminded myself. *Find Ruth*.

Curzon searched through the pockets and haversack of the dead soldier and took a clipped bit of silver coin and twists of gunpowder from his cartridge box. The gunpowder was of more use to us than the gun itself, which would be a heavy burden and useless without lead shot. He held up the man's pocket watch, one eyebrow raised in question. "This is worth a great deal, if we could find someone half honest."

I shook my head. "We dare not." We'd been hoarding coins, both British and Spanish, for the journey homeward, but being caught with a watch such as that could be a disaster. Curzon nodded in reluctant agreement and replaced it in the man's waistcoat with a sigh.

"Any rabbit?" I asked.

"Not much," he admitted. "But we could boil the bones."

I ran my fingertips over the number that told the distance to Charleston. Though it pained me greatly, we had to walk in the opposite direction, to Riverbend. It would be much safer to first seek word of Ruth there than in a city controlled by the British.

Curzon shouldered his haversack. "Which way?"

"The woman said north and northwest from here," I said. "If we keep the Cooper River to our right, we ought come upon the place before dawn."

CHAPTER IV

Tuesday, June 26, 1781

MANY, VERY MANY MELANCHOLY IDEAS HAUNT
MY IMAGINATION UPON THIS OCCASION.
—LETTER FROM ABIGAIL ADAMS TO HER
COUSIN JOHN THAXTER

WE MADE OUR WAY THROUGH THE woods, keeping the river close enough that we could follow its course. As sun set, we fell into our customary rhythm of night-walking. I'd walk in front for a while, then he would. People accustomed to cities require the aid of a lantern to walk in the countryside at night. Their eyes have been burned by the light of too many candles. Not us. Our eyes became sharper in the dark.

I'd expected to be even more alert than usual because we were in the midst of shifting armies and roving militia. But it was Curzon who halted our progress twice, when groups of wagons rattled by on the road. I hadn't noticed, which shocked me.

"Has your fever returned?" he asked, before we started walking again.

"I'm fine," I answered.

'Twas a falsehood. The bees of my melancholy, which had rarely troubled me since we escaped that foul man Bellingham at Valley Forge, were buzzing inside my brain-pan, fast overcoming my customary caution.

I tried to hold tight to the notion of finding Ruth, for that was my true compass heading. I strained to see her in my remembery: the little girl who slept with a doll tucked in her arms, her thumb in her mouth. The grievous truth was that the details of her face had started to fade. Was she missing a tooth from the top or the bottom jaw when she was stolen? Was her chin pointed like Momma's or broad like Poppa's?

What manner of sister was I that I could not remember her face?

Hours later Curzon touched my elbow. "Look thataway," he whispered, pointing through the trees.

The house lay at the end of the lane of live oaks, though the distance and the still-thick cover of night made it impossible to see anything more than a dim shape of the building. Beyond it the river curved hard.

"We're here," he added.

My heart was thumping so loud, I expected every person for miles could hear it. A ghost image of myself ran all the way down the lane and burst in through the front door, ready to tear the house down to its foundations until I found my sister. The rest of me stood fixed to the ground, shaking.

"Don't do anything foolish," Curzon warned. He pointed to the darker shadow of the woods at a remove to our left. "We'll head over there, so the wind will keep our scent from the dogs."

I nodded.

"Swear to me," he said. "Give me your oath that we shall wait and watch until we understand where we might safely approach."

Our habit was to study any house or barn for a full day and night before we drew close and inquired about food, work, or directions. This caution had saved us many times. I pressed my lips together and fought to rein in my frustration. It did no good to let desire and dream race ahead of common sense.

"I swear that if we don't hurry, the sun will rise and expose us," I said.

We walked silently through the woods until we found an ancient sycamore possessed of branches that offered an easy climb. By the time we'd settled in a crook high above the ground, the first robins and mourning doves had begun to sing. From our perch we had a good view of the side of the main house and a hint of smaller buildings behind it. Their muddied shapes slowly took proper form as night faded: rooflines, doorways, chimneys.

A lone rooster called.

"Something's amiss," I murmured. "A place this size ought have more than one rooster."

"Mayhaps the others are asleep." Curzon shifted uncomfortably, his form too large for our crowded perch. "Mayhaps these roosters post one fellow to guard, and the rest stay warm in their beds, until feeding time."

"Beds?" I asked.

"Rooster berths." He drew up his knees to his chin, wincing. "That's what I need, a better berth."

"'Tis called a roost, you ninny. Climb higher if you require more room."

He did so without another word. Since winter he'd grown even taller and more broad across the shoulders. He was near twenty years, but he still thought himself the size of a boy. In his absence the crook was perfect-size for me, as if the tree had seen me coming and grown a special Isabel-shaped nesting place where I could shelter safely through the day and doze until dark. Except I knew there would be no sleep for me. The cool mist rising from the ground brought to mind the last visit I'd made to my mother's grave, back when I was young enough to believe that people held to their promises and the world would treat all children fair. That was the day our journey had truly begun.

Was the spirit of our mother watching over us? Did she know how long I'd been searching?

Fearful questions crowded in. What if Ruth had died long ago? The notion chilled me and made me shiver. I'd worked hard to keep such terrible thoughts away, but they surrounded me now. Would strangers have buried her proper, with a preacher and prayers and weeping? Was there a lonely stone in an empty field to mark her passing? Was her grave already grown over with vine and grass? Or did her bones sleep at the bottom of the sea?

"I smell corn," Curzon said in a low tone. "Meat, too."

The interruption was a welcome one. I gave myself a pinch. *Pay attention. Keep your wits about you.*

A cow mooed. There should have been a dozen calling by now, eager to be milked. The birdsong grew louder, accompanied by the *chirrup* of frogs and the thrumming and buzzing of insects. Lowering clouds made it hard for the sun to rise, but I could see enough to be confuddled.

Where are all the people?

The plantations in South Carolina were all bigger than the plantations of Rhode Island. When I was a girl, my family lived on a farm near Newport with another twenty people also held in bondage, along with a few indentured white servants. As we'd drawn closer to Charleston, the plantations had grown ten times that size and more, with miles of fields, and overseers keeping watch to make sure no one ran off.

The stolen—for in truth, that was the circumstance of every person enduring the condition of slavery—the stolen people had to wake long before the sun. Riverbend should have had at least fifty people on their way to the fields, plus the kind of bustle we'd seen behind other big houses at dawn: women carrying wash water, old men repairing tools, little children chasing one another and kicking up dust. Despite the faint smell of cooking nearby, there were no voices in the air.

Clouds shifted and the sky brightened enough for me to see the house in more detail. All of the windows had been broken. Smoke had stained the bricks above a window on the second floor, mayhaps caused by a fire set to burn down the building. Many of the shutters lay in splinters on the ground. The legs of a fine chair poked from the charred remains of a bonfire at the side of the house.

The war had brought trouble here, too.

"Don't fret," Curzon said. He understood my manner well enough to know I'd be upset by the sight.

"But—" I started.

"Don't fret," he repeated. "We'll wait and we'll watch. Tonight we'll learn what we came here for."

"We'll wait," I muttered.

The sun broke free of the horizon and lit the ground afore us like a giant lantern raised by the largest hand. A tidy building some twenty paces behind the house was the source of the breakfast smells, a summer kitchen with whitewashed walls and gray smoke curling up from its chimney. Across from the summer kitchen ranged small buildings made of rough boards, likely the homes of families, and beyond that, a barn, with the edge of a garden visible behind it. An old dog lay in a patch of sunshine in front of the barn, and a few chickens were pecking in the dirt nearby.

"Look there," Curzon whispered.

A white-haired man, his back bent with age, walked slowly out of the barn. The scrawny lad by his side had his right arm in a dirty sling. He was a child of Africa, but lighter than the old man. He turned and called to someone in the barn to hurry. The dog raised his head to watch them pass, then laid it back on the ground as the two disappeared into the summer kitchen. A plump woman, near as old as the man, appeared at the kitchen's doorway, wiping her hands on her apron. "Come now!" she hollered. "Now or you don't eat till midday!" The words were harsh, but her tone was kindly.

A tall girl, almost a woman, emerged from the barn, a crate perched on her hip. Her hair was covered by a rose-colored kerchief that had bits of straw upon it; her face was tilted down, peering into the box. She carried it to the dog, knelt beside him, and set it on the ground. The creature thumped his tail in the dirt as hard as a maid beating a rug.

I squinted, certain we'd crossed paths with that lass before. Had she been hired out to another farm nearby? No, we'd seen her in a town. Baltimore? New Bern? I rubbed my tired eyes and looked again. I could not place her, but if she remembered us from an earlier encounter, it might make it easier to get the information we sought.

After scratching the old hound behind the ears, the girl lifted a tiny gray kitten out of the box and held it to the dog's nose. The dog licked the kitten and the girl giggled.

My heart stuttered. I grabbed at the branches for balance.

The kitten pawed at the dog's snout and was rewarded with another lick. The girl broke into laughter that sounded loud as thunder in my ears.

The shell that I'd carefully built around my heart cracked open.

I clambered down the tree and jumped to the ground, ignoring Curzon's strangled cries for me to stop. I was totty-headed wrong to do it, but I could not help myself. I walked toward the sunlight, then I ran, and then I flew, fast as a bird who has finally caught sight of home after a dreadful-long flight.

CHAPTER V

Tuesday, June 26, 1781

I SHOULD NOT DARE TO TARRY HERE IN MY PRESENT SITUATION, NOR YET KNOW WHERE TO FLEE FOR SAFETY; THE RECITAL OF THE INHUMANE AND BRUTAL TREATMENT OF THOSE POOR CREATURES WHO HAVE FALLEN INTO THEIR HANDS FREEZES ME WITH HORROR.
—LETTER FROM ABIGAIL ADAMS TO HER HUSBAND, JOHN

THE GIRL LIFTED HER HEAD AND shaded her eyes as I approached. She stood, the kitten clutched to her chest. She looked right at me but made no sign that she knew who I was. To the contrary, her eyes narrowed in suspicion.

I stopped, the dog between us. The buzzing in my head grew louder.

She was Ruth and she was not-Ruth at the same time.

This lass was taller than me, though I could not think of how that was possible. The last time I saw my Ruth, she was so small, I could carry her a good mile before my arms got tired. The features of the girl before me muddled, as if water or a thick fog swirled over her face. Her broad, strong chin and wide cheekbones recollected our father; the beautiful skin and long neck was all Momma. Her eyes were only hers, my baby sister's eyes: warm and brown and filled with questions. There could be no doubt.

"Ruth," I whispered.

"What do you want?" she asked. The manner of her speech was Carolina-tinged, though the tone of it was near enough to mine to be an echo. The question repeated itself over and over in my mind, as if it had been shouted into a dark cave.

I swayed a bit, unsteady on my feet. Of all the times I'd dreamed of this moment, here was the one possibility I'd never considered: that she would forget me.

"I'm Isabel, poppet." I tried to smile. "Your sister."

Ruth scowled and shook her head.

How could this be? She'd been full seven years old when that Lockton witch stole her from me. Until then, she'd slept next to me every night of her life. Every day I had played with her, taken her to the privy, and shown her how to do the work required of us. After Momma died, I did mothering things for her, like sewing dolls and making her wash her hands and teaching her prayers. I was all the family she had in the world. She was all I had too.

I leaned closer. "Don't you remember me?"

She scooped another mewling kitten out of the box and cuddled it against her cheek, avoiding my gaze.

An icy thought shot through me. Had she broken her head? Ruth had been born with the falling sickness. 'Twas my job to watch over her, to catch her before she hit the ground when overtaken by a fit. My biggest fear had always been that one day she'd fall and crack her head on a rock because I wouldn't be there.

"I held you when you were born," I said weakly. "We grew up together, you and me—"

"Don't know you," Ruth said.

"What?" My knees weakened. This could not be real, none of it.

What if it hadn't been a fall? Ruth had not been like other children. She learned things slower and needed to be shown the doing of a task one hundred times instead of one. But when she finally understood the hows of a chore, she never forgot it. A few called her "simple," but our mother did not hold with such language. Ruth was just Ruth, and that was good enough for us.

But how to understand her manner toward me now? Had they treated her so badly that her wits were fully addled, her remembery lost forever? *Why doesn't she know me?*

"Who's that?" The cook stood in the doorway of the summer kitchen. "You there, girl, what's your business?"

The voice startled me into action. "Ruth." I grabbed her elbow. "Come with me."

She pulled away with a frown. Her refusal surprised me as much as her strength.

"Unhand that child!" The cook rushed toward us as I again reached for my sister. Close on her heels came the old man and the boy with the injured arm.

"I've come to take you home," I said urgently. "We have to run!"

I reached for her again and managed to clutch a handful of her skirt.

"Don't touch her," shouted the boy.

The old man hobbled behind him. "You let go of our Ruth!" he called in a high, reedy voice. "Release her!"

The three of them pressed close together like a guard. Ruth spun out of my grip and slipped behind them.

Why doesn't she know me?

The ground under my feet seemed to roll, as if I stood aboard a ship in the middle of the ocean. This almost-grown Ruth thought I was a stranger. My body ached with the pain of it. My heart hung heavy in my chest, not wanting to beat.

She turned her face away from me.

"Please–" I started.

"The soldiers took everything." The old man was out of breath, but he spoke quickly. "I'm sorry, lass, we've nothing left to give. Mister Prentiss is due back soon and–"

"You don't understand," I interrupted. "I'm not looking for food. I'm here for Ruth."

The boy moved so that he stood betwixt us, a spindly fence with long legs. "Don't seem she knows you," he said.

His rude manner sparked my anger.

"Don't seem that's your business," I snapped. "Tell them, Ruth."

Ruth gently shook her head back and forth, denying me wordlessly.

"You ought to leave right away, child," the cook said quietly, "for your own safety. These are unsettled times."

"Fina's right," the man added. "'Tain't safe here. Wait in the woods till dark; we'll bring food. But then you must head out. Last thing we need is more trouble."

"I'm not making trouble!"

"Hush!" The boy locked his hand around my wrist like a metal cuff. "Missus Serafina and Mister Walter want you gone, so gone you gonna be."

I tried to pull away. "Turn me loose, you skulking varlet."

He had the strength of a body used to hard work, but his eyes were red rimmed and bruised from a beating, plus he favored that injured arm. A kick to the side of his knee would free me, but it would not help my cause.

The old man took charge. "Stay out of this, Deen," he ordered.

"Let me walk her to the river." The boy tightened his grip.

I thought again about the kick and shifted my weight in preparation to deliver it.

"Carolina is best known for treating guests with kindness!"

We all turned at the sound of the booming voice. Curzon boldly strode toward us from around the side of the barn. He was skilled at adopting the speech of many places. Now he spoke in flat Yankee tones that fair shouted he was a stranger to the South. "Also known for greeting kin with joy, Carolina is," he continued. "Or at the least, with friendliness."

The boy eyed Curzon's tall, muscular form and wisely let go of me. "We're no kin to you."

"Nay." Curzon took his place beside me. "But that girl?" He pointed to Ruth. "And this girl?" He jerked a thumb at me. "They're sisters."

The cook looked sharply between us. "Sisters?"

"We've been looking for Miss Ruth for years," Curzon said. "Last we saw her was in New York, in '76. The Lockton mistress witnessed one of Ruth's fits and sent her down here. She had Isabel drugged the night Ruth was taken, to make the matter more easily accomplished."

"Not taken." Tears threatened, and I dug my nails into my palms. "Stolen. Kidnapped."

"Is this true?" the cook asked Ruth.

I held my breath. Ruth gently set the two kittens in the wooden box without a word. Could she understand what was happening? Was her mind broken or was there another cause for her stubborn refusal to acknowledge me?

"Well?" the cook asked.

Ruth picked up the box. "Must take these babies to the barn."

"Answer Missus Serafina, darlin'," the old man said. "Is this lass your sister?"

Ruth hesitated, then looked at the boy with the injured arm as if seeking his advice. His nod of permission made me want to pull off his ears.

"Please, child," Missus Serafina urged. "You must tell us."

"She was my sister when I was little"–Ruth lifted her chin and looked right through me with sorrowful eyes–"but she's not my sister now." She set the crate on her hip. "Go home, Isabel."

CHAPTER VI

Tuesday, June 26, 1781

THE ENEMY CAME THERE; HE REPORTS THAT THEY TOOK WITH THEM 19 NEGROES AMONG WHOM WERE BETTY, PRINCE, CHANCE & ALL THE HARDY BOYS BUT LEFT THE WOMEN WITH CHILD OR YOUNG CHILDREN. . . . THEY TOOK WITH THEM ALL THE HORSES THEY COULD FIND, BURNT THE DWELLING HOUSE & BOOKS DESTROYED ALL THE FURNITURE, CHINA, ETC., KILLED THE SHEEP & POULTRY AND DRANK THE LIQUORS.

—LETTER FROM CAPTAIN THOMAS PINCKNEY TO HIS MOTHER, ELIZA LUCAS PINCKNEY, DESCRIBING THE EFFECTS OF A BRITISH RAID ON THE FAMILY'S SOUTH CAROLINA PLANTATION

WHEN I WAS LITTLE, I ONCE WATCHED the slaughter of an enormous ox. The powerful beast was strong enough to kill the butcher, so the man entered the pen armed with a sledgehammer, as well as a long knife. He went straight to work without a word, raising the heavy hammer high in the air, then bringing it down on the animal's huge head. The ox stood, quivering, for a moment. It looked at me, wet eyes stunned with pain and confusion. Then it collapsed in the mud.

As Ruth walked away from me, I felt as if my body and soul had been shattered, like I was that poor ox, frozen in the moment after the dizzying blow of the hammer and before the killing-cut of the knife.

Ruth disappeared into the darkness of the barn.

My knees wobbled again. Suddenly Curzon was at my side, his arm around me to keep me from falling.

"Something's not right," I murmured. "She's been hexed or she's befuddled. I must talk to her. . . ."

"We found her," Curzon said softly. "All is well. Let's talk to these folks, learn about the full circumstances here."

"But . . ." I paused, unable to think clearly, barely able to speak. "But . . ."

"Come with us," the old woman said. "I've seen fatter broomsticks than the two of you. You need to eat."

Curzon's arm gently propelled me forward, and we followed the old couple and the boy into the summer kitchen.

Once inside, Curzon peered out each window, his face grave. "Is it safe for us here?"

"For now," Mister Walter said as he slowly sat on the bench. "Prentiss, he's the overseer, he's gone to Charleston to get more field hands. Won't be back for a few more days 'cause he's got a lady friend down there. You're safe enough for a good meal."

Missus Serafina set bowls filled with rice and beans on the table.

"Very kind, ma'am." Curzon shot me a worried glance and sat down across the table from Mister Walter and the boy. "We are much obliged to you."

I found myself sitting next to him, with no memory of walking to the table, nor taking a seat. My mind had become unmoored from my body, like a rowboat that slipped its anchor or an apron blown off the clothesline in a gale. I kept picturing young Ruth, remembering the feel of her chubby arms around my neck as I pretended to be her horse, galloping across the garden at her command.

"Here you go, dear."

I blinked out of my reverie. Missus Serafina was handing me a mug.

"Thank you, ma'am," I replied.

"Drink it down," she said firmly. "All of it."

The water was straight-from-a-deep-well cold and made my teeth ache, but the first sip made me realize how dry and dusty my insides were. By the time the mug was empty, my head throbbed with the chill of it.

Curzon dug his elbow into my side; Mister Walter was waiting to bless the meal.

I closed my eyes and bowed my head. His heartfelt prayer brought me no comfort. That increased my misery even more, which did not seem possible but was true.

When the prayer was finished, Curzon introduced us properly.

"You married?" the old man asked.

"Friends," Curzon said. "Respectable friends, sir."

Mister Walter stirred his breakfast. "I've been married to my old gal for thirty-seven years now."

His wife scooped dried peas from a barrel. "Thirty-eight."

He smiled at her. "She thinks I forget. This here is Aberdeen." He nodded at the boy with the sling.

Aberdeen glared at us, then went back to eating.

"Where are the rest of your people?" Curzon asked. "What happened here?"

"Patriot militia came through a few weeks back, looted the place good. A few, including Deen, took advantage of the trouble and ran off. Prentiss gathered up some friends and went after them, only left three fellas here to guard the rest of us." He grinned. "A group of rovers came in and finished the work of looting the place. They scared off the guards. A good hundred or so fled to freedom. I pray every night that they all make it."

"Did they run to the British?" Curzon asked.

"Doubtful," Mister Walter said. "British officers stayed here in the spring, guests of Lockton. They treated us just as bad as any of them."

I should be paying closer attention to his words, I thought. *We need to learn all we can before we leave.* But sorrow dulled my mind. Ruth wanted nothing to do with me. I was Isabel, her not-sister. I could think of little else.

"Where were you headed?" Curzon asked Aberdeen.

"Spanish Florida," Aberdeen said before he put a big spoonful of rice and beans into his mouth. "Twisted my ankle running and tried to hide in a tree. Would have made it, but the branch broke. So did my collarbone when I hit the ground."

"Prentiss did the rest," said Mister Walter.

That explained the boy's swollen eyes and the stiff way he walked.

"Fool doesn't have the sense God gave a goat." Missus Serafina put the lid back on the barrel of peas and hit it sharply with a small mallet to make it fit tight. "Couldn't wait for the sun to set that day, had to be the first one across the field. Numbskull."

Aberdeen scowled but said nothing.

Mister Walter took a sip of water, then asked, "See any soldiers close by?"

Curzon briefly described our adventure at the crossroads, giving details about the skirmish and the number of men on both sides. While he talked, I ate the beans and rice, tho' I tasted them not. My sister had denied me. Nothing else mattered.

"I thought all the British were holed up in Charleston," Curzon finally said.

"Been terrible lawless out here since that city fell," Mister Walter said.

I was heartily sick of hearing of armies and dangerous men. I murmured an excuse, stood up, and walked to the open door, where I could watch the barn for signs of Ruth.

"Why didn't you and your wife run?" I heard Curzon ask.

"Too old to move fast enough," Mister Walter said. "Didn't want to put anyone in danger. If our Sirus and Jenny were still alive, they'd have put us on their backs and carried us. Our family would have been the first one gone."

"Long gone," added Missus Serafina.

"But they passed on years ago, and their children . . ." He paused for a moment, then cleared his throat. "We've no way of knowing where our grandbabies are. They were sold away from us. Mebbe that's why we became so fond of Ruth. She filled the hole in our hearts."

No one spoke for a moment. Of all the wretched sins committed by the white people who stole our lives, the breaking of families was the most evil.

I needed to concentrate on the good of this circumstance, lest I lose my reason. Ruth was alive, had been well cared for. This old couple loved her and had raised her like she was one of their own. Indeed, she had become their own.

But did that mean she wasn't mine?

CHAPTER VII

Tuesday, June 26, 1781

MY MIND WAS SORELY DISTRESSED AT THE THOUGHT OF BEING AGAIN REDUCED TO SLAVERY, AND SEPARATED FROM MY WIFE AND FAMILY.
—MEMOIRS OF BOSTON KING, WHO FLED SLAVERY TO JOIN THE BRITISH ARMY

"DON'T STAND THERE IDLE," MISSUS Serafina said, motioning for me to join her at the worktable. "Help me sort these peas."

I wiped the tears off my face, shook my head to clear away the clouds of melancholy, and took my place next to her. Her twisted fingers rubbed each pea slow and careful before she set it in the pot. I realized that her left eye was gone milky, and her right was not much better. Missus Serafina was nearly blind.

"Why don't you sit awhile?" I asked.

"I might just do that," she said, sliding the heavy bowl over to me. "But you make sure to do the job right. No one likes stones in their soup."

"Yes, ma'am," I promised.

Missus Serafina dished out more food for the fellows at the table, then joined them with a bowl of her own. The conversating fell into the weary, familiar subject of the war. The fatigue of the long night fell across my thoughts like a welcome shroud. My hands fell into the rhythm of choosing the good from the bad: *Pea, pea, pebble. Pea. Pea. Pebble. Pea.* I didn't look up until the bowl was empty some time later, startled to find I was alone with the old lady.

My heart pounded. Why was this happening, this dropping out of time and awareness? We were in dire circumstances. I needed to be alert; I needed to understand what we'd walked into.

"Your friend offered to split wood for us." She poured hot water into a basin to wash the dirty bowls and mugs. "We're running low."

The sound of chopping came through the window, and I felt more at ease. Curzon was close by.

"If you have another axe, I can help him."

"The way your mind wanders?" she chuckled. "Cut your foot off, you would. You might could dry a few dishes if you want." She handed me a cloth and pared a few soap shavings into the steaming water.

We worked in quiet, punctuated by the sound of the axe cleaving wood. She waited a bit before she asked the question that I knew was coming.

"How'd you come by that?" She pointed a soapy finger at the scar on my cheek in the shape of the letter *I*.

"Madam Lockton, with the help of a judge in New York." As I spoke that hated name, I realized that Missus Serafina would understand better than anyone, so I continued. "When she told me that Ruth had been sold to the islands, I fought her. She had me arrested, and"–I motioned to my face–"the court took her side in the matter."

Missus Serafina scrubbed hard at rice stuck to the bottom of a bowl. "That woman has a serpent where her soul should be."

"Is she in Charleston?" I asked.

"Madam?" Missus Serafina chuckled low. "She and her mister got tired of the war. They're in London now, waiting for it to end."

"London?" I could scarce credit her words. "London in England?"

"The very same." She chuckled again. "I can just see Madam trying to worm her way into the Queen's parlor, and that old Queen telling a footman to shut the door in her pointy face."

Loathing and rage against the Lockton woman had been the other constant in my heart as I'd searched for Ruth. Just as it had never occurred to me that Ruth wouldn't be happy to see me, I'd never once considered that my greatest enemy had fled over the sea to England. So much of what I thought to be true had been overturned in the course of one morning, I knew not the difference between up and down.

"That when you ran off? When they burned you?"

Missus Serafina's question tugged me back. "No, ma'am. That was in the summertime. I didn't learn that Ruth had been sent to Carolina instead of the islands till after Christmas. That's when I ran." I paused. "That's when we ran."

Before I knew it, I was pouring out our story to her in a way that I'd never done before. I described the frozen January night we escaped New York, then arguing with Curzon for months until the two of us went our separate ways, and the way Fate had brought us together again at the Valley Forge encampment. I explained all we'd endured there and how we'd run from Bellingham, the cursed man who'd tried to claim us as his property. By the time we'd finished the dishes and mixed up a batch of corn bread, I'd told her of the years we'd worked our way to Riverbend and the troubles that had slowed our journey.

Missus Serafina spread the corn bread batter into a spider pan and set it over the glowing coals that she'd raked to the front of the hearth. She slowly stood up and wiped her hands on her apron.

"And you haven't married the lad?" she asked.

My face flushed hot. "Like he said, we are respectable friends, nothing more."

"Do you love him?"

"We are often at odds."

"Sounds like a marriage to me," she said. "How long you plan on staying?"

"Hadn't planned, in truth. I figgered Ruth was in Charleston. Only came here to see what we could learn about her circumstances."

The pain inside my heart reached and clutched at my throat. I was caught in the worst nightmare imaginable, worse than anything I'd ever endured . . . worse than all of it combined. It felt as if the firmament of my world, of my soul, was cracking, and I didn't know how to stop it.

"Child?" Missus Serafina hobbled over to me. "What is the matter?"

I cleared my throat, forced out the words. "I . . . I never thought she'd forget me. She must have been so scared, she was so little then. I . . ." My voice was raw and ragged. "I'm so grateful, ma'am, so blessed that you and your husband cared for her, you love her and . . ."

My heart and my dreams broke at the same time. I sobbed loudly as I fell apart into countless pieces. The old woman wrapped her arms around me and pulled me close. She rocked me gently as I cried and cried and cried. Just as I thought the storm within me had ended, that motherly voice quietly whispered, "Hush now," and I broke out in fresh sobs.

When finally the well of my tears ran dry, she sat me at the table, made me drink a mug of milk sweetened with honey, and gave me a clean rag to wipe my face with.

"You been too strong," she said firmly. "I know about that. Strong starts out being the right thing. Your hands grow strong enough for your work. Your back strengthens under your burdens. Soon your mind becomes strongest of all; has to be to get through the hard days. You were mighty strong to come so far after our Ruth. That is a blessing indeed. But you haven't cried like that in a long time, have you?"

I shook my head, feeling like a child.

"Don't forget how to be gentle," she warned. "Don't let the hardness of the world steal the softness of your heart. The greatest strength of all is daring to love. Now, you remember I told you that."

I took a sip of sweet milk. "Yes, ma'am, I shall. Thank you."

She dipped a rag in the hot wash water and rubbed at the worktable. "Where do you go from here?"

"Home," I said. "To Rhode Island."

"Your kin there?"

I paused. "We just have each other. Our parents died a long time ago."

"Then why go back?"

"It's home."

"You own a house there? A big farm, with chickens that Ruth can fuss over?"

"Not yet," I said. "But I will. I'm smart, strong, and I work harder than most. I'm a fair hand when it comes to needlework, too. I can take care of her."

Her gaze met mine, but I did not understand the expression on her weathered face. Outside Curzon's axe fell regular as the pendulum on a windup clock.

"I can see that she has a home here," I said quietly. "But she needs to come with me."

Missus Serafina rinsed out the rag in the bucket. "I agree."

"You do?"

"Course, I do. I wanted her to run off with the others, but she wouldn't leave us." She hung the rag from a peg on the wall. "Ruth is the most stubborn child ever walked, except maybe for you."

"She acts like you are her family."

"We are." A tear escaped from the corner of her blind eye. "That means you are part of our family too." She smiled. "That's why I can tell you how you ought live your life."

"She . . ." I paused to swallow the lump that kept bobbing up in my throat. "She told me to go away."

"I'll talk to her." Missus Serafina rested her hand on mine. "Then we'll assemble the things you'll need."

"Need for what?"

"You're leaving as soon as dark falls. All three–"

Aberdeen flung himself through the door, dust covered and gasping.

"Horses!" he cried. "Prentiss is back!"

CHAPTER VIII

Tuesday, June 26, 1781

WELL, NOW COMES THE DAY OF TERROR.
–LETTER FROM ELIZA WILKINSON OF SOUTH CAROLINA
DESCRIBING SOLDIERS INVADING HER HOME

"HOW FAR?" MISSUS SERAFINA ASKED. "How many?"

"Two strangers and Prentiss," Aberdeen panted. "Just turned down the lane."

"Get them in the loft," she said, hurrying to put away the clean mugs and bowls. "Ruth is already in the barn. Stay with them up there."

"But he'll ask–"

Missus Serafina crossed the floor quicker than I thought possible. She grabbed the front of Aberdeen's shirt. "You and Ruth ran off days ago, that's what I'll tell him. Stay hid in the loft till we come for you."

She stopped. The sound of pounding horse hooves drew closer. The old dog in the yard gave a loud *woof!* and loped toward the front of the house. Curzon appeared in the doorway, ready for trouble, the axe still in his hand.

"Follow me," said Aberdeen.

We crossed from the summer kitchen to the barn so fast, our feet barely touched the ground. By the time my eyes had adjusted to the darkness inside the barn, Curzon was helping

Aberdeen move a rickety ladder to the loft. Ruth rose with a puzzled look, holding a kitten in each hand.

"Deen?" she asked.

"Prentiss is come back early," he explained, reaching his hand out to her. "He's got men with him. Fina says we have to hide."

Ruth set the kittens down and dashed up the ladder, disturbing the chickens that had been dozing up there. I followed close behind. She grabbed some empty gunnysacks at the edge of the hayloft and scurried to the far corner, where the hay was piled deep, clucking all the while to calm the birds.

Loud laughter came from the direction of the house. The dog began barking like his tail was on fire. I prayed the noise would cover our movements.

"Isabel!" Curzon hissed.

He and Aberdeen passed up pitchforks to me, then climbed the ladder and pulled it up behind them, setting it close to the wall. The four of us silently burrowed into the hay; I loosed my hatchet and held it ready in my hand.

We lay still as the dead–Curzon, Aberdeen, Ruth, and me.

Aberdeen placed a gunnysack against the wall in front of us so it covered the gaps between the boards and acted as a shield. The rest of us did the same, moving slow so as not to upset the chickens. Now we could peer through the loose weave of the cloth to the ground below. Anyone looking up at the barn would not see us. A large, slovenly white man dressed in muddy breeches came into the barnyard, followed by two British redcoats, who also seemed worse for wear. Their unsteady gait made them look as if they walked on the deck of a ship rolling on the waves.

"Ruth!" bellowed the man.

My sister started shaking. I turned, afraid she'd been seized by a fit.

"Ruth!" he repeated.

Though only twelve years old, Ruth resembled more a maid of sixteen.

"I wished ye coulda seen her, a fine lass, she is," Prentiss slurred. "She was. Food for the gators now, I reckon. Damn that girl."

His companions said words too faint for us to hear, and they all three laughed like fools. 'Twas not yet midday, yet they were already muddy in drink.

Prentiss had a notion to harm her, that was clear. 'Twas fear of that odious man that caused her to quake, not the falling sickness. I reached out my hand to her, thinking to pat her shoulder. She shied from my touch.

Missus Serafina hurried from the summer kitchen carrying a tray with sliced ham and pickles. The men gave a drunken huzzah at the sight of the food and followed her into the house. Shortly after the door closed behind them, Mister Walter appeared, leading three horses to the barn. I waited until he and the animals were inside, and started to rise, thinking to steal a few words with him. Ruth grabbed hold of my skirt and pulled me back down. She laid her hand on my lips, then pointed to tell me I should again lie flat and stay hidden.

"Oh, yes, what a day!" called Mister Walter loudly. "What a long day already for these fine horses." The sound of buckles and leather straps indicated that he was removing the saddles. "Need to rest up and prepare for the next long journey, don't you, my good friends?"

One of the horses snorted. Mister Walter gave a laugh that sounded hollow and false.

"No sense in fussing, you old thing," he said, curious loud. "Any noise you make is gonna bring Mister Prentiss to investigate. That man deserves a good meal and as much rum as he can hold. So you horses, you just stay quiet and peaceful. Soon as Mister Prentiss and his companions are settled, I'll see you fed and watered and ready for your next trip."

Aberdeen raised his eyebrow a bit. Curzon and I both nodded to show we understood. Mister Walter's message was meant for us.

We stayed silent and still long after Mister Walter went back to the house. A chicken fluttered across the loft and settled in front of Ruth. She reached out and stroked the feathers on its throat until the creature closed its eyes.

Aberdeen and Curzon exchanged a few words, so low that I couldn't hear them, though we were lined up right next to one another. Aberdeen then turned so he could whisper to me.

"He says you need to sleep."

"Don't need sleep," I lied.

"You'll be leaving soon as it's dark enough. Gonna need sleep to move quick," Aberdeen said. "Gonna need to run miles before sunrise."

Curzon raised himself up enough that I could see him. The worried and determined expression on his face said more than any words could have. He was right; we needed rest. But I needed time to soften Ruth's manner toward me, time to help her turn from being a tall stranger to being my little sister.

Even if we'd had the rare luxury of time, I had no idea how to make such a transformation possible.

CHAPTER IX

Wednesday, June 27, 1781

We fight, get beat, rise, and fight again.
—Letter from Patriot Major General Nathanael Greene to the Marquis de Lafayette

'TWAS FULL DARK WHEN I AWOKE. I blinked, trying to recollect where I was and how I'd come to be there. The truth of the matter sprang upon my senses in a rush: We were hiding and in the gravest form of danger. I lay without moving; that was Ruth to my left, and beyond her the boy, Aberdeen, with Curzon on his other side.

I listened.

A few mice scurried through the hay at the far end of the loft. The roosting chickens above muttered in their sleep. Night insects whirred in the darkness outside, but no owls called, no wolves. Then I heard a door close. Footsteps approached the barn from the house.

Ruth gave a start, instantly awake. The boys were both tensed, hands clutching axe and pitchforks. I gripped my hatchet. We were prepared to fight our way out if we had to.

I heard a woman humming loudly, Missus Serafina making her slow way to the barn. The tune recollected a hymn we used to sing in Rhode Island.

Ruth's face relaxed.

Missus Serafina hobbled past the barn as if making for the privy, then she stopped humming and came back, her feet almost silent in the dirt. She crept into the barn a moment later, stood still, then whispered to us to come down from the loft. The boys went down the ladder first. Ruth tucked a sleepy chicken into her skirt before she descended.

"Don't," I said.

She ignored me. By the time I reached the ground, she had taken a large basket from a hook on the wall and settled the chicken in it. Missus Serafina motioned for us to stay silent and follow her. We slipped out the back door of the barn one at a time and hurried past the summer kitchen. From there we dashed to the welcoming darkness of the woods, where Curzon and I had perched at dawn.

Once we'd reached the safety of the trees, Missus Serafina had to stop. She leaned her hand against a tree trunk, breathing heavy, like she'd been running miles instead of steps.

Ruth rushed to her side. "Are you poorly?" she whispered.

The old woman smiled weakly and patted Ruth's cheek. "Just a little spell, nothing more. Don't you worry about me."

An owl called from the darkness. The wind blew the clouds away from the face of the moon and rustled the leaves above us.

"Walter's coming," Missus Serafina said quietly. "I have to go back to the house, Ruth. Don't want that Prentiss coming out to look for you."

"Don't want him bothering me," Ruth agreed.

Missus Serafina took my sister in her arms, held her tight, and whispered in her ear. When she pulled away, tears were rolling down the old woman's cheeks.

"You are very poorly, Fina." Ruth wiped away the tears with her sleeve. "I'll walk with you."

"No, sweet girl." Missus Serafina straightened up. "I need you to walk with Walter." She pointed to the form of her husband, standing in the shadows. "Swear to me, my dear Ruth. Swear by the name of our Lord that you will walk with Walter and Isabel and the boys. You have a long way to go."

Ruth frowned. "Don't want to. Ghosts in the dark."

My sister did not grasp our true circumstances or intent. That was for the best. We needed to get her far away from Riverbend before we told her the truth.

"You must be brave for me," Missus Serafina said. "Aberdeen will keep the ghosts away, you know he will. Swear that you will do everything Walter asks of you."

I held my breath. If Ruth got stubborn now, all was lost.

"If you want me to, I swear," Ruth said. "By the Lord."

"Thank you, child. Now I'll be able to sleep at night." She looked at me. "May God bless you all and keep you from harm." Her voice wavered. "You take good care of her."

Before I could reply, Missus Serafina turned away from us and limped back to the house. I wanted to call after her to thank her, to pour out my gratitude at her feet. I owed her everything, for she had loved my sister as much as our mother had. But we had no time.

The owl hooted again.

"This way," whispered Aberdeen.

Mister Walter led us along the river, pausing once so we could gather the supply-filled haversacks he'd hidden hours earlier. After we'd walked a long ways, we turned north onto a narrow path that led around the edge of a murky swamp. He didn't stop walking until we were curtained on all sides by great sheets of hanging moss.

"Why are we here?" Ruth asked. "The cow needs milking soon, and I have to help Serafina."

"I'll take care of Fina, darling." Walter pulled a cloth from his pocket, wiped the sweat from his brow, and looked past Ruth at us. "I'm fair certain that Prentiss believed our story, that she's already been gone for days. Deen, too. His mind is on the new people arriving tomorrow. Your real danger will be from the scoundrels and rogue militia units."

He pointed. "Another mile or so, the path forks left. That's what you want, Deen, head west a fortnight, then south. Stay well away from Savannah, and try not to fall out of any trees."

"Where you going?" Ruth asked Aberdeen.

The boy busied himself with retying his sling instead of answering her.

"What about us?" I asked.

"Stay straight north, don't turn west with Deen," Mister Walter said.

"If you had the choice," Curzon asked, "which direction would you go?"

"West and northwest to the mountains takes you to open territory, but plenty of settlers out there are as dangerous as the bears. Southward will get you to the Spanish lands eventually, but there's terrible fevers along the way. If I were you, I'd travel north, plumb north. 'Tain't perfect, but your chances are better. Keep to the edges of the swamps, they'll thin out the farther away you get."

"Gators in swamps," Ruth said. "Don't like them."

"Me neither," Curzon said. "But don't worry, Isabel will kill any gators that bother us. Once we get to Rhode Island, we'll find a cobbler who will make us gator-skin boots."

"Rhode Island?"

"Rhode Island," Curzon repeated. "That's where we're going."

I felt a stab of frustration with Curzon's rambling mouth. There was no need to tell Ruth our plans, that would just muddle her mind more and make it harder for her to leave.

Ruth's mouth opened as the arrow of truth hit home. "You all running?"

"*We* are running," Curzon corrected. "You and me and Isabel."

"Not me," Ruth said quickly. "I belong here, with Missus Serafina and Mister Walter."

I pressed my lips tight together. Her reaction was exactly what I had feared.

"Not anymore, dear." Mister Walter paused to clear his throat. "Isabel and Curzon are taking you home."

"This is home," Ruth insisted. "I'm your sweet girl, you both say that every morning. You need help polishing, and Missus Serafina can't see good. She has swoons. I help her."

The strong sentiment in her voice moved us all to tears.

"You can't stay," I said gently. "You're coming north with us. We're going to live free in Rhode Island. You won't have to be afraid anymore."

"I'm not afraid." The moonlight caught the stubborn set of Ruth's chin and the temper flaring in her eyes. "You can't make me run with you."

We needed months to accustom her to the idea, time so she could work through the hows and the whys and be settled about it. But we only had time measured in a few heartbeats.

"You must," I said firmly.

"Scolding her won't help," Curzon said.

"Sweet-talking won't either."

"Go away!" Ruth turned her back on me.

Mister Walter sighed deeply. The sound filled me with shame. I had said the wrong thing again, taken the wrong tone.

"What if I come with you?" Aberdeen asked Ruth.

"But you're going–" I said.

"Hush, girl," Mister Walter said to me. "Ruth."

She turned around slowly.

"Will you run with them if Aberdeen goes too?" Mister Walter asked.

Ruth's eyes filled with tears. "Don't want to leave you."

"Isabel is right. You must go," Mister Walter said fiercely. "If you stay, Prentiss will hurt you. Fina and me, we couldn't bear that."

Ruth covered her ears with her fists.

Mister Walter gently pulled her hands down and held them in his. "We talked about this before, remember? We don't want you to leave, poppet, but you must. 'Tis the best thing for you. The best for you makes us happy and proud. I know you want to make us happy and proud, don't you?"

Tears began to trickle from Ruth's eyes.

"Mind your sister," Mister Walter continued. "Mind the boys, too. Stay close to them."

Ruth shook her head back and forth, the tears now washing unchecked down her face. I sniffed and dabbed my eyes on my sleeve.

"Be still and silent when you're told to." Mr. Walter's voice got caught in his throat for a moment.

"I want to go home," Ruth whispered. "I want to go home with you."

"Keep home in your heart, where no one can steal it." He kissed her forehead. "Keep Serafina and me in your heart too, and in your prayers. You are our sweet girl, darling Ruth. Nothing will ever change that. Hold us in your heart and you will never be alone."

CHAPTER X

Thursday, June 28–Thursday, August 23, 1781

ALL I HAD EVER HEARD OF LIONS, BEARS, TIGERS, AND WOLVES NOW RUSHED ON MY MEMORY, AND I SECRETLY WISHED I HAD BEEN MADE A FEAST TO THE FISHES RATHER THAN TO THOSE MONSTERS OF THE WOODS.
—JOURNAL OF SCOTSWOMAN JANET SCHAW AS SHE TRAVELED IN THE SOUTHERN COLONIES

THE FIRST WEEKS AFTER WE FLED Riverbend were painful hard on our bodies and our spirits. The air clung to our throats like hot wax as we skirted the edges of nameless swamps. Our clothes dripped heavy with sweat. Battalions of troublesome insects drew blood, despite our coating our skin with mud and fanning ourselves with palmetto leaves. We were all of us afflicted with every sort of misery and fear.

But nothing felt as bad as the fact that Ruth would not look at me.

She'd take food from Curzon and put her boots back on if he asked her to. (She had rarely worn shoes at Riverbend and did not like the feel of anything on her feet.) When sadness overtook her and the tears ran down her face, she'd let Aberdeen pat her on the back gently. She stuck as close to him as a thistle in lamb's wool. He was the only one allowed to hold the chicken basket when Ruth had to answer a call of nature. If I stepped too close, she'd stop dead, crossing her arms over her chest and refusing to move until I walked away.

In the first days I worried that the fatigues of the journey would be too much for Ruth, that we'd have to slow down or take days of rest. But she endured the hardships as good as any of us, without a word of complaint. Her tenacity impressed me so much that one day I tried to compliment her on it, to explain what a remarkable lass she'd become. She turned away from me, but I followed her, determined that she should know that I was proud of her. She closed her eyes and covered her ears. When I tried to pull down her hands—gently—she spat in my face and ran to Aberdeen.

Curzon drew me away from them. "Come help me with the fire."

He needed no help, of course, but I followed him all the same. We collected dried pine needles and twigs in silence, then crouched next to a bare spot of damp ground.

Curzon pulled his flint and steel striker from his haversack. "She needs time to accustom herself to you, to all these changes."

"'Tain't natural," I whispered as I piled a handful of the needles on the ground. "She treats me like her worst enemy."

"You won't change her sentiments by being forceful." He struck the flint shard against the small steel bar. Tiny sparks flew but did not catch. "You're making the matter worse."

He was right, though I was loath to admit it. I was in the company of my sister. I had what I'd wanted, what I'd sacrificed everything for, but nothing was the way I'd thought it would be.

"What if she doesn't change?" I asked.

"Patience," he said, continuing to hit the steel.

"I have none."

He spoke harsh. "Find some."

Every day that had passed, Curzon had grown more and more short tempered. The reason was painfully clear. He had stayed with me only because of his debt. I'd saved him from certain death in a British prison back in New York, so he, in turn, had vowed to help me find my sister. Now that the debt was paid, our time together would soon end. He wanted me to get along better with Ruth so he could leave us without worry.

The thought of him leaving caused a curious ache within me.

A spark finally caught in the needles. I bent forward to blow on it gently, but it went out.

"We're lucky Deen is with us," Curzon said. "Let Ruth turn to him; they're friends."

"I'm afraid she'll run off with him."

"Now you're talking like a looby." He scowled as he poked at the needles.

"They're too damp," I said.

He struck the flint and steel together again. "No, they're not."

"Yes, they are." I stood up. "I'll go back and find something drier." I brushed dirt from my skirt. "And you're wrong. I'm certain they're planning to go off on their own, though it would mean death if they did."

"Don't conjure disaster," he grumbled. "Just find tinder."

We walked in the hours just before sunrise and just after sunset, resting during the middle of the day and the middle of the night. We moved steady and quiet except for the occasional sound of Ruth sniffling back her tears and for the clucking of her chicken, which rode like a queen in the basket she carried. Half of the time Curzon took the lead on the path, half of the time 'twas me. Whenever we came across clean water, we'd drink all our bellies could hold, fill the gourds Missus Serafina had put in our haversacks, and move on. When the time came to rest, we'd scout a ways off the trail, make beds of moss or pine boughs, and try to sleep. I always took the first watch. Curzon took the second.

Years of dangerous, shared travel had heightened our senses. Curzon and I both noticed the instant when the bats overhead vanished, or when the smell of a distant cook fire reached us; we noticed the snap of broken branches, or the sudden swirl of the mist rising off the swamp water that heralded the approach of a large creature or a rowboat. We'd signal to the others and move off the path, sometimes wading deep into the foul water, holding our haversacks above our heads, until we were sure it was safe. The first time this happened, Aberdeen scorned us, for there had been no danger. The second time—after a frightful trio of banditti passed by—he apologized.

The land itself became our enemy. The heavy miasma that hung in the air was crowded with ghosties and restless haints bent on terrifying us. Thunder-gusts would suddenly boil into violent summer storms. Once we saw a spear of lightning set fire to a cypress tree so close by that we were forced to run from it.

But the moon waxed fatter, and that made our navigation northward easier. The night it shone bright and full, we walked a good fifteen miles, by my reckoning. After that, it shrank as if it were being whittled away by a sharp paring knife, until there came the night of no moon, in which we traveled barely two miles. Before we slept that night, we ate the last of the dried meat.

The goods that Missus Serafina and her husband had given us were so useful that I suspected the others whom they'd helped run for freedom had succeeded in their quest. We had hooks for catching fish, a small pot for boiling water, and peas and grits stored safe in extra gourds. Along with flint and steel, we had two knives with fresh-honed blades, small blankets, three needles, and a quantity of good thread. We still had our small collection of coins but had vowed to hoard them until we reached the place where we'd settle. Even if we had been inclined to buy something, there were no markets or tradesmen in the swamp.

Hunger was a stern master. After we ate up the grits, peas, and meat, we collected whortleberries, mulberries, and chinquapin nuts, which we ground into a paste. Aberdeen proved a deft hand at catching catfish with a hook attached to a braided length of thread. One night he surprised and captured an opossum. Roast opossum tastes much like a well-fed pig.

Ruth's chicken, now named Nancy, produced one precious egg each day. We took turns eating it. On those days with no food other than that egg, we'd crack it into the pot of boiling water to share between us four. The chicken itself would have made the best meal imaginable, but Curzon and I agreed to consider that only if we were truly desperate. Long as most days brought fish, berries, or nuts, Nancy would live, for she alone could stir Ruth out of her deep melancholy.

Living in a city or a town, you accustom yourself to the names of the days and the activities they promise. Sundays are church days. High Street market in Philadelphia is open on Tuesdays. The oyster sellers in New York are best visited on Fridays. The days grow into weeks and then months as recorded in an almanac or noted atop the page of a newspaper.

In the wilderness days shed their names. The only measures that have meaning are the phase of the moon and the degree of emptiness in your belly. How much strength remains in your legs. How much sorrow crowds your heart.

I thought I knew how to shoulder the burdens of journeying. I'd certainly been tired before. I'd walked so long that I'd fallen asleep only to wake as I was tumbling to the ground. I'd walked until the blisters on my calluses grew blisters of their own. But I'd never known such bone-crushing fatigue as I did in those endless weeks of north-going. My mother used to say, "Heavy hearts make heavy steps." I wish that she would have told me the remedy for that.

In the first weeks of our journey my mind raced with notions about rebraiding the memories that might join Ruth's heart to mine. I dreamed of cooking her oyster stew and berry cobblers, and singing the songs our mother had taught us. I ached to tell her all I could remember about Momma and about our father, who'd been killed when she was a baby. But the moon grew full again, and her manner toward me did not change, not even by the smallest bit. I said "Sweet dreams" whenever she lay down to sleep. She always turned her back to me without a word. Instead of the loving sister who'd walked through hell to rescue her, Ruth saw me as the loathsome stranger who had stolen her away from her heart-kin, Missus Serafina and Mister Walter. That hurt me more than anything I'd ever suffered in all of my life.

I longed to talk this over with Curzon, but as the miles passed, he grew as silent and distant as Ruth. His manner to me, on the rare times he did speak, had become formal, as if we'd just met each other and knew not what to discuss. I might have put his strangeness down to hunger or an imbalance of humors, even a mild, remitting fever, but he was always ready to talk with Aberdeen and went to great lengths to cheer Ruth's spirits by carving her small birds intended to keep company with Nancy Chicken.

It was only me he avoided.

After weeks of walking, the swamplands slowly turned into woods thick with oak, walnut, hickory, and ash trees, and mercifully free of alligators. Some nights the air grew cooler, which made travel easier. As the moon waned again, the oak forests became dotted with pine, laurel, willow, beech, and birch. We spotted wild turkeys and parrakeetos, and often heard partridges in the brush, but could never figure a way to catch any of them.

As we drew farther away from Carolina, Curzon and Aberdeen took to conversating more when we paused to eat or sleep. Their confabs were quiet but so tense you could near see sparks flying. They were arguing about the war. Aberdeen favored the British on account of Lord Dunmore's proclamation that runaways who reached British lines would be freed. Curzon, of course, sided with the Patriots. He tried to convince Aberdeen that a country that declared all men to be created equal was a country more inclined to free its slaves. Aberdeen laughed at him.

I stuffed moss in my ears and tried to sleep.

For three nights we passed through a pine barren, an eerie, stinking landscape of enormous, scarred trees that wept tears of sap. We came across a friendly chap there, name of Huntly, who had liberated himself and his wife from a farm in Georgia after the Savannah battles. He was living rough, earning a bit of coin by collecting pine sap and tending the tar-burning kilns, which gave the air its stink. His wife lay buried by a laurel tree with their baby boy, born dead after his mother labored three days and nights to bring him into the world. Huntly said his wife died of a broken heart hours later.

He offered to trade us an old axe for Nancy Chicken. We turned him down but gave him that day's egg, which he enjoyed mightily. Using a stick, he scratched out a map in the sand to show us the safest way through the rest of the barren, detouring us around a collection of unsavory folk. Then he offered to marry me, should I be so inclined to stop my journeying.

I thanked him politely and declined his offer.

CHAPTER XI

Friday, August 24–Sunday, August 26, 1781

ONE OF THE MEANS OF PREVENTING INTERMITTENT [FEVERS] IS *WARMTH*. PERMIT ME TO RECOMMEND IT TO YOUR WHOLE FAMILY, IN CLOTHING, BED CLOTHES, AND IN LARGE AND CONSTANT FIRES.
—LETTER FROM DR. BENJAMIN RUSH TO ABIGAIL ADAMS

WEEKS OF HARD TRAVEL HAD WEAKened and wearied us all. Ruth had been limping for days on account of a twisted ankle; though, of course, she would not let me tend to her. Curzon had a ragged cough, and my bowels had declared rebellion. Added to all that misery was Aberdeen, that half-witted looby, that fool slubberdegullion, who had begun to doubt our course. He suddenly wanted us to head west, away from the war and everything that wanted to chase us. He and Curzon argued the merits and weaknesses of his plan ceaselessly, dogs scrapping over a meatless bone.

I feared that if Aberdeen left, Ruth would follow him, but I knew that the scrawny lad would more likely listen to Curzon than to me. I strode ahead on the path, my gaze flitting from tree to tree like a sparrow, hoping to spot an apple tree heavy with ripe fruit. I fought a yawn and lost. Curzon had taken to making each day's journey longer and our time for sleeping shorter. 'Twas another sign of how anxious he was to be quit of us.

"Ruth!" Aberdeen suddenly yelled.

I spun around. The boys were kneeling next to Ruth's twitching form, sprawled on the ground. She'd been seized by a fit.

I ran as fast as I could, cursing myself with every step for walking too far in front. By the time I got there, the fit had ended. Ruth lay still, eyes closed, her breath coming regular. I saw no blood nor sign that she'd hurt herself in the fall. If she were still a child, I'd have cradled her head in my lap and spoken quiet and sweet to her until she'd come back to herself. Fits confuddled and sometimes alarmed her. But I hung back, unsure of how she would react to me. It was Aberdeen who brushed the leaves from her kerchief and cupped his hands around her face, her eyes still closed.

He looked up at me in horror. "She's burning up!"

We made camp right there.

At first it just seemed a pestilent fever. Ruth slept deeply but woke if pinched hard on the neck. Each time I roused her, Aberdeen or Curzon would get her to drink water until she slipped back into sleep. She had a few more shaking fits but never opened her eyes. Her body gave off the sour smell of illness, as if the fever were slowly burning its way through her. She slept an unnatural sleep all that night and the day after that.

This was my fault, all of it.

I should have stayed by her side no matter how much it vexed her. I should have slowed the pace of the journey. No wonder Ruth couldn't abide me. I was a wretched, impatient, horrid sister. I knelt next to her, bowed my head, and prayed without cease, but it did not seem to help.

At dawn we moved her to an abandoned shack near a stream. It was more of a hovel than a shack: three leaning log walls with a few roof beams but no roof, and a fire pit instead of a proper hearth and chimney. The boys engineered a sort of roof by laying densely leaved ash and oak branches over the beams. I covered the far corner of the hovel with pine needles and dry leaves and then spread a blanket on top of it all so Ruth could lie in a spot both soft and dry.

She did not notice. The fever had pulled her down to insensibility. She lay like a rag doll, not moving at all if pinched.

After some discussion we left Aberdeen to keep watch over her whilst Curzon and I scouted a bit farther afield, both to measure the safety of the place and to look for food. He looped around and around the hovel in ever-growing circles and found no sign of other people. I moved back and forth between the stream and the hovel, bringing water, wild grapes, and a handful of grubs for Nancy Chicken.

On the last trip I ranged as far upstream as I dared and was rewarded with the blessed sight of a willow tree. Willow bark could bring down a fever and strengthen the sick.

Thank you, Lord, I prayed as I cut the slim branches. *Thank you for your protection and wisdom and guidance. Thank you for this wonderful tree and that remarkable shack. Please forgive my . . . well, forgive me for everything that I've done wrong, including ending this prayer in haste. Ruth needs me. Amen.*

Aberdeen had a fire going by the time I returned.

"Any change?" I asked as I scraped the bark from the twigs.

He shook his head sorrowfully. "She hasn't even moved."

"Are *you* feeling feverish?" I asked him. "Pain in the belly? Does your head hurt?"

"Don't worry about me," he said. "I can take care of myself."

He watched as I brewed a pot of willow bark tea, then tried to get some of it into Ruth. She would not wake enough to swallow. I dared not pour it into her mouth for fear she would choke.

"Seems like we might be here awhile," he said.

"Nay," I lied, trying to mask my fear. "She'll be on her feet again tomorrow."

He looked at me for a long moment without speaking. A fever that came on this hard and fast could be fatal; everybody knew that. *I might lose her again. I might lose her for good.*

"A wash-down always makes a sick person feel better," I said hoarsely. "Can you fetch more wood for the fire?"

Soon as Aberdeen left, I tore a strip off the bottom of my shift, dunked it in the cooling tea, then gently washed Ruth's face. The rag was quickly stained with weeks of dirt and sweat. I rinsed the rag, then cleaned her neck. Heated more water, then washed her arms and her hands.

Aberdeen returned, built up the fire, and fetched more water. Once it was ready, I untied and pulled off her left boot. Her foot smelled hideous. It was so filthy that it required another two pots of water to clean it proper.

Curzon looked in. "Wouldn't it be easier if we carried her to the stream and washed her there?"

I shook my head. "The shock of the cold would harm her. Sick bodies require comfort and moderation in all things."

Sick bodies require proper bed rest, I thought, *covered with clean blankets and under a proper roof.*

I pulled on the reins in my brainpan to stop the progress of my thoughts. It would do no good to stray into melancholy or to fuss about the things we did not have or could not do. I set a fresh pot of water on the fire to warm, then unlaced Ruth's right boot. It refused to slip off as easily as its mate had. In fact, it was necessary to fully loosen the laces and tug hard as I could. Before I could wonder at the cause of this, the boot finally came off.

I dropped it with a gasp and clapped my hand over my mouth in horror. The stench of death filled the air.

CHAPTER XII

Sunday, August 26–Monday, August 27, 1781

WHEN A WOUND IS GREATLY INFLAMED, THE MOST PROPER APPLICATION IS A POULTICE OF BREAD AND MILK, SOFTENED WITH A LITTLE SWEET OIL OR FRESH BUTTER.
—*DOMESTIC MEDICINE*, BY DR. WILLIAM BUCHAN, 1769

CURZON AND ABERDEEN RUSHED IN. I pointed.

Aberdeen gagged and hurried outside.

"Dear Lord," Curzon murmured.

Ruth's heel was cut open with an ugly, festering wound. The foot and the ankle were swollen and hot. Injuries such as this could be as fatal as musketballs and cannon fire.

"How did it happen?" I asked.

"Four days ago I caught her walking barefooted again," he said. "Only noticed on account of she was limping."

"You didn't tell me? You didn't think to check her feet?"

"I told her to put her boots on, and that was that." He glanced at the wound again and rubbed his hand over his head. "That must have hurt like the Devil. She's a tough one." He paused and motioned for me to follow him outside.

I went reluctantly, afraid of his next words.

The three of us stood around the small fire.

"You know what we must do," Curzon said.

The thought of it sickened me. I shook my head furiously. "We can't."

"We must," Aberdeen said. "That foot smells of poison. Only one way to cure it."

Curzon pulled his knife from his belt and set the blade in the fire. "We've got to burn it out."

"Nay." I shook my head again. "I won't allow it."

"You want to see her dead?" he asked.

"Of course not." I wrapped my hand in the bottom of my skirt, snatched the knife from the fire, and dropped it in the dirt. "But I know better than you what the pain of fire can do to a person. She's already terrible weak. It could kill her."

Curzon studied me hard, then dropped his eyes to the knife. He'd been in that crowd outside the court in New York. He'd witnessed everything I suffered the day they marked me.

"But–" Aberdeen started.

"Hush," Curzon said. "This is for Isabel to decide."

"We'll try it my way first," I said. "Just for today. But I'll need your help. She'll fight me."

As I heated another pot of water with willow bark, Curzon found a supple oak stick as big around as his finger. I tore another wide strip off the bottom of my shift, ripped it into three rags, and boiled them in the pot. As I lifted the first one out with the handle of my hatchet, Curzon placed the stick in Ruth's mouth, giving her something to bite upon. She stirred but did not wake. Aberdeen followed my directions and crouched to hold Ruth's legs. Curzon put his hands on her shoulders.

"Ready?" I asked.

They nodded.

I said a quick prayer, then pressed the hot poultice against the festering cut.

Ruth awoke with a strangled scream.

The boys gripped her tight. I quickly wiped away the dirt, pus, and blood. She screamed so loud, I thought my ears would burst. I dashed out of the hut and pulled the next steaming rag from the pot. I waved it quick to let it cool a bit, but not too much, for we needed the heat to draw out the poison. The boys had been talking to her the whole time, explaining the circumstances and begging her to be strong.

I dared not look her in the face for fear that it would weaken my resolve. Folding the rag, I pressed it against the cut hard enough to force out more blood and pus.

Ruth shrieked, arching her back, then collapsed into blessed unconsciousness. I took advantage of this and pressed the hot rags even harder, until the wound wept only blood and her foot was as clean as possible. Aberdeen staggered outside to retch and was a long time in returning.

That evening Curzon again scouted the area as the sun was setting, to make sure our hiding place was still secure. The two boys slept outside. I lay alongside Ruth but could not sleep. I held her as she shook with fits and with fever, then rocked her gentle side to side, quietly asking her to forgive me, telling her how much I loved her, and begging her not to die. Every time the poultice on her heel cooled, I fetched a hot one.

She did not wake.

Curzon entered the hovel at first light.

"Has she said anything?" he asked. "Opened her eyes?"

I shook my head.

"Are you crying?"

I sniffed back the tears. "Nay."

He felt Ruth's forehead. "Can't tell if she's cooler or hotter."

"She's as fevered as she was yesterday," I said, "but no more. And her foot seems less swollen."

"She's strong," he said. "She's already survived much."

I wiped my eyes on my sleeve. His kindhearted words could not cheer me or even offer hope. I felt sucked into the heavy mud of a pestilent swamp, trapped and unable to move. I had failed in the only thing that mattered: taking care of my sister, keeping her safe, free, and happy.

Curzon squatted. "If we had all of the King's riches at our disposal, what medicines would you want from the apothecary?"

"We don't have time for foolish games," I muttered.

"'Tis neither a game nor foolish," he said. "Is there anything that could help her?"

I tried to rub the crick out of my neck. "Peruvian bark is the best for fevers, but only those caused by miasma. If she would just rouse enough to swallow proper, I could get some willow tea into her. That would cut the fever much as any physician's decoctions or tinctures."

I stroked Ruth's limp hand. Her fingers were longer than mine and thinner. More than anything, she needed food. "With the King's riches I'd order my cook to make a sweet pudding with cardamom and a pot of beef marrow broth with barley. I'd bake loaves of soft bread for her and churn the butter myself. And honey; I'd send a maid to market to fetch some honey for the bread."

I stopped. The fantasy was painful.

"It's foolish to talk about impossible things. We have no

riches at all, much less the King's. All we have is worry and pine needles."

"And willow bark, and your fortitude and cleverness, and . . ."

Ruth's fingers curled a bit, holding on to mine. I held my breath. Ruth's chest continued to rise and fall, and then she uncurled her fingers. I raised her hand and rubbed it against my cheek.

"Isabel," Curzon said softly. "I want to find a farm or market, use our money to buy the victuals she needs. She needs proper food to strengthen her."

"All we've seen are forest and a few tobacco fields."

"Fields mean farms. Farms mean food."

"Farms mean trouble." I rested her hand at her side. "You show up, they'll put you in chains, set you to work in that tobacco."

"Think back on what Huntly told us in the pine barren." He spoke slow, like he was explaining the matter to a befuddled child. "We're only three or four days from the sea, and I'm near certain we're in Virginia. It won't be hard to find a town, buy some food."

I shook my head. "It's too dangerous."

"There are more free blacks here than in Carolina, more room for justice. I'm a free man and I defy anyone who tries to prove me different. I have papers."

He spoke with an uncommon tone of defiance. I lifted my head and met his gaze. He looked older. He was turning into someone I barely knew.

"You'll be caught," I said. "They'll throw your papers in the fire."

"Seems it's my choice," he said. "Not yours."

The only sound was the very faint noise of Ruth's breathing.

"Doesn't matter what I think," I finally said. "You're leaving."

"Aye." He paused. "But it didn't seem right to go without saying good-bye."

"Will you come back?" The question flew from my mouth before I had time to consider it.

He frowned. "What sort of fellow do you take me for? Of course I will. I've convinced Aberdeen to stay. He'll help keep watch and maybe have some luck with fishing."

He stood in the doorway. The light shone in around his form, causing his face to disappear in shadow. "I'll be gone awhile. Five days, likely. If I'm not back in a week's time, you need to move on without me."

He left without waiting for my response.

CHAPTER XIII

Monday, August 27–Monday, September 3, 1781

I AM CONSCIOUS THAT I HAVE THE FACULTY OF IMAGINATION, THAT I CAN AT PLEASURE . . . REVIVE THE SCENES, DIVERSIONS, SPORTS OF CHILDHOOD, CAN RECALL MY YOUTHFUL RAMBLES, TO THE FARMS, FROLICKS, DALLIANCES, MY WALKS, LONELY WALKS, THROUGH THE GROVES, AND SWAMPS, AND FIELDS.
—DIARY OF JOHN ADAMS

RUTH SUFFERED ANOTHER SHAKING fit shortly after Curzon left. When it was over, I looked up to see Aberdeen watching close.

"Can you help me?" I asked. "She has to drink this tea to bring down the fever, and . . . well . . . the truth of the matter is that she's more fond of you than me."

"You want me to try to rouse her?" Aberdeen asked.

"Please."

It took a long time, but Aberdeen—by teasing, shouting, telling jokes, and pinching Ruth's ears—was able to get her to come to the surface of awakeness long enough to take a few sips of willow tea. Then the fever pulled her back into a deep sleep. It was a small improvement, but 'twas an improvement all the same.

I settled Nancy Chicken close to Ruth's side, then followed Aberdeen out to the fire.

"She looks worse," he said, his face creased with worry.

"She drank some," I said. "That's a good sign. Thank you for your help and for your kindness with her."

He grunted and poked at the small fire with a stick. "How do you know she won't die?"

Because I cannot allow myself to think that, I thought.

"If she dies, she can no longer torment me," I said, trying to shove a false note of good cheer into my words. "She'll want to live for that reason alone."

He did not smile. "The way she looks in there?" He pointed at the hovel with his stick. "That's what she looked like when she first come to Riverbend."

I sat on a log. "You were there?"

"Aye. She came in a wagon from Charleston with a load of carpets from over the sea. Missus Serafina tried to get her to eat something, but Ruth just laid herself in front of the hearth and stared into the flames. Hardly ate a bite. Wouldn't move from the spot. Folks said she'd soon be measured for her grave. Did Fina tell you any of this?"

"We didn't have time for stories," I said.

He took off his sling and slowly stretched his arm above his head, then to the side.

"One day," he continued, "an old hound dog wandered in and lay down next to Ruth. She reached out and petted it. The dog stuck by her side after that. Then Ruth started to eat more, and she gained her strength. Mister Walter saw that she liked critters, so he put her to work helping with the horses, cows, and everything else in the barn. Some folks said Ruth had hexing ways, but they was wrong. Ruth was just patient; part patient and part stubborn. She'd wait out a horse or a duck till it calmed. Then she'd be its friend."

He rubbed his collarbone, nearly mended now, and then

his shoulder. Soon he'd be able to make his own way in the world too.

"She tried running away at first, though she'd never say where she was going or why. She'd just sneak off, cause all kinds of worry. That's why the old folks put the fear of ghosts in her. To keep her safe, Fina filled her head with scary stories about haunted woods and devilish ghosts. That stopped Ruth from running."

He ended the story abruptly.

The expression on his face helped me realize something I'd not seen before. "Are you sweet on her?"

"No." He poked at the fire, sending sparks into the air. "Yes. Mebbe. She's always been my friend, ever since . . ." His voice trailed off to nothing.

I picked up a willow branch, took out my knife, and started scraping the bark. "Ever since when?"

He gave me a hard look. We had never talked like this, the two of us. Never talked about things that mattered.

"It's just that I don't know her," I explained. "I don't know my own sister. I don't even know how often she has fits or what makes her laugh. I can't tell if she remembers anything about me, or about her life before Riverbend. I don't mean to pry into your business, but if you can help me understand her, that would be another kindness."

"Critters make her laugh, and silly songs." He started breaking bits of a dead branch into small sticks for the fire. "She doesn't have as many fits as she used to."

He stopped and stared into the fire again, like he was seeing young Ruth there. Mayhaps young Aberdeen, too. He stared so long, sat so silent, I was certain he'd forgotten I was there. I wanted to keep him talking so I could hear the stories of the years I'd missed with Ruth.

"Were you born at Riverbend?" I finally asked.

He shook his head, stood up, and walked to the pile of dead branches and brush. "Got sold to Riverbend the year afore Ruth turned up, at hog-butchering time. I was eight years old." He brought his boot down hard as he pulled up on a branch, snapping it cleanly. "So when butchering time came round again, I was in mighty low spirits. I missed my parents and my brothers something terrible. Ruth found me crying in the loft. She sat down next to me and patted my back, gave me a cloth for my nose. I told her my whole story about where I'd come from and who my family was. Things I hadn't told anybody, because it just hurt too much to say their . . ."

His voice cracked and my heart went out to him. No wonder he was close to Ruth; they'd both been stolen away from everything they knew and loved.

He cleared his throat with a sharp cough. "It hurt too much to say their names, so I didn't talk much. Anyway, Ruth listened, sweet as could be. When I was done, I asked after her people."

"What did she say?" I asked.

"That she didn't remember nothing."

"Did you believe her?"

"No." He fed another branch to the fire. "But I kept asking. Different days, different questions. She always said she didn't remember a thing in her whole life before that mangy dog lay down next to her by the kitchen fire."

I looked down at my hands, one clutching a willow twig, the other the knife, and was again enveloped in sorrow.

"Mayhaps she hit her head," I said quietly. "Mayhaps it destroyed her remembery."

"In that case, I guess, she's lucky," Aberdeen said. "She's got you here. You can tell her all the things she forgot."

"She won't even look at me," I said. "She doesn't want to hear anything I have to say."

"Don't seem to me like she'd argue right now." He tossed the branches on the fire and brushed off his hands. "Going fishing. I'll be back afore dark."

I watched him disappear, then brewed up more willow tea and tried to get Ruth to drink it. She wouldn't wake, lost again in a place I could not reach. I rinsed her handkerchief and soaked it in the willow tea, then replaced the cold poultice on her foot with the warm one. She stirred a little but did not wake. Sweat had beaded on her brow, but I had no rag to wipe it.

My shift had reached the end of its ability to offer up cloth, so I opened my sister's haversack, a treasure that she had closely guarded during our journey. Inside I found the rough-hewn birds that Curzon had carved, a few pinecones (these would have made for great fire starters, but I did not filch them), colorful pebbles, and a small handful of buttons that had been fashioned out of seashell. The buttons had been wrapped in a handkerchief that held clumsy girl-stitches; Ruth's first sewing, I guessed.

At the bottom of the bag, wrapped in a pair of stockings that were too small to fit her, I found a soft doll made of scraps of faded cloth that smelled faintly of clove and nutmeg. I buried my face in it and pictured Missus Serafina and Mister Walter, filled with so much love that they could send Ruth away from them. I tried to imagine what Aberdeen had described, the Ruth of five years earlier, weeks after she'd been taken from me in New York. She'd arrived at Riverbend in the hottest part of the summer. Her first friend had been a dog; her second, a boy as scared and lonely as she.

I repacked her haversack, except for her half-embroidered

kerchief, which I took outside to rinse in willow tea. When it had cooled, I took it into the hovel and sat next to Ruth's still form.

"I don't know if you can hear me," I said, "and I feel like a right fool talking to you this way, but at least I know you can't cover your ears or storm away from me." I wiped the sweat from her brow. "Let me tell you about the day you were born. . . ."

Every waking moment of the next two days and nights I told Ruth her stories. I told her about the colors of the quilt that Momma had wrapped her in and how happy Poppa had been when Ruth smiled at him for the first time. I reminded her of all the animals she had known in Rhode Island and the taste of Momma's cooking. I tried to conjure the smells of the farm: the dirt after a spring rain, bluebells blooming in the July sun, ripe apples on a cold October breeze, and the smoke from the chimney as snow piled deep around the house.

Some stories I told in order of when they happened; the day we buried Miss Mary Finch, followed by being sold to the Locktons, followed by the dreadful trip aboard the ship from Newport to New York, followed by our first encounter with Curzon.

(I suffered an odd pain when I spoke his name, and changed the course of that tale.)

Other stories grouped themselves together, like sorting peas from pebbles. Talking about our father led me to his stories about the country marks on his face, the scars he was given by his elders in a ceremony in the village over the sea where he'd been born. How he'd been kidnapped from his parents, his brothers and sisters, and all his friends.

This spun itself into the telling of the few stories I knew of Momma's mother, also born over the sea. She was stolen from her home when she was full grown and taken from her husband and children there. I told Ruth how our Momma carried Jesus in her heart always, and about the differences between our Congregational church and the Catholics and the Quakers, and the little I knew about the folk called Jews, and the folk called Mussulmans, who prayed five times a day. Why some people born over the sea paid special respect to springs of clean water, and how they greeted the sun with reverence each morning.

I'd run down one thread of the stories that I wanted her to remember, then chase back up it so I could travel down another thread. Back to Momma; her songs, her kindness, her rules. Back to New York; the rooms of the Lockton house, the sunflowers that grew outside, and Becky Berry, who cooked there. Back to Rhode Island; how I tried to teach her the letters and numbers, how she'd fed chipmunks, how she'd woken afore anyone every morning of her child days.

I took short breaks to eat the tiny fish that Aberdeen caught in the stream, taking care to set aside the longest bones that could be used as pins. He sat and listened in as I told Ruth about snow, how it fell like frozen feathers from the sky, how it could be formed into balls and thrown at a sister, how icicles grew like frozen giant's teeth off the edge of the roof, and how everything melted into water and mud when spring took winter's place. Aberdeen did not believe me about the snow. He wanted me to tell every story I knew about the great ships that crowded the wharves of Newport and New York, how far they journeyed, and what it sounded like when the wind filled their sails and pulled them from the harbor toward the endless sea. So I told those stories too. He wanted to hear about England and Scotland, where there was a city named Aberdeen. Said he fancied a trip there one day.

I talked until my voice was rough and raw, all the while keeping up a steady application of hot poultices on her dreadful cut, as well as a constant stream of prayer to God and supplication to the ghost of our mother.

Late the second night Ruth regained enough awareness to drink some tea and eat a few bites of egg. On the third morning she woke enough to drink a full pot of willow tea. That afternoon I had to help her take care of a call of nature, which was a momentous jolly occasion, for it meant that her insides were working proper. The next day I noted a resolute change in her wound; the skin around it had cooled and the swelling had much receded. She ate an entire egg as well as a handful of grapes. Best of all, she complained that the grapes were sour. Aberdeen laughed out loud and said that if she was restored enough to be peevish, then she was well on her way.

Once she was fully awake and returned to the land of the living, I stopped telling her stories. I had enjoyed the telling, but when Ruth regained her senses, she became wary of me again. The unsettled sensation betwixt us flared. Her eyes narrowed when I stepped close to her, as if she were a cat who'd just spied a snake in the grass. She did not argue or turn away. She even conversated a bit, asking for water for Nancy Chicken or if there was anything left to eat. That was an improvement, to be sure, but any hopes I had of my sister arising from her sickbed with newfound love for me were soon crushed.

Four days and nights had passed and Curzon had not

returned. I worried about his absence ceaselessly. Aberdeen shared a tiny bit of my concern, but he was younger and more inclined to hopeful thoughts. That night Nancy Chicken wandered off whilst we slept and did not return. Ruth understood the meaning of this tragedy as well as we did. She lay on her back and cried quiet, with her hands covering her face.

And then the fifth day passed, a day when Aberdeen and I ate nothing. The fish had vanished, we'd plundered all the grapevines we could find, and we'd lost our source of eggs. Ruth could walk a bit, but only with one arm over Aberdeen and the other round me. I counted it as a victory that she was willing to lean on me without shrinking from my touch. But it would take weeks before she could walk for hours on end, and then only if we could find some food.

Aberdeen and I did not talk about this. We did not discuss Curzon, either, because to do that we'd have to entertain the notion that he'd abandoned us or he'd been captured, and I could not decide which would be worse.

And so the sixth day passed too.

I woke the morning of the seventh day to find Ruth staring at me, the tip of her nose almost touching mine.

"I hear a donkey," she said.

"Donkey?" I asked, startled by this strange declaration. "Are you certain?"

She nodded.

I cautiously peered outside. A thin finger of smoke rose from the ashes of the fire. Aberdeen was nowhere in sight. I held my breath but heard only the wind in the trees and the burble of the stream.

"There is no donkey," I told Ruth.

She looked at me with pity, as if my ears did not properly work. "It's coming closer. Sounds like a nice donkey."

A voice bellowed from the woods: an exuberant, loud, comforting voice. "Is anyone to home?"

CHAPTER XIV

Monday, September 3–Saturday, September 8, 1781

THE GENERAL DOES NOT MEAN TO DISCOURAGE THE PRACTICE OF BATHING . . . ; BUT HE EXPRESSLY FORBIDS, ANY PERSONS DOING IT, AT OR NEAR THE BRIDGE IN CAMBRIDGE, WHERE IT HAS BEEN OBSERVED AND COMPLAINED OF, THAT MANY MEN, LOST TO ALL SENSE OF DECENCY AND COMMON MODESTY, ARE RUNNING ABOUT NAKED UPON THE BRIDGE, WHILST PASSENGERS . . . ARE PASSING OVER IT . . . : THE GUARDS AND CENTRIES AT THE BRIDGE, ARE TO PUT A STOP TO THIS PRACTICE FOR THE FUTURE.
—GENERAL ORDERS OF GEORGE WASHINGTON

RUTH MOVED ACROSS THE HOVEL ON her backside and sat in the doorway.

"Donkey," she said to me. "Told you."

Curzon emerged into the clearing very slowly, tugging behind him a reluctant donkey attached to a small cart. He didn't look any worse for having been gone from us for a week; indeed, he looked better, smiling easily and seeming quite pleased with himself.

"Egads!" he exclaimed at the sight of Ruth. "Lazarus is a lass."

I helped her to her feet as Curzon brought the donkey closer. The astonishment and joy in his face had me grinning like a fool.

"Her fever broke on the third day and the cut is beginning to heal," I said. "Where did you—"

"It's a long story," Curzon said in a rush. "But I've got apples, bread, and cheese in the cart, enough to feed us all for days."

The possibilities all of this offered us—plentiful food and a way to transport Ruth—cheered me more than anything had in ages. "That is the finest boon I've ever seen."

"What's a boon?" Ruth asked.

"A boon is a nice thing that makes Isabel smile," Curzon said. He chuckled and tugged on the lead rope.

The shock of seeing him again, along with the sound of his laughter, set my belly to wiggling, as if toads had begun hopping within it.

"Don't pull so hard," Ruth scolded Curzon. "He don't like that."

"Consarned beast thinks I am the Devil," Curzon answered cheerfully. "Mayhaps he'll like you better."

Ruth tilted her head and looked the donkey over like a fine lady measuring the worth of a racehorse. To me the poor thing looked like a collection of sticks wrapped in a moth-eaten hide.

"What's his name?" she asked.

"He wouldn't tell me." Curzon took a small sack from the back of the cart. "He is fond of biting folks. We could call him Gator."

He pulled an apple from the sack and handed it to Ruth. Instead of eating it herself, she set it on her palm and slowly extended her hand, offering the treat to the donkey. The creature gave a great snort before biting into the apple.

"You've already captured his heart!" Curzon said. "Every time I try to do that, he bites my fingers."

Ruth regarded the creature with a practiced eye. "His name is Thomas."

"Thomas Donkey?" I suggested.

"Don't be silly," Ruth said. "Thomas Boon."

While we feasted, Curzon shared all the news he'd gathered. We had indeed reached Virginia, where the British army had treated the countryside wickedly for months, burning crops and stealing livestock. Curzon thought we'd best make for Richmond, the new capital of the state. We could seek work for the winter there and push farther north come spring. I argued for traveling on to Philadelphia and finding work with the Quakers.

Our destination remained undetermined, but we agreed that we needed to move.

To travel with a cart, we needed to travel by road. That meant we ought make ourselves more respectable looking. We took turns washing our bodies in the stream as best we could, with handfuls of wild mint having to substitute for soap. I boiled more mint in the pot and poured the water over our ragged clothes in an attempt to make them smell less foul. The purchase of the cart and the foodstuffs had taken every last shilling we owned, so it was going to be a while before we could buy anything new to wear.

We headed for the road at dawn and reached it by midday. Curzon was confident that we were far enough north to travel safely in daylight. I was unsure, but we could certainly move faster when the sun was shining. Ruth drove the cart, which kept her occupied after the sad disappearance of Nancy Chicken. Having spent years on a farm, Ruth was well acquainted with the short and perilous lives of chickens, and she quickly transferred her affection to Thomas Boon.

He was fond of her, too, and would do her bidding long as the boys kept their distance. He could not abide anything dressed in breeches.

I pulled the thin shawl from my haversack and kept it handy. On the few times that we encountered other travelers, I used it to secure my hat on my head and to hide the scar on my cheek from view. The folks we passed paid us little heed. They were either driving a slow wagon filled with children and furniture or galloping at top speed on a lathered horse. Everyone was fleeing the war best they could.

After five days of walking the war found us, despite my fervent prayers. A company of Patriot soldiers, moving twice as fast as we were, overtook us on the road. Their officer called a halt and hailed us loudly, asking us to stop as well.

"Don't say a word to anyone," I told Ruth.

She stuck her tongue out at me.

Curzon strode up to the officer, slipping back into the soldierly way of speaking to a fellow of higher rank. Aberdeen stayed with Ruth and me, his hand resting protectively on the cart. The soldiers, sitting in the shade and drinking from their canteens, were as bedraggled as we were. Some walked barefooted; all of them were exhausted and filthy. Most of them were white, but a few conversated and joked freely with the black lads of the unit. This eased my mind some.

"What do you think they want?" Aberdeen asked.

"Mebbe food," I said, happy that we'd already eaten all of the bread and cheese and most of the apples.

Curzon and the officer finished their confab and approached us, striding quickly. Thomas Boon flattened his ears back.

"It's not much of a cart, sir," Curzon said.

The officer reached out to grab the donkey's reins from Ruth.

"Don't!" Ruth cried.

Thomas Boon brayed loudly and kicked, missing the officer's legs by a whisker.

"This wretched beast is terrible fearsome," Curzon said. "The bane of my existence. You are welcome to him."

Another soldier approached and tried to reach for the reins. Thomas Boon brayed even louder and snapped at the man with his yellow teeth. He succeeded in tearing the sleeve of the fellow's jacket. Both of the soldiers now took two cautious steps back.

"Except for his biting and kicking," Curzon said, "he's capable enough. He has worms in his bowels, of course, but you must expect that in a beast this old. Whatever you do, don't let him haul gunpowder. He does have a tendency to rear up when startled. He takes great pleasure in dumping everything onto the ground."

"What say you, Pearce?" the officer asked the soldier with the torn sleeve.

"More trouble than it's worth, sir," the man answered, scowling at Thomas Boon. "If we hurry, we'll make Williamsburg by dark."

"Williamsburg, sir?" Curzon asked. "I thought the army was encamped at Richmond."

"Cornwallis has holed up at Yorktown, a day's march from Williamsburg," the man said. "The French army is already there, waiting for the rest of us." He put on his hat. "Best of luck with this beast."

Pearce yelled, "Rouse yourselves! Time to march!"

We waited until they were well ahead of us, then resumed our journey. A few miles later we paused outside a ramshackle tavern that sat at the crossroads; Richmond to the northwest, Williamsburg to the southeast.

Curzon, with his gift of the gab, went inside on a scouting mission. He returned with the facts geographical and military that we needed. American troops and their French allies were indeed camped near Williamsburg, and the British at Yorktown. Both towns lay on a finger of land that jutted into the Chesapeake Bay, and were separated by miles of farms and marshes.

The news discomfited me.

"We'll be trapped," I said after he'd finished. "Surrounded by water on three sides, with not just two but three armies, counting the French? We'll be like partridges driven into a net."

Curzon held up his hand and counted off the advantages of Williamsburg on his fingers. "One: Where there is an army, there is work. Two: We're far enough north to not fear the Locktons. Three: With so many folks of all sorts there–black, white, Indian, slaves, free people, indentured folk–we'll be able to fold ourselves into crowds with ease. Four: It's harvesttime, so there will be food. Five: We're worn down. Injured. Broke. A month in one place would do much to restore our strength and spirits."

I opened my mouth to argue but closed it without saying a word. He was right. We were hungry and weak. We had no money, nor prospects to earn any in the open countryside. The road to Williamsburg was safer, if only by one small peppercorn. It felt like we were marching ourselves straight into trouble, but I could not think of a better course.

CHAPTER XV

Sunday, September 9, 1781

I AM NOT SORRY THAT THE LINE OF CONDUCT SEEMS NOW CHALKED OUT, . . . BLOWS MUST DECIDE WHETHER THEY ARE TO BE SUBJECT TO THIS COUNTRY OR INDEPENDENT.
—KING GEORGE III, WRITING TO HIS PRIME MINISTER, LORD NORTH, NOVEMBER, 1774

THE ROAD SWELLED LIKE A SPRINGtime river as we neared Williamsburg. Countless muddy boot prints and deep ruts carved by the wheels of heavily loaded wagons overflowed into the fields on both sides, cutting down the corn and wheat nearing harvest. We found ourselves in the company of more travelers than we'd seen in all the weeks since we fled Riverbend: sutlers with wares to sell, drovers leading herds of cattle, highborn gentlemen riding fine horses, farmers with wagonloads of hay, common folk on their way to work for the army or to enlist. Ruth watched all with wide-eyed fascination. Curzon took the measure of every man he met, conversating with some and keeping a distance from the rest.

After years of keeping to the shadows, it unnerved me to walk in the sunlight, surrounded by so many strangers. I stayed close to the cart and gave myself a strict talking-to, on the inside, where no one else could hear: *Chin up, walk proud. Chin up, walk proud.* Free people didn't dart their eyes fearfully, as if waiting for a blow or accusation. We had as much business on that road as anyone else; more, mayhaps, for we were honest people, seeking only work and safety.

Chin up.

Midway through the hot afternoon we crested a long hill and stopped, agog at the sight below. Thousands of dusty white tents were pitched in arrow-straight rows on both sides of the road, an encampment that stretched a mile or so from the base of the hill to the houses of Williamsburg.

"What regiments are those?" I asked.

"I do believe we're looking at the army of the French king Louis number sixteen," Curzon said.

"Lord save us," I murmured.

"Seems the French have come to take care of that." Curzon grinned. "Pardon the blasphemy, Country."

I smiled despite myself. He had not used my old nickname for a very long time. It cheered me to hear it again, and to see his face alight with excitement.

As we progressed, the road filled with French fellows laughing, talking, and shouting, all of it in their curious tongue. The French uniforms were vastly superior to the rags that the Americans had worn at Valley Forge. The men around us wore white breeches and shirts, with white jackets trimmed in blue. Nothing was ever truly white in an army encampment, of course. Mud and blood and the sundry stains of daily life put paid to that. But the high-spirited fellows around us nonetheless looked fresh, strong, and ready for a fight.

The sound of French spoken by so many recalled to me the months we spent at Valley Forge, a bleak and sorrowful time. I'd been forced back into slavery by an odious lickspittle named Bellingham, a rich man trying to become richer by befriending the Continental army. He made me work at Moore Hall that winter, where General Greene conducted business and kept company with friends and his wife, Caty. The dashing young French general, the Marquis de Lafayette, dined there often and spoke French with Missus Caty, who flirted more than was seemly for a married woman. The marquis was always kind to serving folk, be they paid servant or enslaved. He took the time to thank me for ordinary tasks like pouring wine or removing stains from his waistcoat, and he was never rude nor frightening, the way some men could be. His gentle politeness made me rather fond of the sound of French words on the air.

Curzon took hold of Thomas Boon's bridle and walked with his shoulders back and head held high, as if he were again in uniform. I stayed along one side of the cart, with Aberdeen on the other, his head turning back and forth staring at the canvas city on both sides of us, his eyes as wide as Ruth's. He'd been strangely quiet since we turned southeast to Williamsburg.

Our pace slowed to a crawl, then the crowd ahead of us halted. The breeze from the east blew a terrible stench in our direction. We had an unfortunately direct view of a line of soldiers pissing into a trench dug into the ground for that purpose. Ruth stared.

"That is not for your eyes," I said to her. "Look away."

"I need a privy," Ruth said. "I can go there."

"You can't use that one, it's for soldiers," I said, stunned that she had spoken to me direct. "We'll find a necessary in town, behind a tavern or some such. There are no bushes with suitable modesty here." I stood on tiptoe but could not see why we'd stopped. "What is this delay?"

Curzon hopped on the back of the cart. "Cannons are

blocking the road, well and truly stuck in the mud." He jumped back to the ground.

Ruth squirmed a bit. "I can go behind a tent."

"Patience," I replied, ignoring the angry look she shot at me.

"Go round the west side of the crowd," Curzon said. "Down that lane between the tents. There's a big building beyond them, has the look of being a public place, not a house. See the weather vane atop it?" He handed the donkey's lead rope to me. "I figger you'll find a privy at the back."

"Wait." I hesitated before I took the rope from him. "Aren't you coming with us?"

He exchanged a glance with Aberdeen. "We're going to scout around the camp and then the town." He bit his lip, as if he was going to say something that he knew would displease me. "There'll be a market hereabouts. We'll meet up with you there."

His words puzzled me. We were to split up in this crowd of military strangers? It went against all of our habits of safety and caution. This was not just a foolish notion, this could be dangerous.

"Meet us when the bells chime eight," Curzon continued.

"In the dark? What if we can't find each other? What if–"

"Trust me," he said, his eyes scanning the crowd.

I was puzzled about his sudden shift of mood and confused about his intentions. "What are you scheming?"

"In search of work, nothing more," he protested, his eyes still not meeting mine. "It'll be easier for us to move about without lasses attached."

And with that, he disappeared into the crowd, with Aberdeen at his heels.

CHAPTER XVI

Sunday, September 9, 1781

THE INCREASE OF OUR SICK WITHIN THESE FEW DAYS PAST . . . MAKES ME ANXIOUS TO STATE TO YOUR EXCELLENCY OUR SITUATION WITH RESPECT TO BLANKETS; THE HOSPITAL IS ENTIRELY WITHOUT THIS ARTICLE . . .
–LETTER FROM JAMES CRAIK, CHIEF HOSPITAL PHYSICIAN OF THE CONTINENTAL ARMY TO GEORGE WASHINGTON ABOUT CONDITIONS IN THE WILLIAMSBURG HOSPITAL

I WAS SO SHOCKED BY THE SUDDEN turn of events, I stood there like a statue as Thomas Boon pawed at the ground and bared his teeth at a soldier who brushed too close.

Did they just leave us here? In the middle of two armies?

"I have to go!" Ruth called.

The urgency in her voice recollected me to myself. We had to get away from all these uniformed fellows.

"Come, Thomas." I dragged the reluctant beast to the right and down the rough path between two rows of tents. A number of French soldiers smiled and nodded at us. One even bowed in Ruth's direction. I paused to look at her with a stranger's eyes. Her face was both delicate and strong, and her form was that of a woman, tho' she was in many ways a child.

"Ignore those men," I warned her. "Those are alligator smiles."

She frowned and shifted anxiously on the seat of the cart.

"And stop that," I said. "You'll get a splinter in your backside."

"I need a privy," she said. "Or a bush."

I pulled harder on Thomas Boon's rope. The donkey seemed determined to move as slow as possible. Ruth gave a little moan and gritted her teeth. We were all three of us in misery until we made our way clear of the French encampment and reached the large brick building. As we went around the back of it, a tall woman, yellow haired and pink faced, came out a door carrying a basket overflowing with stained linens. When she caught sight of us, she set the basket on the ground.

"You certainly took your time," she said with a frown.

Ruth bounced up and down on the seat, eyes desperate.

"Pardon me, ma'am," I started. "It's just that my sister needs–"

"Mister Wickham contracted for a full-size wagon. Do those women not know how much washing we have here? Dozens of lads puking. Half of 'em are French and I can't understand one word. But they puke same as our boys."

"Please, ma'am," Ruth interjected. "Privy?"

The woman jerked a thumb at a small building just visible beyond a well-trimmed boxwood hedge. Ruth scrambled off the cart, limping toward her goal as fast as she could.

"Many apologies for her rude tone," I said.

The privy door slammed behind Ruth, startling a flock of sparrows that had been hiding in the hedge.

The woman grunted. "We've all been in a similar state, one time or another. Ten thousand lads make these matters even more difficult than they normally are."

From the large building came a great roar of pain, suddenly extinguished.

"Poor sod," she muttered.

"Is this the hospital?" I asked.

She looked me over and then the donkey and the cart. "Not from here, are you?"

"Newly arrived." I met her gaze briefly. My toes curled in my boots. Was she good-hearted or evil? You could not tell that just by looking at the outside of a person, that was a sad truth. I crossed my fingers for luck in the folds of my skirt. "We're here to work but still learning our way around the town."

She nodded. "This was called the bedlam house. They built it as a hospital for those who lost their reason. The war has filled it with sick soldiers who have smallpox, the bloody flux, or broken limbs. Filthy creatures, all of them."

A harried-looking white man stepped out of the building carrying another basket of bloody linens. "I thought we'd arranged for a proper-size cart," he said roughly.

"Aye, but in this, too, we shall have to make do. Needs must, Mister Wickham, needs must. I'll have a word with Widow Hallahan on the morrow, impress upon her our circumstances."

The man muttered something low, set down his basket, and returned inside.

She motioned to me. "Give me a hand, lass."

I grabbed the other side of the biggest basket, and together we lifted it into the cart, then set smaller baskets beside it. As we finished, the privy door opened and Ruth emerged, looking much relieved. She hobbled back to us and climbed onto the seat without a word.

"Bess!" the man shouted from a window. "You're needed!"

"As always," she responded. "Don't set your breeches afire." She turned back to me. "Tell Widow Hallahan to hire a larger cart or send you girls round twice a day, every day. Ain't right to make these lads lie in filth like sickly hogs."

"Yes, ma'am," I said. "I shall make clear the severity of your need."

Ruth clucked her tongue and Thomas Boon walked. She waited until we were well clear of the woman's hearing before she said with wonderment, "Five seats in the privy. Never seen such a thing."

CHAPTER XVII

Sunday, September 9, 1781

TOOK A WALK TO TOWN WITH A NUMBER OF OUR GENTLEMEN AND TOOK A VIEW OF THE TOWN AS IT IS THE METROPOLIS OF VIRGINIA. THERE ARE SOME VERY ELEGANT BUILDINGS, SUCH AS THE COLLEGE PALACE, CAPITOL OR STATE HOUSE, IN WHICH IS ERECTED A STATUE OF MARBLE THE IMAGE OF LIEUT. GEN. BERKELY, GOVERNOR OF THE STATE OF VIRGINIA, &C.
—JOURNAL OF LIEUTENANT WILLIAM FELTMAN,
FIRST PENNSYLVANIA REGIMENT, ON ARRIVING
IN WILLIAMSBURG IN SEPTEMBER 1781

WILLIAMSBURG WAS MORE A TOWN than a grand city like Philadelphia or New York. One long street, wide enough for two carriages to pass each other with ease, ran from the hospital building at the west end, past the Governor's Palace near the center of the town, to the capitol building at the far end. Beyond the capitol camped Continental regiments mixed with militia units. When we reached that encampment, we turned around and passed through the town again. I was getting anxious, for I'd seen no signs of a laundry.

The street bustled with horse-drawn carriages and oxen pulling wagons filled with barrels, firewood, and supplies for the army. The smells of roasting meat and fresh bread made my nose twitch and my belly grumble. The tang of the burning charcoal of the blacksmith's forge and the stink of freshly deposited horse dung could not compare. Men and women hurried along the sidewalks on their errands to the print shop, the market, taverns, and coffeehouses. Those who bothered to take notice of us saw what they wanted to see: two slaves on a master's errand, one leading a mean-eyed donkey, the other riding a cart held together with pine tar and hope. I knew enough to use their blindness to our advantage. Our free papers would be given more weight the farther north we traveled, but they guaranteed nothing if we encountered evil and unscrupulous folk. The swamps and the mountains contained different dangers than cities, but in truth, I'd grown more comfortable with them.

In addition to the worries presented by the town, my troublesome mind kept drifting back to Curzon's strange manner. The farther north we'd traveled from Carolina, the quieter and more distant he'd become. He had returned to us with the donkey and cart, true enough, but mayhaps that was just a sign of the goodness of his heart; he'd not abandon us to starve. Mayhaps he'd been waiting for a place where I could find work and shelter before he went off on a journey of his own making. Was he already headed for Richmond or Baltimore or the wilderness mountains in the west?

The answers did not present themselves. Nor did the laundry.

On our third trip through town I began to worry that our presence was becoming conspicuous. As we passed the market, a short serving woman in a green and yellow striped bodice and green skirt motioned to me to follow her to a quiet spot under a linden tree, away from the hearing of others.

"You seem lost," she said quietly as she set down a basket heavy with green beans. Her speech was flavored with the notes of an island. Jamaica, mayhaps.

"Kind of you to notice," I said with relief. It went against all of my cautious habits to speak openly with a stranger, but the peril of our circumstance was quickly growing. "We're to deliver that washing to Widow Hallahan's, but I don't know where it is."

"Whole town is topsy-turvy," she said. "You're wanting to go east a block, turn left at the brick shop with the red door. One street later you'll see a tavern with the sign of a fat pig out front. Go along the alley behind the tavern, and you come to the laundry. Old Missus Hallahan runs the laundry, her son owns the tavern."

I studied the woman closer. Her hair was covered by a dark green kerchief and above that a straw hat. She wore a necklace of two pierced cowry shells around her neck, and her hands showed the strength that comes with constant labor.

"Is she a good mistress, Widow Hallahan?" I asked.

"Better than some," the woman answered. "You been hired out to her?"

"My sister and me, we're looking to hire ourselves out," I said. "We've been long on the road and need a safe place to work and restore ourselves."

Ruth watched us wordlessly.

The woman picked up her basket, watching the folks passing by, and taking their measure with skill. She waited until we were again in relative solitude, then leaned close to me.

"Do not linger here. The confusions of these days might seem in your favor, but they are not. With so many running for freedom, white people hereabouts are eager to steal the liberty of newcomers. Best take your chances with the British, if you can."

Without waiting for a reply, she quickly turned, her skirts flaring, and headed back to the market. I wanted to call out, to ask her name and to thank her.

I dared not, and that left me heartsore.

Once we'd been advised of the location, the laundry was easy enough to find. The one-story brick building with two windows on each side of the door was separated from the back of Gray Boar Tavern by a courtyard crisscrossed with ropes that were filled with drying clothes. I led Thomas Boon and Ruth under the flapping shirts and breeches and stopped in front of a pipe-smoking, wrinkle-faced white woman.

She put down the torn gray shift she was mending and stood, drawing on the pipe and blowing smoke from her mouth and nose. She scowled as she examined the baskets in the back of the cart. A strong smell of lye came from the open laundry door behind her.

"Are you Missus Hallahan?" I asked politely.

"That's what folks call the daughter-in-law. I'm the Widow Hallahan." Her nostrils quivered as she bent her face toward a basket. "Where's this lot from?" she demanded.

"The old bedlam house." I hefted a basket. "Where shall I set them, ma'am?"

She sighed. "By the door, with the rest of them."

Through the open windows behind her I could see steaming cauldrons big enough to bathe a cow in. Along the wall stood baskets heaped with dirty shifts, breeches, and all other manner of clothes. I spotted two that contained tidy stacks of clean linens, ironed and folded.

I lifted the next basket. "Miss Bess has more dirty linens waiting."

"I promised that woman nothing. Had another flibbertigibbet lass run off yesterday, all on account of a handsome soldier."

I carried another basket and nodded, which seemed to encourage her.

"What's the point of that?" she continued. "Soldiers are as dirty as they come, plus they drink all their pay, when they get paid, which is rare. Who wants that sort of trouble, I ask myself?"

I set the last basket on the ground. Ruth had climbed down and limped over to pet Thomas Boon between the ears.

"Miss Bess mentioned you might need some new help."

"Did she, now?"

"We could fetch her linens and do more besides." I swallowed to keep the nervous tone from my voice. "My sister and me can chop wood, haul water, work on the scrubbing board. I'm a fine hand with a needle as well."

"You're not from here," she said after a pause.

"No, ma'am." I thought quickly. "From the north. After our parents died, we came down here to find our aunt and uncle, but they'd moved on."

The woman's eyes had narrowed against the tobacco smoke. "Just arrived?"

"This very day." I kept my gaze steady, feeling her eyes on my cheek. The shawl could disguise the mark from a distance, but this close it was easily noted.

"The look of your hands tells me you know how to work," she said. "But that mark on your face gives me pause. How do I know you're not run away from your rightful owners?"

I slipped into the story that I'd repeated so many times, it had become a sort of charm or prayer. "Born free in the sight of God, ma'am, and into the arms of our parents, also free people. We have papers to testify to that."

I pulled the folded oilcloth from my haversack, unfolded it, and withdrew the free papers I'd written for us. She took them from me and held them upside down, at arm's length, pretending to read them. After a moment spent frowning at the words, she looked me over.

"How did you come by that mark, then?" she asked. "Caught thieving?"

"No, ma'am. It's proof that running with a red-hot poker is a foolish thing to do. Since the year of seventeen and seventy-six I've taken to calling it my country mark, for it resembles the letter *I*. *I* for 'Independence.'"

The woman's laughter made her choke, then cough. "Foolish notion, that is."

Before I could embroider more details on my story, two French soldiers come across the courtyard carrying more overflowing baskets. They walked straight into the laundry, which erupted with the loud protests of a young woman. "Oh, no, you don't. Take those right back to your monsir, you tell him we don't have time to wash your nasty drawers. You tell him–"

The old laundress interrupted her in a surprisingly powerful voice. "Be still, Elspeth. I got you some help. We can take them French togs." She returned the papers to me. "Two meals a day and you can sleep inside. Can't pay cash until the army pays me, Lord knows when that will be. But I'll only take you on, not your sister. She's sickly."

"She's stronger than she looks," I said hastily. "And the

donkey will only listen to her. What if she drove the cart and took care of the delivering and picking up of the baskets? Would that be worth feeding her, too?"

Widow Hallahan scratched her chin with the stem of her pipe and pondered a bit before saying, "Might could work. You"–she pointed the pipe at Ruth–"take yon cart back to the hospital for the rest. Tell Bess you'll bring the clean bandages and blankets to her tomorrow."

I caught my breath. Ruth couldn't drive the cart around alone. She'd see a chicken that looked friendly and chase after it, or turn down the wrong street and run into horrid circumstances. It didn't matter how hungry or tired or desperate we were. It didn't even matter that Curzon and Aberdeen were on the edge of leaving us on our own. This would never work. Our employ at the laundry had ended before it had begun.

"Pardon me, ma'am, but–" I started.

Neither Ruth nor the widow paid me any attention.

"Where the privy has five holes?" Ruth asked.

"Only one in town," the old woman said. "Go direct there and come straight back. Don't talk to no soldiers, and don't let them touch that donkey. They'll steal him in a flash, thieving varmints that they are."

"I'll go and come back," Ruth repeated, frowning, "ma'am, after I feed Thomas Boon. He's terrible hungry."

The old woman watched Ruth scratch Thomas Boon's neck. "I'll feed that donkey and you, long as you go and come back without tarrying."

Instead of agreeing straightaway, Ruth persisted with questions. "What will you feed him?"

I held my breath while Widow Hallahan studied first Ruth, then Thomas Boon, then Ruth again.

"Same grub as our horses—hay, oats, and mayhaps a few carrots when you get back from the hospital."

I smiled with relief. The old laundress had found the best way to guarantee Ruth's speedy return.

"I'll go direct and come straight back," she vowed solemnly. "On my honor, ma'am. Donkeys have a fondness for carrots."

CHAPTER XVIII

Sunday, September 9, 1781

The Brigade Commissaries are to apply forthwith to their Brigadiers or Officers Commanding brigades, and with their approbation respectively, fix upon a plan for collecting all the dirty tallow, & saving the ashes for the purpose of making soft soap for the use of the army.
—General Orders of George Washington

AFTER THOMAS BOON WAS FED, RUTH ventured off with the cart whilst I tried not to run after her. *Chin up*, I reminded myself. *All is well. It's a small town. She won't get lost. Keep stirring.*

My first task was to stir the great cauldron of boiling shirts with a stick the size of an oar. The two other lasses working for Widow Hallahan, Kate and Elspeth, were mean-spirited snipes, but I was too worried about Ruth to pay any heed to them.

All is well. Keep stirring. All is well. Keep stirring.

My nerves jangled and clanged loud as alarm bells until Ruth returned from the hospital, the cart full with more dirty laundry. I was certain that I'd suffer a collapse if Ruth was sent out again, but Widow Hallahan put her to scrubbing at stained linens with a horse-bristle brush. Thomas Boon was tied to a fence post, where he produced a prodigious amount of dung, which I had to clear away with a shovel.

Ruth giggled each time this occurred.

When not hauling donkey dirt, I took the dry laundry down from the line in to Widow Hallahan for ironing, then took the shifts and breeches out of the boiling rinse water, twisted them to remove as much water as possible, and laid them on the wash lines and across the hedge to dry.

It was hard and heavy work, but it made the time fly.

At the end of the day Widow Hallahan sent us to the tavern's back door to get our meal: sour stew scraped from the bottom of the pot, dried bread crusts, and water that smelled of fish. We ate outside. Kate and Elspeth ate meat pie in the kitchen, at the table with chairs. They each received three meals a day, not two, and they had proper sleeping quarters and a bed to sleep on in the tavern's attic. Widow Hallahan was another snake-souled woman; happy enough to take our labor, but too evil to treat us fair.

As the sun began to set, Kate and Elspeth went off, tra-la-la-ing about the fellows who'd been courting them. It fell to me to haul out the ashes and bring in enough wood for the morrow's fires. As soon as I laid out the damp-smelling sleep pallets on the flagstone floor, Ruth lay down, curled on her side, and fell asleep without a word to me.

I sat with my back against the wall and watched as she slept. The events of the day had unfolded themselves so quickly and altered our circumstances so dramatically, I could scarce begin to make sense of them all.

Church bells tolled seven times. (How strange it was to be marking time by the ringing of church bells again! Our clock had long been the setting sun, the rising moon, the hoot of hunting owls, and the chirp of lonely frogs.) I waited as the bells announced the passage of each quarter hour, pondering how many days we ought stay in Williamsburg and if it was truly safe to allow Ruth to venture forth alone in her cart again. Widow Hallahan had explained that most of the washing she did was for officers and gentlemen of the army. She had great hopes for the convenience of Ruth and a delivery cart, which meant my sister would be venturing out among strangers every day.

By the time the bells gave the count of eight of the clock, my list of worries was long and fretful. Atop it sat the possibility that Curzon had already abandoned us. I grimly wrapped my scarf to mask my scar, secured my hat, and locked Ruth inside the laundry, praying that she'd stay deeply asleep until my return. I also asked the Lord to forgive me for bothering Him so frequently, but these were indeed trying times.

I took the quieter back streets to the market, staying clear of the strolling groups of soldiers and officers already muddy in drink. Noise and candlelight spilled from windows open to catch the cooling breeze. Certain words and names streamed through the air like dark ribbons: "Cornwallis," "York," "battle," and "soon."

I found Curzon and Aberdeen standing at the edge of a boisterous crowd that surrounded a pair of mud-covered wrestlers. Curzon had evidently been watching for me, but Aberdeen was concentrating on the match. Curzon tapped him on the shoulder and said something, pointed toward the shadows behind the print shop.

"Ruth sleeps," I said as they joined me. "I dare not tarry."

"Indeed," Curzon said.

We quickly exchanged our stories of the day. After I shared both the good news and the bad about our prospects at the laundry, Curzon explained he'd found a blacksmith in need of a fellow who knew his way around a forge and hammer. Aberdeen boasted that he'd found work at a butcher in the French encampment, then he blathered on overly much about how much food he'd soon be eating. There was something about the way his eyes moved and the nervous manner of his hands that made me certain that he was lying.

"So Williamsburg is filled with rewards for us all," Curzon concluded.

"Nay," I said. "We cannot stay here. Ruth will never see danger if it crosses her path while she is out in the camp. We need to keep moving north, to Baltimore mebbe, though Philadelphia would be best."

"We can't," Curzon said flatly. "Not until we've earned coin and put some meat back on our bones."

"We must," I said. "A good-hearted woman in the market warned me. So many slaves have fled the farms hereabouts that their owners are desperate to replace them. We're in grave danger of being snatched up, all of us."

"The army will shelter us," Curzon said.

"The same army that handed you back to Bellingham?" I reminded him.

He shook his head. "All that has changed. The army has even more black soldiers now than it did at Valley Forge. It's desperate for skilled laborers like me. Williamsburg would be unsafe for us in ordinary times, but with the French and Continentals here, it's likely the safest place for us in the whole country."

"A pox on the blasted army," I muttered.

"I can help." Aberdeen interrupted our argument. "I can go with Ruth on her deliveries."

"How?" I asked. "You'll be up to your knees in cow carcasses every day."

Aberdeen glanced over at the wrestling crowd, where a loud "Huzzah!" had gone up, indicating a victory. "I'll find a way."

Curzon nodded. "Ruth listens to him better."

"Not always," I said.

"Yes," Curzon said. "Always, at least, thus far. Aberdeen will take good care of her, he's proved that. Mayhaps if she spends some time with him, and then some time with you each day, it will help soften her manner toward you."

I crossed my arms over my chest. It was hard to stay angry with Curzon when he made sense.

"You swear you'll stay by her side every step?" I asked Aberdeen. "You won't leave her on a whim?"

"What kind of scoundrel do you take me for?" he asked.

"Think of how happy she'll be," Curzon added.

That was part of my concern, though I did not want to say it aloud. Ruth's fondness for Aberdeen had grown steadily during our journey. The day would soon come when he would go his own way, of that I was sure. The sooner I could wean Ruth from her affection toward him, the better. But having him escort her through the camp for a day or so whilst I calculated our next move would keep her safe and occupied in a useful manner.

"All right, then," I said.

"I'll be there at sunup. I'll bring a treat for that ornery critter of hers too." Aberdeen studied the crowd again and nodded to someone distant. "I need to talk to that fellow yonder. Good night to you both."

CHAPTER XIX

Monday, September 10–Friday, September 14, 1781

THERE IS TO BE SOLD A VERY LIKELY NEGRO WOMAN AGED ABOUT THIRTY YEARS WHO HAS LIVED IN THIS CITY, FROM HER CHILDHOOD, AND CAN WASH AND IRON VERY WELL, COOK VICTUALS, SEW, SPIN ON THE LINEN WHEEL, MILK COWS, AND DO ALL SORTS OF HOUSE-WORK VERY WELL. SHE HAS A BOY OF ABOUT TWO YEARS OLD, WHICH IS TO GO WITH HER. THE PRICE AS REASONABLE AS YOU CAN AGREE. AND ALSO ANOTHER VERY LIKELY BOY AGED ABOUT SIX YEARS, WHO IS SON OF THE ABOVESAID WOMAN. HE WILL BE SOLD WITH HIS MOTHER, OR BY HIMSELF, AS THE BUYER PLEASES. ENQUIRE OF THE PRINTER."
—ADVERTISEMENT IN BENJAMIN FRANKLIN'S NEWSPAPER, THE *PENNSYLVANIA GAZETTE*

ABERDEEN WAS AS GOOD AS HIS WORD, to my surprise. Every morning he showed up at the laundry as if he'd nothing better to do than to escort Ruth and her donkey around town and the encampments. The whiff of deceit still clung to him; I was certain that he was not being honest about all of his doings. But he made Ruth giggle with his comical gallantry and led Thomas Boon about as if the creature were a prize-winning stallion. Ruth returned safely each evening; that was what I cared about the most. I asked no questions about his job with the butcher.

One night Ruth was so excited, she forgot to be sour with

me and told how they'd seen a group of soldiers racing crabs they'd caught in the river. The winning crab wore a crown of braided daisies and was paraded to great "Huzzahs" until it pinched the hand of the fellow holding it. 'Twas a rare delight to listen to her. Most days I was lucky if I heard more than a dozen words from her mouth, though she always spoke polite to Widow Hallahan and Miss Marrow, the tavern's cook, who made our meals.

I did not see Curzon in the days that followed. I tried to fool myself into believing that it did not matter. When asked about him, Aberdeen acted as if he did not know where it was Curzon worked or slept. When I pressed him for further information, he mumbled something nonsensical and hurried away. My suspicions about Curzon's curious behavior on our journey from Carolina—his sudden silences, his odd way of studying me when he didn't think I was watching him, and the dark moods that overtook him like a storm—shadowed me constantly.

Hallahan's did not wash the filthy clothes of ordinary soldiers. That work was done in the encampments by the soldiers themselves or their wives, who were hired by the army to wash and cook and mend. We cared for the clothing and bed linens of French and American officers, government men, and travelers in town to supply the army, and of course, the disgusting rags sent in by the hospital. The bundles and baskets arrived faster than we could manage them.

My days started before dawn. First the dirty water from the day before had to be hauled out of the kettles, bucket by bucket, and dumped outside, though not too close to the laundry or the tavern, or in the yard between the two, else we'd be tracking mud all day and increasing the chances that a stray shift or pair of breeches would fall to the mud and need washing all over again. Then came the refilling of the kettles with water pulled up, bucket by bucket, from the well. After the clean water had been poured into the kettles, I again built fires under them. Proper laundering required boiling-hot water and lots of it.

Kate and Elspeth always arrived late and yawning. They rarely spoke to me direct, but from their confabs I learned they were both indentured servants; Kate from Scotland, Elspeth from Ireland, and they had three years of labor left to pay off their voyage to America. They reveled in gossip and rumor and thought themselves superior to me. 'Twas tempting to tell them what I thought of them, but our situation was too unsettled. My best course was to work hard and pretend that they did not exist. I contented myself with dreaming of the days to come, when I'd be mistress of my own house, my own farm, on land I owned in Rhode Island, whilst they'd still be toiling for others, likely with a passel of lemon-faced brats holding on to their skirts.

The work of the washing took ages to complete. White shirts and underdrawers, stockings, neckerchiefs, and handkerchiefs needed to be sorted and washed separate from those that were dyed blue, brown, green, or red. To loosen the dirt, the clothes were first boiled in the massive copper kettle. Then they were scrubbed with lye soap made from ashes and pig's fat. Sometimes this was done with a brush, other times against an old scrubbing board that liked to take the skin off a girl's knuckles. Stains—and near everything had them—were treated with lye or pipe clay and then soaked in soapy water. To lighten the marks of sweat, ink, and muck found on shirts and underdrawers, we'd use scalding-hot milk, vinegar, or fresh piss. After another good boil with soap the clothes would be rinsed and rinsed and rinsed again in cold water, twisted hard to remove as much water as possible, then hung on the lines in the yard.

White clothes were dried in the sun, dark clothes were dried in the shade to preserve the color. We spread them on hedges and hung them on tree branches and on the ropes that crisscrossed the courtyard between the laundry building and the back of the tavern. When heavy with shirts, shifts, and, breeches, the yard seemed a massive ship with sails made of billowing laundry ready to pull us all across the sea to unknown lands.

Once everything was dry, we'd check the hems and seams to make sure all the lice had been drowned. Elspeth did most of the mending, and Kate's specialty was ironing. Though I could have done both of their specialties, Widow Hallahan made sure that the chopping of firewood fell to me.

The fair weather of our first days in Williamsburg turned foul just as we lay down to sleep on Thursday night. We'd already brought in the dry clothes from the lines, thank heavens, and we slipped into sleep to the playful tune of rain on the roof tiles.

Hours later we were jolted awake by the heaviest clap of thunder I'd ever heard. Ruth awoke with a shriek. Thomas Boon gave a mighty bray outside, echoing the nervous whinnies of the horses stabled nearby. I heard a bit of shouting in the street and went to the door to see if a house had caught on fire or, worse still, if the sound had actually been British cannons firing on the town. A lad running in the rain assured me that thunder was the only cause of the unholy racket. Another mighty rumble and blast of wind sent him dashing away.

I closed the door against the driving rain and sopped up

the puddles by the threshold. Ruth had already burrowed back under her blanket and was snoring softly. The wind howled and rattled the windowpanes. There would be no more sleep for me, that much was clear.

I spent the rest of the night emptying the cool dirty water and refilling the kettles, then tending the fires, so that the water was near boiling by the time Kate and Elspeth arrived the next morning. They had to start work right away instead of indulging in gossip for an hour, and it made them even more peevish than usual.

Their glum faces cheered me.

Widow Hallahan didn't arrive until Ruth and Aberdeen left to deliver clean shirts to the officers of the Virginia regiment. She bustled in faster than I'd ever seen her move.

"Pray tell me, lass," she inquired of me breathlessly, "are you accustomed to kitchen work? Assisting a cook and the like, keeping up with a mighty tide of dirty pots? These sluggards"–she pointed at the scowling girls–"are barely skilled enough for the laundry. Don't dare trust them to work in the mister's tavern."

I thought quickly. I'd learn more from tavern talk than the idle gossip in the laundry, though I would be more visible to anyone seeking me out.

Widow Hallahan's cheeks were flushed crimson and her hands were shaking. "Well? Can you do the work?"

"Indeed, ma'am, yes, I can."

"Hie yourself to the tavern, then. General Washington arrives today!"

CHAPTER XX

Friday, September 14, 1781

OUR FORCE IS DAILY GROWING STRONGER, AND I FLATTER MYSELF WE SHALL VERY SOON CIRCUMSCRIBE CORNWALLIS WITHIN NARROWER LIMITS THAN HE HAS LATELY BEEN ACCUSTOMED TO.
—LETTER OF VIRGINIA GOVERNOR THOMAS NELSON JR. ABOUT THE TROOPS GATHERING AT WILLIAMSBURG

MISS MARROW, A PALE WOMAN OF middle years with a nose that had been broken more than once, looked me up and down, handed me a scrub brush, and pointed to the collection of dirty pots. "More's a'coming. Make haste."

The tavern had been hired to supply an officers' dinner to celebrate the arrival of General Washington and the rest of the Continental and the French armies. In the interest of profit Mister Hallahan decided that the tavern should also serve customers as it did every day, so Miss Marrow was burdened with her daily tasks in addition to preparing the feast. She did not stop moving, flying from table to hearth to larder to smokehouse to cellar and then back again. Her commands to me were sharp and short: "Peel them taters. Shuck them oysters. Wash out that pie plate. Knead that dough. Pluck them pigeons. Slice the ham thin."

Shucking oysters gave my belly an unexpected turn. The

innards of an oyster look like a massive snot sneezed out of an ogre's nose. But there was no time to indulge in queasiness. When the oysters were shucked, I had to beat dozens of eggs for the cakes.

The smells of cinnamon, rising bread, and roasting meats were a vast improvement over the stench of dirty breeches and lye that hung in the laundry. The speed of the work was much faster, but 'twas a welcome relief to be away from the sharp-tongued nattering of Kate and Elspeth. Miss Marrow gave me leave to eat all of the ham and brown bread, and drink all of the cider, that I wanted, long as I kept working whilst I ate. Thus properly victualed for the first time in months, I felt strong enough to cook for the entire army.

By midday the front room was crowded with gentlemen and officers shouting in excitement and demanding meat pies and ale. Miss Marrow gave me a clean apron to pin atop my skirt and thrust a heavy serving tray into my hands.

"The mister will show you who gets what. Don't say nothing to nobody, and hurry back."

The rest of the afternoon I fair ran between the front room and the kitchen, serving the gentlemen, clearing away their dirty plates and mugs, and taking care of the washing up, while Miss Marrow continued to cook up the parade of dishes that would be served at the officers' feast. The men were so excitable about the prospect of battling the British in the days ahead that they paid me no mind, long as the food and drink kept coming. To my frustration, all the talk was about the newly arrived troops, mostly arguments about how many soldiers were there. For all the shouting and huzzahing, no one said anything that helped me understand better if Williamsburg was a safe place for us, or if we should flee as soon as darkness fell.

Late in the day the front room emptied as the gentlemen hastened to the encampment to be a part of the ceremonies honoring His Excellency George Washington. Miss Marrow and I both jumped out of our shoes at the monstrous sound of twenty-one cannon blasts. Mister Hallahan hurried in to tell us 'twas just a salute for the great general and his French friends, not an attack by the redcoats. Shortly after that, a fine wagon pulled up to the front door. We packed the food into crates and boxes, which were carried out to the wagon by handsome French soldiers. Several crates of wine were also loaded into the wagon.

After it drove away, Miss Marrow filled a plate with two slices of peach pie and set it on the kitchen table in front of me, saying simply, "You done good work. Thank you."

She ate in the front room with only Mister Hallahan for company. In truth, I felt bad on her account. First time all day she'd been able to sit herself down and take a bit of ease, and she had to listen to the pompous twit boast about the money and good fortune the war had brought to his establishment. Seemed to me he was sweet on her, though he had a wife at home busy with five children, according to Kate and Elspeth. I peeked through the door and saw Miss Marrow hastily eating her well-deserved meal, whilst the mister held forth about how he much preferred to work for the French, as they paid in coin where the Patriots paid mostly in promises. The poor woman was so bedraggled, she could scarce keep her eyes open, much less pretend to be interested in what he was saying.

I knocked and entered the front room.

"Pardon, miss," I said. "But I've finished with the washing up. Is there anything more you'd like me to do?"

Before Miss Marrow could answer, Mister Hallahan turned and looked me over. I gave a shudder, feeling as if a goose had walked across my grave.

"Who did my mother hire you from, girl?" he asked.

"She hired me on my own account, sir," I said, chiding myself for not waiting until he'd gone. "I'm freeborn, sir."

"She has papers, the missus told me," Miss Marrow added.

Hallahan sipped his mug. "She helped you in the kitchen, as well as serving out here?"

"Couldn't have done it without her," Miss Marrow said. "Go on back to the laundry, Isabel. And thank you again."

I found Widow Hallahan snoozing by the fire, a basket of buttons and a shirt in her lap, and no sign of Kate or Elspeth anywhere. I cleared my throat loudly. The old woman blinked the sleep from her eyes and sucked at her teeth.

"Done already?" she asked, as if I'd been gone a few moments instead of the entire day.

"Yes, ma'am," I said. "The French fellows came for it all in a big wagon. Mister Hallahan seems most pleased." I looked around the laundry. The fires under the washing kettles had gone out, but the ashes and cinders had not been removed. "Where are Kate and Elspeth?"

"Ugh." She shook her head. "Making cow eyes at the soldier boys, of course. Why are lasses so bedazzled by a uniform, can you tell me that? More Frenchies, I hear, in addition to our boys. You know what that means, don't you? More white uniforms to clean. Why do the Frenchies stick their lads in white uniforms? Do they not know that the business of war is filled with mud, blood, and dung?"

She stood and put her hand to her back. "Least our boys wear sensible togs, them that has uniforms. We can take some pride in that, we can." She yawned. "Your sister went off too."

"Beg pardon?" Fear stabbed at me. "Ruth isn't out delivering with Aberdeen?"

"Nay, the boy brought her back early. Said the whole camp's a hullabaloo what with all the new folks a'coming and a'going, and His Excellency parading about, and redcoats hiding behind every bush–"

"Ruth left," I interrupted her. "You let her wander off on her own?"

"Work for the day was done, not my place to tell the girl to stay or to go." She studied me hard. "Some reason you don't want her out there? Somebody looking for her, mayhaps?"

I grabbed my hat and scarf from the peg by the door and dashed outside without answering.

CHAPTER XXI

Friday, September 14, 1781

HIS EXCELLENCY GENL. WASHINGTON ARRIVED IN CAMP THIS AFTERNOON IN CONSEQUENCE OF WHICH 21 CANNON WERE DISCHARGED FROM THE AMERICAN PARK, THE WHOLE ARMY PARADED AND PAID HIM THE HONORS DUE TO HIS RANK.

—DIARY OF EBENEZER WILD,
FIRST MASSACHUSETTS REGIMENT

I MOVED THROUGH THE CROWDED streets as fast as I could without breaking into a run. *She's gone to watch the parade,* I tried to convince myself. *She'll want to see the fine horses that the officers ride upon.*

Scarier possibilities galloped into my brainpan. *What if she's been kidnapped, what if she's lost, what if she's hurt?!* . . .

I stopped thinking and simply prayed: *Please keep her safe, please keep her safe, please keep her safe,* the words matching the hasty beat of my boots on the cobblestones.

The army was now so large, it spilled over Williamsburg from end to end and miles beyond. I had to slow down as I reached the thick crowd of townsfolk who had come out to gawp at the new arrivals. The sun was sinking into the low-hanging, dark clouds to the west. The wind snapped the regimental flags with a sound like distant musket fire. Sergeants shouted orders to their men. There were thousands and thousands of soldiers, spread over miles of camp. I needed help.

I needed Curzon.

I pulled away from the crowd of townspeople and hurried into the middle of the encampment. Lanterns were being lit; pork and beef were roasting over fires. Fiddles and pipes played. Men and boys laughed and sang and called to one another as sparks from hundreds of campfires rose into the darkening sky. I followed the sharp smell of charcoal burning on a forge, seeking the regimental blacksmiths. None of them had seen a lad matching Curzon's description. Or hired one.

I couldn't find her. Or him, and he had lied about working at a forge.

Panic clawed its way up my throat. I wanted to scream Ruth's name over and over again, but that would bring unwelcome attention that could harm us all. Shouting for Curzon would do me no better. *Should I seek out Aberdeen? Should I go back to the laundry? Should I inquire with a Continental officer, or would I have better luck if I spoke with a French gentleman?*

What if I never see her again?

Suddenly I heard the loud braying of an irritated donkey. A familiar, annoying donkey whose noise seemed to my ears like the trumpeting of a host of angels.

Thomas Boon!

I turned my head to locate the source of the noise, then followed it past four rows of tents to a clearing that had become a small village of its own, with sutlers selling their wares whilst soldiers ate, conversated, and played at cards and dice. At the far edge of the clearing Thomas Boon had his ears laid back and was showing his teeth at a tall soldier dressed in Continental dark blue. The man laughed loudly, grinning, as did Curzon, who slapped the fellow on the back.

The most momentous shock came from the sight of my sister. Ruth was sitting in the donkey cart and laughing with the two as I had not heard her laugh since she was seven years old. Whatever the cause of the mirth, she laughed hard enough to clutch her belly and wipe a laugh-tear from her eye.

I hurried over. "What possessed you to run off like that?" I asked Ruth. "You scared me to death! Don't you know how dangerous–"

"Hold up there." Curzon touched my elbow. "She didn't run off. I stopped at the laundry just as she returned from her delivery. Told the old lady with the pipe to tell you we'd be with the First Massachusetts Regiment, near the sutlers."

"You swear you told her that?"

He gave me a look of frustration. "Have I ever lied to you?"

I arched an eyebrow in reply.

"About anything important, that is," he added. "Ruth has been with me the whole time. She didn't run off. You want to holler at someone, then holler at the old woman, though she'll probably throw you out on the street if you do."

"Apologies," I said to Ruth. "I didn't mean to shout at you." I reached for the lead rope, feeling confuddled and out of sorts. "We need to go back."

"Wait, wait," Curzon said. "There's no rush, no danger. Don't you remember Ebenezer?"

"Good evening to you, Miss Gardener." The tall soldier bowed. "Is it still Miss Gardener? Or have you become a married lady?"

I gave him a quick study. His sleeves stopped short of his wrists, and his coat was not big enough to be buttoned over his broad chest. His freckled face was smudged with dirt, as were his hands. He looked like a thousand other soldiers I'd seen, except he was a full head taller than most. But when he flashed a gap-toothed grin, I knew him in an instant: Ebenezer Woodruff, Curzon's friend from the battlefields of Saratoga, who'd helped us escape Valley Forge.

"Good evening, Mister Woodruff." I inclined my head a bit, unsure of what else to do.

"He's Sergeant Woodruff now," Curzon said with a grin of his own.

"Sergeant," I said politely. "Congratulations."

"'Tis a delight to find you here"–Ebenezer gave the hint of a second bow–"and to make the acquaintance of Miss Ruth. Seems you have many adventures to tell."

His courtly manner surprised me. The Eben Woodruff I remembered was a rough-cut and bumbling farm boy, though stouthearted and loyal. Didn't seem possible he could grow up into a sergeant.

"This is not the best time nor place to tell about them," I said.

"Indeed," Eben said. "Mayhaps I could come round some eve. We could go for a stroll." His eyes darted to Curzon. "All of us, of course."

I had the oddest sensation that he was trying to be charming to me. The notion so flustered me, I could not think clear for a moment.

"Have you heard how General Washington fooled the British into thinking he was about to attack New York?" Curzon asked me with delight. "Ebenezer and the rest of the northern army have been racing down here to meet up with the French. 'Tis the best strategic maneuver ever!"

He looked more like his old self than he had in months–alert but at ease, a half smile on his mouth. Despite his bad experience with the army, he was always in the highest of spirits when it was close by.

The note of longing in his voice pierced through me. It didn't matter if he worked for a regimental blacksmith, or drove a supply wagon, or armed himself with a shovel and worked as a laborer; the dream proclaimed by the bigwigs in Philadelphia of a nation built on freedoms excited his mind like nothing else. Curzon had paid his debt to me. It was clearer than ever that this was where he wanted to be.

The encampment seemed darker, as if the fires were all burning low. I shook once with a chill, feeling very alone even though I was surrounded by thousands of souls. I forced a false, polite smile. "I'm afraid that's a tale best saved for another time. We need to get back to the laundry."

"No, we don't," Curzon argued.

"You don't," I corrected, "but Ruth and I do. Get back in the cart, sister."

Ruth crossed her arms over her chest and sulked.

"I'd be honored to escort you," Ebenezer offered.

"Not necessary, you rogue," Curzon said. "I'll see them safely out of the camp. You should see if there's any supper left."

"There's never enough supper." Ebenezer smiled ruefully. "I was mistaken when I told you that eating was the best part of soldiering, wasn't I? In any case, good evening to you all. Stop by later, old friend, and I'll tell you more about . . ." He glanced at me and seemed to temper his words. "About what we discussed earlier."

Curzon was a regular Mister Ramblemouth as we made our way back through the town, nattering on about all the news he'd learned from Ebenezer: the army's lightning-quick march from New York, the defeat of the British in West Florida by the troops of the Spanish king, and tales of their old friends from Valley Forge. As we passed the market, he turned and caught me staring at him.

"Why the glum face?" he asked. "Aren't you excited?"

I waited until we'd walked clear of a thick knot of people before I answered. "Why should I be excited?"

"His Excellency has come to town!" he replied, as if the answer were an obvious one. "The better part of our army is here, ready to fight shoulder to shoulder with the French, who care even less for the British than we do. I can taste the victory, I tell you."

"You hammer horseshoes," I said, "or rather, you would be if you were, in fact, working for a blacksmith. You lied about that, didn't you?"

"There are many ways to help the cause of freedom," he began, puffed up and putting on air as if he were a statesman or other sort of fool.

"A pox on your ridiculous notions," I said.

Ruth slapped the reins to make Thomas Boon walk. She began humming a fife song that had been played near Eben's campfire. Curzon and I walked the next block without speaking.

We used to argue endlessly about the Revolution. He was a firm believer in the Patriot cause. He loved to prattle on about the Declaration of Independence and how the United States of America promised to be a new sort of nation. I was forever reminding him that we'd been enslaved by both Patriots and Loyalists, and that neither side was talking about freedom for people who looked like us. Things had grown so heated that we'd had to agree not to discuss it.

"What if I said I was thinking of enlisting again?" he asked.

And now the conflict had cracked open in our laps once more, stinking like a rotted egg.

I stopped. "I'd say you were an addlepated fool."

He acted as if he hadn't heard me. "If we can defeat Cornwallis, it could well mean the end to the war. Now that the French are openly helping us, King George fears he'll lose his islands in the Caribbean, as well as America. General Washington needs all the skilled soldiers he can get." He threw back his shoulders. "Like me."

I snorted. "Where was the good general when the army handed you over to Bellingham? Did His Excellency intervene because of your fine soldiering skills? Of course not. He owns hundreds of slaves himself. The Patriots fight only to be free of British taxes. They don't care a whit for your freedom, nor mine."

"That's changing," he argued.

"Balderdash," I replied.

Ruth's gaze went back and forth from my face to Curzon's as we argued. Her hum changed to a loud whistle.

"Did you not see how many sons of Africa are soldiers in uniform back there?" He pointed back toward the encampment. "Black men make up a goodly portion of it, as many as one in five or one in four by some counts. In fact, your beloved Rhode Island has a regiment with fellows earning their freedom by fighting as Continental soldiers."

"'Earning,'" I pointed out. "Not 'earned,' which means by the end of the war, if they survive, some varmint judge could well clap them back into chains. We'd be better off running to the British."

My words shocked him like a slap to the face. "Have you lost your senses?"

"Actions speak louder than words," I said. "The redcoats don't promise a soldier's uniform or battlefield glory, they just put fugitive slaves to work. But they work in freedom and can leave whenever they wish."

"The blasted British want to enslave our entire country!" Curzon yelled.

His voice was so loud that heads turned. A small group of soldiers clustered at a tavern door shouted a hearty "Huzzah!" and lifted their mugs in approval of his sentiments.

"You are a muzzy-headed blatherskite," I muttered.

"And you're a vexatious cabbagehead," he replied.

"Stop fighting," Ruth said. "I don't like it."

Neither did I, though I was not prepared to say it aloud, not when Curzon was afloat on his patriotical fantasies of war.

We walked in silence until the sign of the Gray Boar Tavern came into view. Curzon halted the donkey just beyond the reach of the light that spilled out of the windows. "I have something to say."

I put my shoulders back and tried to present myself in a calm manner, ready for his apology, prepared to ask forgiveness for my own sharp tongue and to have a proper confab about how we could get away from this danger-soaked place.

"I'm listening," I said in a gracious tone.

Curzon removed his cap. "I enlisted three days ago."

I was so stunned, I could not speak for a moment. The distance that had been growing between us suddenly became a separation. He had torn the cloth of our friendship in two.

"You have a bizarre attachment to a cause that cares nothing for you," I finally said.

He cast down his eyes and scuffed at the dirt with the toe of his boot. "Figgered you'd say something like that."

Thomas Boon shook his head. Ruth leaned forward and patted his rump. Curzon cracked his knuckles.

"You must choose a side, Isabel," he said softly. "Rebel or redcoat."

"I am my own army," I said. "My feet and legs, my hands, arms, and back, those are my soldiers. My general lives up here"–I tapped my forehead–"watching for the enemy and commanding the field of battle."

"This is not an occasion for jesting."

"I am dead serious," I said. "Neither redcoats nor rebels fight for me. I see no reason to support them."

He stared at me intently. "What do you fight for, then?"

"I don't want to fight anymore. I want to be as far away from armies and war as possible. I want to live the rest of my days without fear."

He frowned. "No one wants to be in a war. But that is our circumstance. You must choose a side, else you become a target for both."

I hesitated. If we'd had this conversation the previous winter, I might have added that I wanted him at my side. I might have confessed that he'd make a fine husband for me, and that I would be a fantastical good wife. But between us now lay a poisonous swamp of misunderstandings, arguments, hurt feelings, and sadness.

"What do you fight for?" I asked.

"Freedom." The firm resolve on his face made him look like someone I barely knew. "Freedom for everyone. That's a cause worth dying for, don't you think?"

"You can't help anyone if you're dead," I said.

"At least I care enough to try."

"What do you mean?"

"The rest of the world can go hang, for all you care."

"The rest of the world hasn't done me any favors."

"What about me?" he demanded.

"You've done your share, as I did for you."

"So the accounts between us are balanced?" he asked in a raw voice. "You are well satisfied that I owe you nothing, having helped you recover Ruth? I can tell you that you owe me not a single thing. Done and done."

I swallowed hard. "Is that how the columns add up to you?"

"Indeed they do, Miss Gardener." He stepped away from me, his eyes hard and angry. "I shall take my leave of you now."

"Do as you wish," I said, trying to ignore how badly his words hurt. "You need not trouble yourself with us anymore."

"Don't you worry, Country," he said in a voice that cut through me. "I shall never trouble you again."

CHAPTER XXII

Saturday, September 15–Wednesday, September 26, 1781

AMONG THE PLAGUES THE BRITISH LEFT IN WILLIAMSBURG, THAT OF FLIES IS INCONCEIVABLE. IT IS IMPOSSIBLE TO EAT DRINK, SLEEP, WRITE, SIT STILL OR EVEN WALK ABOUT IN PEACE ON ACCOUNT OF THEIR CONFOUNDED STINGS. THEIR NUMBERS, EXCEED DESCRIPTION, UNLESS YOU LOOK INTO THE 8TH CHAPTER OF EXODUS FOR IT.
—LETTER FROM ST. GEORGE TUCKER TO HIS WIFE, FANNY TUCKER, JULY 11, 1781

CURZON WAS TRUE TO HIS WORD. DAYS passed, some filled with cold rain, others with an unwholesome, stifling heat, but none of them brought any sign of him.

He ended our friendship, I told myself firmly. *He chose his own path.*

I stirred boiling pots of breeches and shirts. I carried trays in the tavern. I split wood, hung laundry, heated irons, and hauled water, taking on extra tasks in a effort to tire myself out and drive the thoughts of him from my mind.

I worked and worked and worked to quiet the sorrowful truth.

He chose the war over me.

More French and American soldiers arrived each day. The air filled with dust and the noise of thousands of men practicing their musket firing and maneuvering drills. Hundreds of wagons heavy with supplies and tools crowded the roads. Animals, too: horses for pulling the wagons and carrying officers; and cattle, sheep, and pigs destined for the butcher's corral. To round out the rations, countless barrels of flour, cornmeal, salt, beans, and peas were unloaded from boats at the river landing.

The tavern was so busy that I was often sent there to serve at mealtimes, and sometimes to help with the washing up as well. Mister Hallahan promised to pay me extra for my tavern work as soon as the Continentals settled their accounts with him. I gladly took on the work.

'Twas much easier to learn of the circumstances of the war in the tavern than in the laundry. A captain eating bean soup at the Gray Boar loudly proclaimed that the encampment held more people than the great city of Boston. The other men argued with him, but the captain had seen the muster rolls, and the numbers did not lie, he said. Mister Hallahan poured a steady stream of ale, wine, and rum for his customers. Miss Marrow prepared pots of barley soup, roasted rabbits, and onion pies, and I carried all of it to the tables. Messengers rode in and out of the town in anxious clouds of dust, sometimes stopping at the Gray Boar to quench their thirst. Everyone was starved for the latest news from Richmond and Philadelphia, including me.

When I could, I smuggled newspapers under my skirts and read them in the privy. Spain and the Netherlands had promised to help America. The third son of King George, a young fellow called Prince William Henry, was in the British-held city of New York. I thought mayhaps the redcoats might crown the lad King of the United States. I was not certain if that would end the war or guarantee that it dragged on for generations.

In the same newspaper I found the word "Aberdeen," referring to the city in Scotland. I tore it out to give to our Aberdeen the next day, so he could learn the spelling of his name. Though I still did not trust him entirely, he was as regular as a well-wound clock, and it cheered Ruth to be in his company. I vowed to watch him closer, to see if I could figger why it was that she so preferred him to me.

Our second full Sunday in Williamsburg, Widow Hallahan reluctantly gave us leave to attend church. We walked slow, for it was a glorious day: bright skies, gentle breeze, no stained breeches to scrub. I considered not going to church at all, but Momma would not have approved of that. She'd taken us to a small, clapboard-sided Congregational church when Ruth was a baby. They didn't have churches like that here. Aberdeen had heard of a man named Gowan who preached in the Baptist manner to slaves and free folk. I wanted very much to hear this Baptist manner, but the congregation met in a grove miles away, and I could not afford the time nor the risk of searching for it.

We headed for the big brick church in the center of town, Bruton Parish Church. I studied Ruth's gait as she walked. Her foot was healing rapidly—helped, no doubt, by being able to eat every day and sleep soundly each night. I still didn't have a good measure of her abilities. One day I'd think certain she had the mind of a child of five; the next I'd see a flash, a spark that made me suspect she understood quite a bit more. She was clever enough to know when Elspeth tried to give her extra chores. She would tell the kinds of falsehoods that an ordinary lass of twelve might tell, pretending she hadn't eaten the last of the bread, or that she had no idea how the ashes had been dumped just outside the door instead of in the ash barrel.

When I confronted her about her small lies, she simply crossed her arms and stared over my shoulder. She'd talk to the donkey, to Elspeth, Kate, Aberdeen, Widow Hallahan, and even the old lady's friends who dropped by with a small bit of washing, but if I entered a room, she'd like as not snap shut her mouth like an irritated turtle and crawl into her shell. Even on her best day she rarely spoke more than a few handfuls of words to me. But as we walked to church, she cheerfully greeted every cat, dog, pig, and sparrow we passed.

Outside the church we watched as gentry and army officers entered, the gentlemen doffing their hats, the ladies smiling. If we joined them, we'd be required to walk up narrow stairs and sit in the upper gallery. That was the only place for black-skinned folk. When we lived in New York, I'd thought that being in the gallery meant our prayers would get to God first because we sat closer to heaven. I was wrong. All it meant was that the white people in church wanted to chain our souls as much as our bodies.

Instead I positioned Ruth and myself under a mulberry tree at the edge of the graveyard, close enough to the church that we could hear the prayers and hymns through the open windows. A scraggly, half-grown hound bounded between the gravestones and rolled on his back so that Ruth could scratch his belly.

I leaned against the trunk of the tree, delighting in the luxury of a moment's peace. Had it been only two weeks since we arrived in Williamsburg?

The minister's sermon floated on the breeze. "Pray for the happy period when tyranny, oppression, and wretchedness shall be banished from the earth; when universal love and liberty, peace and righteousness, shall prevail. . . ."

I bowed my head. Most every person sitting upon the fine pews in there owned people who had been kidnapped from their families or held in bondage from birth. The foul hypocrisy of the sermon made me want to scream loud enough, long enough, to make the church, the Governor's Palace, the laundry, even the building used for a hospital, crumble like the walls of Jericho. Maybe then the walls around their hearts would fall too.

The congregation entered into song, praising God and His mercy.

I prayed. I thanked God for leading me to Ruth. I asked Him to help me in my constant struggle to hold my tongue and control my temper and become a patient person. I asked Him again to soften Ruth's manner toward me and to help me show her how much I loved her. I tried to pray for Curzon's safety, but my confuddled sentiments had me thinking that he deserved to be shot in his backside, and that made me feel the worst sort of devil. My mother and the Lord Himself would be disappointed in me for such thoughts. I sighed at my failure.

Ruth looked up. "You poorly?"

"Nay," I said.

"You sound like a sick horse." She imitated my sigh in an overly dramatic fashion.

"Time to go back," I said, starting for the road. "And I am not a horse."

She muttered something that sounded like "'Tis a shame."

I began to hope that the coming battle might continue to be postponed. I cared not what would cause this; wet gunpowder would suffice, or an outbreak of the bloody flux suffered by both armies. If the American and French would stay content in Williamsburg, and the British holed up ten miles away in Yorktown, for just a few more months, winter would arrive. Armies rarely fought once the winter winds began blowing. We would benefit from such a circumstance, Ruth and me. Mister Hallahan would surely have the coin to pay my tavern wages, and our continued work in the laundry would pay for our lodging and meals. By spring we'd be in fine fettle and ready to walk home to Rhode Island.

I amused myself by imagining that one day I might serve General Washington his chicken pie. I'd offer the suggestion of the army overwintering in Williamsburg, and he'd see it at once as a brilliant military tactic, and he'd give me a Spanish silver dollar for being so clever.

Such thoughts were proof that I was much in need of sleep.

CHAPTER XXIII

Thursday, September 27, 1781

I NOW PERCEIVED THAT MY CASE WAS DESPERATE, AND THAT I HAD NOTHING TO TRUST TO, BUT TO WAIT THE FIRST OPPORTUNITY FOR MAKING MY ESCAPE.
—BOSTON KING, WHEN A LOYALIST MILITIAMAN THREATENED TO REENSLAVE HIM

JUST WHEN IT SEEMED THAT THE countryside could not hold another soldier, musket, or canteen, General Washington declared it was time to fight.

"We all knew this day would come," Widow Hallahan said as we gathered in the courtyard. "You two." She pointed at Kate and Elspeth. "I expect you want to visit your lads."

The girls nodded, faces flushed and eyes wide.

"Don't forget your modesty," the widow warned them, "and be back by dark."

Ruth unhitched Thomas Boon from the wagon. Aberdeen headed for the water pump, buckets in hand. Widow Hallahan studied me.

"You need to help with the serving," she said. "Tavern's full to bursting with sutlers. But when you're done with that, take the rest of the afternoon off, you and your sister. Mind you get back in time to serve the supper." She reached into the pocket of her apron and pulled out a tarnished coin, which she handed to me. "Buy yourself something nice."

"Thank you, ma'am." I curtsied and hurried away before she changed her mind.

After I'd finished in the tavern, I made my way with Ruth and Aberdeen through the crowded streets to the baker's. Ruth was determined that we should eat gingerbread, and indeed the smell of it was enticing.

"You can only buy a small loaf for that coin," the baker's lad said.

"That should be enough for the largest loaf, enough for six people," I protested.

"War troubles make everything more costly," he explained.

"Allow me." Aberdeen pulled a small handful of shillings and pence from his pocket. "We'll take the largest loaf you have, if you please, sir."

As if that weren't startling enough, Aberdeen then led us to a merchant that sold all sorts of sundries, and there he bought a child's toy fashioned of wood. It was a stick with a cup at one end, and a ball attached to a string on the other. The trick of the thing, he explained, was to catch the ball in the cup. 'Twas much harder to do than it seemed.

He handed it to Ruth with a dramatic flourish. "For you, Miss Ruth."

She giggled and took it with a shy smile.

"She needs new stockings more than a child's frippery," I said.

"Isabel don't like fun," Ruth told Aberdeen.

"Let's go to the river," he said. "Mebbe that will lift her mood."

As we walked down the well-worn path, the wind swirled, bringing first the sweet smell of the bake ovens, then the stink of rotting hides and offal from the slaughtering pens, and finally, the heavy stench of fish. I had a rare longing for the smell of the ocean, the clean salt air that would sometimes roll all the way to our door at the farm where we had been children.

Ruth walked ahead of us, nibbling on the gingerbread and watching the hummingbirds, thrushes, and meadowlarks flitting through the trees. When we reached the water, she settled herself upon the grass and played with her new treasure. Aberdeen and I sat in clear sight of her, but far enough away that she could not overhear our words. It was the first truly private moment we'd had since we entered Williamsburg. I sensed that he had planned all of this. His aim was to hold a confab with me, not just to delight Ruth. Coming after his display of coin in the shops–coin that no butcher's boy could possibly have earned in a few weeks' time–I found myself mighty suspicious.

I looked around to confirm that no one could hear us and then spoke plain. "Where did you get that money?"

Aberdeen plucked a long blade of grass and chewed the end of it.

"Have you turned thief?" I demanded.

He acted as if he hadn't heard me. "You still aiming for Rhode Island when all this rot is finished?"

"Stealing will land you in jail or a grave. And yes, Rhode Island is our destination. Our home."

"Is it true what Ruth said"–he leaned back on his elbows–"that you want the British to win?"

I narrowed my eyes, even more wary than before. "Why would Ruth say that?"

He gave a snort. "Watches you like a hawk, she do. Tells me all kinds of things about you: the way you say you ain't hungry, then give her your supper; the way you turn the other cheek when those looby laundresses are rude to you. She also says you want the British to win."

The sun bounced off the river, throwing sparkles into the air. Ruth happily played with her new toy. She was content in that moment, smiling. The calm peace on her face recollected the way she'd looked as a small child, before our lives became fear-filled and muddled.

"Does she say why she's mad at me?" I asked.

He ignored my question again. "Is that true? Do you favor the British cause?"

I studied him close. He'd grown a bit over the summer too. There was a fine cut on his chin and a patch of whiskers by his ear, signs that he'd begun to shave his face with a thin-bladed knife or the sharpened edge of an oyster shell. His shirt was new and his sling gone, for his broken collarbone was healed. If he'd been nine when Ruth arrived at Riverbend, then he was fourteen years old now, a difficult age in the best of circumstances.

"Did you rob a Frenchman?" I asked. "That butcher you claim to work for?"

He spoke quieter. "I work for the army, Isabel. I count the enemy's men and guns. I listen outside tavern windows when they are muddy in drink." He again patted the coins in his pocket. "The army pays good money for secrets."

"You're a spy?"

He nodded, excitement glowing in his face.

"You are an addlepated lackwit," I said. "I was a spy once. It ruined our lives."

"Mayhaps you chose the wrong side."

"I chose the same side as you and Curzon." Saying his name aloud caused a bewildering ache in my chest. I cleared my throat. "I spied on the British on the orders of a Patriot captain who promised to help Ruth and me escape New

York. He betrayed us. They'll betray you, too. Might as well put your legs in chains right now."

Aberdeen eyed me calmly. "Didn't say I spied for the Patriots."

I paused as the meaning of his words sank in.

"You work for"–I whispered the last words–"the British?"

He grinned.

"They're just as bad!" I declared.

"Slaves running to the British get freed," he argued.

"Only if owned by Patriots," I added. "Loyalist slaves are returned."

"So you lie to them. They won't know, not around here. The redcoats just want hard workers. Fight for them, and you get to be your own master."

"They don't fight for us," I insisted. "Neither army does."

"Now you're just talking foolishness," he said. "You and Ruth need to join me, you do. When we win, we gonna sail to Scotland. Gonna find the city what's got the same name as me, like in that newspaper you showed me."

His eyes were filled with dreams of glory, an affliction common to boys who had never been soldiers.

"They promise you that?" I stood and shook out my skirts, too upset to stay at the side of such a fool. "Did they promise that they had jobs for me, for someone like Ruth?"

"You need to listen–" he started.

"Army promises are only useful in the privy, when you need to wipe your backside."

"Sit yourself down." He nodded his head slow, as if I were a child and he were a wise, old granddad. "You're just sore on account of being so tired."

I wanted to pitch him in the river. "Come, Ruth," I called. "We must go."

Aberdeen stood up and spoke quickly. "You did me a good turn, helping me come this far. So listen: First chance you get, head to Yorktown. Half day of walking and you come across rice fields. Once past them, cut through the woods on the left side. Go through the woods to the river, walk downstream to the town."

"We're not going to Yorktown."

"Tell the guards that you and Ruth can sew and cook. Talk fancy-parlor good. I know you can."

"I don't trust the British," I said.

"So you staying here?"

"Now, Ruth!" I called. "Don't want to make the widow angry at us."

Aberdeen leaned forward. "You'll stay here and support the rebels?"

"I don't trust the Patriots, either," I said. "The winner of this ridiculous war matters not to me."

"The battle's coming, Isabel," he insisted. "You must choose a side."

CHAPTER XXIV

Thursday, September 27, 1781

IT IS POSSIBLE THE SLAVE MAY HAVE FALLEN INTO YOUR HANDS, THO' HE HAS PRACTICED EVERY STRATAGEM TO CONCEAL HIMSELF BY DENYING HIS MASTER'S NAME, & CHANGING HIS OWN & HIS DIALECT; BUT THE MARKS ON HIS SHOULDERS CANNOT BE REMOVED.
—LETTER FROM JUDGE EDMUND PENDLETON TO VIRGINIA CONGRESSMAN JAMES MADISON, WHO LATER BECAME THE FOURTH PRESIDENT OF THE UNITED STATES

THE CHURCH BELL WAS TOLLING ELEVEN of the night as I closed the back door of the tavern. I wove my way past the maze of damp laundry in the courtyard. The final day of the army's presence in Williamsburg had brought more work than anyone had counted on. I was tired of being tired, and I was cold to the bone. All I wanted to do was to sleep without worrying about my sister or Aberdeen or any soldiers at all. I picked up a few sticks of wood for the fire, already thinking about how lovely it would feel to lie down.

As I entered the laundry, something crunched under my foot. I knelt and squinted in the half-light. Muddy boot prints dirtied the floor. Man size. Kate or Elspeth had allowed one of their soldiers to visit and had been too lazy to clean up after him.

I'd wash the floor in the morning.

Ruth snored loudly. I cleared the ashes from the hearth and set them in a tin bucket, another task left undone by the lazy girls. There were a few scraps of unburnt paper in the ashes, which was odd. Mayhaps Elspeth had had her lad start the fire. The buffoon must have used newspaper instead of hot coals.

I stacked kindling, then added smoldering coals from the wash kettle fire to set them ablaze. I sat on the stool in front of the fire and took off my shoes and stockings. The loud crackling and popping of the wood made Ruth stir in her sleep, but she did not wake. Few could best her when it came to sleeping.

As the flames rose, I looked about the laundry. The dried boot prints tracked across the floor several times, then retreated to the door. 'Twas a pity these girls did not seek the affection of fellows accustomed to scraping their boots before they entered a place.

Then my eye caught the glint of something stuck between the floorboards: a small button carved from shell. I did not remember seeing one like it on any of the washing we'd cared for. It most resembled the few that Missus Serafina had given Ruth in her haversack. Ruth cherished those buttons, as she did all things given to her by the old couple. She would never have treated them with such neglect.

I searched and found a second shell button in the corner, along with a scattering of dried seeds. Such was the power of my fatigue that I sat dumbfounded in the firelight, staring at the tiny objects in my hand for several moments before the truth of their origin crashed upon me like thunder.

I leapt to my feet, dashed the length of the building, and scrambled up the small ladder to the loft in the north end of the room. I felt my way in the gloom past the crocks of soap, vinegar, and lye, taking care not to overturn or break anything, searching for our haversacks. They were not where I had carefully stored them on a high shelf, but shoved into a nest of tattered wicker baskets.

I slung the haversacks over my shoulder, quickly made my way back to the firelight, and dumped out the contents. Ruth's sack contained a gourd, buttons, pins, and the embroidered handkerchief that Miss Serafina had given her, along with the stockings that no longer fit, wrapped around the cloth doll.

My haversack was a complete jumble. My hatchet and knife were both there but had been thrown in carelessly. More upsetting was the state of my collection of seeds; I'd collected and protected them so carefully over the years, carrying them for thousands of miles safe in the dampproof pockets I'd fashioned out of oilcloth. Less than half were safe in their covering. The rest were heaped together at the bottom of the sack.

Ruth rolled onto her back. Her hand opened, showing another shell button in her palm. She must have done all of this, but why? Was she going to be mad at me forever?

Then I realized what was missing. Our free papers.

Gone!

In defiance of Widow Hallahan's rules I lit a candle and carried it back to the loft, heart in my throat. I picked through the pile of broken baskets, moved aside the dusty spinning wheel, and peered into the soap crocks. I unrolled moldy, ancient rugs. I emptied a crate of old rags and balls of twine.

All I found were mouse droppings and a few tiny bones.

I returned to the hearth. It couldn't have been Ruth. Could it? She knew our position here was perilous. She knew those papers were our only security. That is to say, I thought that she knew it. Had she tucked them under her pallet? Hidden them in her pocket? Had I, in my own fog of fatigue, moved them and forgotten it?

A gust of wind crept in under the door. The fire sputtered. I absently used the tongs to rearrange the wood so that it would burn better.

Paper. *Paper!*

I overturned the tin bucket of ashes and spread them on the hearthstones, then plucked out the singed bits of paper. Two were smudged with the marks of dirty fingers. The third showed the careful script of my handwriting. I'd written *clared to be fr.*

"Wake up!" I shook Ruth roughly. "Did you do this?"

She blinked, sleep-muddled, and sat up on her pallet.

"Did you use the paper in my haversack to start the fire?"

She gazed out the window. "'Tis not morning."

"Morning or night, it matters not!" I picked up the shell button that had fallen from her hand. "You took down the sacks and you played with the buttons."

She nodded.

"Did you play with your doll?"

She nodded again.

"And my seeds?"

She hesitated, then gave a little nod.

"What about the papers? In my sack?"

She shook her head. "Don't holler."

"Did you use them to build up the fire, mayhaps? It's a cold night."

She looked at the hearth, then shook her head again.

"Don't lie to me."

"Mister Walter doesn't like lies. You're mean. You're mean and ugly."

"This is more important than if I'm mean! Did you burn the papers?"

She yawned. "Mister burned the papers."

"No, he didn't, he's not here! Why are you so foolish!" I yelled. "You did it, didn't you? You've ruined everything! Again!"

The brokenhearted look on her face stopped me like a pitcherful of cold water had been thrown at me.

"I'm sorry," I said. "I'm tired. You didn't understand, it's just–"

Two tears traced a salty path down Ruth's cheeks. She lay back down on her pallet and pulled her blanket over her head.

CHAPTER XXV

Friday, September 28, 1781

VIRGINIANS ARE QUITE CRUEL TO THEIR SLAVES.
–JEAN-FRANÇOIS-LOUIS, COMTE DE CLERMONT-CRÈVECOEUR,
FIRST LIEUTENANT IN THE AUXONNE REGIMENT OF THE
FRENCH ARMY AT YORKTOWN

I DID NOT SLEEP WELL, CHASED BY shadows until finally woken by a strange noise. Sweat-soaked and bewildered, I sat up. What was that sound? Something I'd not heard before, of that I was certain.

I rose and checked the door. The latch was undisturbed. I took a flatiron from a shelf and stood by the open window. A thunder-loud roll of drums beat in the distance. It startled me so much that I almost dropped the iron. The sound of shrilling fifes cut through the dark, and then I understood.

The army was on the move.

I unlatched the door and stepped outside. The hot air was thick with damp, like wet wool lifted from a boiling kettle. The entire town seemed awake in the darkness. Cattle bellowed, townspeople and soldiers hurried through the streets, horses pulled wagons, tossing their heads and whinnying.

I closed the door again.

How many more days would the Hallahans keep us on? Without the armies, they'd have no need of our help. Where would we go? How could we go anywhere in safety? I needed paper—costly paper—and a pen and ink to forge new free papers for us. I had neither money nor friends. Curzon had chosen his own path, and that pained my heart more than I thought possible. 'Twas unlikely we'd see Aberdeen again; the army he needed to spy upon was on the road.

I watched my sister sleep. As soon as she woke, her scowl would return, or maybe a look of hurt. On account of my temper the state of our sisterhood had again sunk into a dank bog of misery. I seemed incapable of doing anything right when it came to her. 'Twas no wonder she couldn't abide me. More and more, I could hardly abide myself.

I lay back down and stared at the darkness overhead. There'd be no more sleep for me. I rolled up my pallet and set to work.

By the time the steam was rising off the wash kettles, Widow Hallahan had not yet appeared. Neither had Kate nor Elspeth, which was curious. I peeked across the courtyard but saw no signs of life. Ruth woke, washed her face and hands in the basin, and tied a dark blue kerchief over her hair. She said nothing to me.

"Aberdeen stopped by whilst you slept," I lied so as to spare her feelings. "He can't escort you to the hospital, on account of the army moving out. I shall take his place."

She nodded, then went out to the courtyard. Thomas Boon nickered a greeting, and she spoke to him quiet enough that I could not hear her words. I swept the laundry, taking care to remove all the dried mud, carried in more firewood, and, finally, crossed the courtyard to the tavern, puzzled by the change in our routine.

The back door of the tavern stood open to the breeze. Widow Hallahan and Miss Marrow were sitting at the kitchen table, their breakfast of porridge, apples, and cheese in front of them. A newspaper was on the table too, folded in a most untidy manner.

I rapped lightly on the doorframe. Both women looked up, startled by my appearance.

"Didn't John come by to fetch you?" Widow Hallahan asked.

"No, ma'am," I said, confused. "Am I to work at the tavern today?"

The women exchanged a glance.

"Nay," the old lady said. "He, uh, he said you need to drive a wagon for him today."

"Drive a wagon?"

"Not ascared of horses, are you?" she asked.

"Not at all, ma'am. Does the hospital have extra washing?"

Again they shared a look of mystery.

"Might could be he wants you to drive the hams out to the French regiment." Widow Hallahan cut a slice of cheese. "They believe in a proper midday meal, even when marching. Indeed, he said something to that effect."

That sounded like a falsehood. The French army had their own wagons. They would have sent it to fetch the hams in the night. But Mister Hallahan's need to lie to his mother was not my concern.

"Kate and Elspeth have not turned up," I said. "The kettles are ready to boil."

"Gave them girls the day off." She began peeling the apple with the thin blade of the knife. "Figgered they'd be caterwauling and boohooing and the noise would grind my patience to dust."

The fire in the hearth crackled. The tavern felt hollow without the raucous noise and bustle of guests.

"Should we fetch the laundry from the hospital while waiting for the mister to return?" I asked.

"No need," Widow Hallahan said.

I blinked. "Pardon me, ma'am, but there's still plenty of puking and bleeding going on. They've more than three hundred sick fellas."

Miss Marrow rose from the table, took the boiling pot of water from the fire, and poured it into the basin on the sideboard.

"Ruth and me can get to the hospital and back in a flash."

I held my breath, praying first that she wouldn't complain about me walking with Ruth, and second that she wouldn't dismiss us on the spot, seeing as there was little need for us in the absence of the army.

"Nay, best you stay close by," Widow Hallahan said. "All is amuddle, what with the soldiers heading into war. What a world!"

The cook darted her eyes at me strangely, then started scrubbing at a crusted pie plate with a rag.

"If I may, ma'am . . . ," I swallowed hard. "How long do you figger that you'll need Ruth and me to work for you?"

"Well, that's the thing you need to talk to John about." She cut the long, dangling apple peel and it dropped to the plate like a ribbon. "He'll be here in a flash. Went off before he finished reading the paper."

I felt sure that meant our time at the laundry was finished. What should I do now? Ask at the hospital for work? But there was all sorts of sickness there. We needed work that would pay us enough for food and a roof to sleep under, but not if the place would be the death of us.

"What of my wages?" I asked boldly. "Mister Hallahan said I'd be paid cash for my time working in the tavern."

"Another topic to discuss with himself."

Something was amiss. Widow Hallahan had the head for figures in her family. I'd seen her counting out their earnings at the kitchen table at night. She dealt with the sellers at the marketplace and decided on the prices for food and drink in the tavern. I'd heard her complain about how her grown son had the head of a child when it came to numbers.

Unease fluttered in my belly like a butterfly trapped under a jar.

"Do we have any mutton pie left, Jane?" Widow Hallahan asked.

"A whole pie, big enough for two fellows," Miss Marrow answered.

"Given the unusual circumstances of the day," Widow Hallahan said, spearing an apple slice with the tip of her knife, "the army hullabaloo and all, what say you to a proper breakfast, Isabel, mutton pie and cider?"

"That would be fine, ma'am," I said. "Much obliged."

"You want I should fetch the cider?" Miss Marrow asked.

"First check the street," Widow Hallahan said. "Look for the mister and his friend there who promised to bring the wagon. The way he runs hither and thither is just like his father, Lord bless the old goat's soul."

The cook left the room, still clutching the scrubbing rag and dirty pie plate in her hands, which made no sense to me. None of this made sense. The two women were acting unnatural, as if they were reciting lines from a book, which was a foolish notion, for neither woman could read.

I glanced at the newspaper on the table, my eyes hungry as ever for words on paper. Mister Hallahan did spend long hours reading, seeking information that might help him turn a bargain. Though he never did any real labor in his tavern, his hands were forever stained with ink.

The cook came back in. "No wagon, ma'am."

Widow Hallahan grunted and took another bite of apple. She chewed a moment, then pointed the knife at me. "Would your sister like some peach cobbler?"

"Indeed she would," I answered, careful to keep my tone polite.

Standing behind the widow, the cook stared at me with wide eyes, blue as the summer sky. She held the crusted plate and rag so tight, her red fingers blanched to the color of bone. The intensity of her gaze and her strange manner gave me pause.

My remembery stirred to the night in '76 when Madam Lockton had tricked us with sweets, playacting with kindness to hide her evil intent. The night she stole Ruth.

I saw in my mind the muddy boot prints in the laundry, the disarray of our haversacks, our free papers torn up and burned by dirty hands. Not dirty; held with ink-stained fingers.

The heat in the room threatened to choke me. The truth of our peril rang so loud, I was sure the entire town could hear it. Widow Hallahan was not acting out of kindness; she was seeking to detain us. The man with the wagon was coming for us. To kidnap us. Steal us. Sell us.

I forced myself to draw a long, slow breath and resist the urge to run out the door. I could not let her know I understood her evil plan. To play a fool in front of a devil is often the wisest course of action.

I gave a shy smile and a false nod of gratitude. "Ruth does love peach cobbler, ma'am, and cider, too. That is most generous of you."

Widow Hallahan smiled, preening, ever proud of herself.

"May I fetch her?" I asked, pretending that I would not move without her permission. "It'll only take a moment to clean her up. She's been shoveling donkey dung." I stretched an alligator smile on my face. "I'll wash her hands and scrape the filth off her boots too. Wouldn't do to track that nastiness in here."

"Fine notion, that," Widow Hallahan said. "Jane will have a proper meal laid on the table here by the time you get back."

I forced myself to curtsy, chin lowered, eyes down. In the distance the fifes shrilled again, louder than the birds and the drums.

We had been forced back into war for our liberty.

CHAPTER XXVI

Friday, September 28, 1781

ANY PERSON MAY APPREHEND A SERVANT OR SLAVE,
SUSPECTED TO BE A RUNAWAY, AND CARRY HIM
BEFORE A JUSTICE OF PEACE.
–A BILL FOR APPREHENDING AND SECURING RUNAWAYS,
BY THE COMMITTEE OF THE VIRGINIA ASSEMBLY,
JUNE 18, 1779

I STROLLED SLOW ACROSS THE COURTyard in case the widow was watching me out the window. The heat rose from the earth and made the air shimmer, yet I shook with cold fear. I tried to whistle, but my mouth was too dry. My legs wobbled like I was walking on the deck of a ship lost on a stormy sea.

Where could we go? How far did we have to run? Was it safer to head past the hospital or down to the river landing? Could we risk the main road to Richmond, or should we hide until darkness, then head due north?

Widow Hallahan had been surprised to see me, that was clear. Their plan had surely been to capture us at first light. The sun had been up for near an hour already. The movement of the armies had likely caused the delay, but the wagon and the awful men in it could be just paces away.

I entered the laundry, then closed and latched the door behind me. I could not stop shaking.

Ruth sat on a stool by the open door that led to the street, practicing tiny stitches on her best handkerchief. She looked up at me, then returned her gaze to her work.

I crossed the room in three strides, flew up the ladder, and grabbed our haversacks. I tied the old leather reins around my waist as a belt, then tucked my knife and hatchet into it and quickly descended the ladder.

"Ruth," I said softly. "We're leaving. Come with me."

She shook her head.

"Aberdeen is waiting for us." 'Twas another lie, but told in the cause of our safety. "We must hurry."

I stole two fresh-washed shifts from a basket of clean laundry and added them to my haversack. I paused, then added a small crock of soap. I rolled and tied our blankets and grabbed two hickory washing bats. If captured, we'd fight as long and hard as we could.

I snuck a look out the window. There was no movement or sound from the tavern. How long until Widow Hallahan grew suspicious?

Ruth studied the cloth in her lap, frowning.

"Put your boots on," I said. "Make haste."

"Don't want to." She set down the needlework, crossed her arms over her chest, and shook her head again. "I hate boots. You're mean."

"Please," I insisted. "We might need to run on rocky ground."

Ruth picked up her sewing. "Not running. You hollered at me."

A dog barked in the street. A distant drum rattled. Three women walked by with heavy baskets in their arms, chattering like mockingbirds. A pair of horses appeared, pulling a wagon driven by a round, red-faced man in a tattered straw hat. I froze.

Was this the man sent to kidnap us?

The man slapped the reins on the rumps of the horses, urging them to hurry. He did not glance at the laundry. The horses pulled harder, and the wagon, piled high with casks and crates, rolled past.

Ruth pulled her needle slowly through the cloth, innocent of the dangers that were chasing us, mouths wide, fangs bared. I needed her to understand and follow my instructions. There was no time to explain, or apologize, or mend the broken parts of her heart.

But I had to try.

I crouched next to her. "Heed my words, I beg you." I leaned close to her ear. "Mister Walter and Missus Serafina told you to listen to me. So listen: Bad men are coming for us this very moment."

"Bad?" She drew back a bit and studied me, her frown cutting deeper lines in her brow. "Like Prentiss?"

The name of the Riverbend overseer on her lips startled me. The stark fear in her eyes made me want to hold her tight, but we didn't have time. I nodded with great vigor.

"Yes! Like Prentiss. Very bad men who will hurt us." I lifted her foot, slipped her heavy boot on, and quickly tied it. "But Aberdeen can help us. Only we must be quick and silent." I put her other boot on whilst she stuffed her sewing into her haversack. "Are you ready to run, sister?"

She nodded. "Aye, Isabel."

We shouldered our sacks and put on our hats. I peered out the door, made sure there were no strangers with wagons waiting there, then grabbed Ruth's hand in mine.

"Now!"

CHAPTER XXVII

Friday, September 28, 1781

IF THE ENEMY SHOULD BE TEMPTED TO MEET THE ARMY ON ITS MARCH, THE GENERAL PARTICULARLY ENJOINS THE TROOPS TO PLACE THEIR PRINCIPLE RELIANCE ON THE BAYONET.
—GENERAL ORDERS OF GEORGE WASHINGTON, SEPTEMBER 28, 1781

A GREAT COLUMN OF RED DUST ROSE in the sky to show me the path to safety.

Near twenty thousand soldiers on the march, plus their wagons and horses, threw up such a gigantical red cloud that King George over in England could have spotted it himself. It would be easy to hide in such a maelstrom of confusion. Before that moment the thought of hiding in the middle of the pack of soldiers would have seemed to me as safe as hiding in the mouth of a serpent.

But we had no choice.

We hurried down alleys and slipped through the narrow spaces betwixt buildings. Ruth shushed the barking dogs and startled chickens we encountered. I forced my feet to walk steady, feigning a calm I did not possess, until well beyond the extent of the town itself, then we ran as if we were speeding to catch up to our company.

We soon reached the end of the long line of men and

supplies, the lumbering wagons filled with spades, shovels, axes, tents, flour casks, and iron kettles. I checked over my shoulder one last time but saw no sign of Hallahan, nor a wagon in pursuit of us. In fact, we had walked so far, so quickly, that I could no longer see any sign of Williamsburg.

I slowed my pace. "Does your foot hurt?"

Ruth matched her steps to mine and gave a quick shake of her head. "When we gonna find Aberdeen?"

"Soon," I said with a confidence I did not feel.

We walked along the edge of the road, overtaking the slow wagons one by one. No one remarked about our presence. I noted the air of purpose with which the people around us walked. I imitated it, acting like I knew exactly where I was going and was certain that I would get there soon.

As my fear of Hallahan faded a bit, my apprehension about what to do next grew. We had to eat. We needed a safe place to sleep. Mayhaps we could work for the French; they paid with silver coins. We could leave as soon as we earned enough to get to Philadelphia. But what if Aberdeen was right? What if the British won the coming battle? Should we, in fact, make our way to Yorktown and seek him out?

The image of Curzon's face drifted across my mind. I gave my head a good shake to get rid of it. I wouldn't ask for his help, not ever again. I didn't even know what regiment he belonged to. Before I turned to Curzon, I'd seek out Ebenezer Woodruff. He'd find us work among trustworthy fellows.

As the sun reached the middle of the sky, we caught up to the drovers herding the cattle and sheep that would feed the army. I tried to step with care, but the dung on the road could not be avoided. Ruth would have happily lingered with the animals, but I urged her forward until we came to the ragtag band of women and children that I knew would be walking at the rear of the mass of troops.

They were called "women of the army" or "camp followers"; wives of soldiers who had permission to accompany the troops so long as they cooked and cleaned and mended and cared for the sick. They were a rough sort, used to a life of hardship. A few carried babes on their backs, but several walked with children pulling at their skirts. A few lads of six or seven helped their mothers by carrying sacks of dried peas. They would have been babes themselves when the war started. If it didn't end soon, they'd be shouldering muskets and fighting alongside their brothers and fathers.

"Good day!" I called to a group of women closest to us. Acting cheerful was a part of my disguise.

The three of them turned back to look at me. They were all white, one no older than me, the other two of middling years.

"May we walk with you?" I asked.

The older women studied us in an unfriendly manner, but the youngest, dressed in a blue jacket and a much-patched skirt, grinned broadly, showing the absence of several teeth.

"Sure enough," she said. "Lasses needs to band together, keep usselves safe from redcoats prowling in the brush!"

"Follow me," I said to Ruth.

Ruth refused, shaking her head.

"No shenanigans," I hissed. "Please!"

She shot me a look that could have stopped a bear in its tracks, then sighed and clomped behind me.

"Name's Rachel," the youngest girl said when we caught up to the women. "You get left behind?"

"Indeed," I said, shaking my head with feigned rue. "My sister, she come down with a terrible flux of the bowels. Slept in the privy, she did. But she's all cleaned out now."

The older women grunted, nodded their heads, and commenced to arguing about the best remedies for ailments of the belly and bowel. Ruth glared at me but said nothing, thank all of the angels in God's heaven.

"How much farther till Yorktown?" I asked.

"Not far." Rachel shaded her eyes with her hand. "See that rice field and the woods ahead? My man says them woods, that's a sign we's close. Bloody lobsterbacks hiding in the trees, he says, ready to pick us off one by one."

The women on the other side of Rachel interrupted their doctoring argument and laughed.

"Pshaw!" said one. "Them lobsterbacks are all holed up in Yorktown, wetting their breeches in fear and hoping for a rescue boat. Only thing to be afraid of in them woods is skunks." She tilted her head some and gave us a close looking-over. "Where do ye hail from?"

I swallowed hard, not daring to respond. If she questioned me too close, she'd know in an instant that we didn't belong with the army. I did not know enough of the life of camp followers to bluff my way into their midst. If we were found out to be imposters, we could find ourselves captured and headed to the auction block. The thought near made me retch.

There was only one path left to take: to the British.

"Oh, gracious!" I said loudly.

"Are you poorly too?" Rachel asked.

"Nay, but my sister here, she's got that look on her face again. Methinks I ought find a spot of privacy for her in the woods. Many thanks for your company."

I grabbed Ruth's arm and pulled her with me, half running for the woods.

"Should we wait for you?" called Rachel.

Her friendly tone caused a pang within me. I looked back at her over my shoulder. "You best move on."

CHAPTER XXVIII

Friday, September 28, 1781

About 700 Negroes are come down the river [with] the smallpox. I shall distribute them about the rebel plantations.
–Letter of British general Alexander Leslie to Lord Cornwallis about his decision to spread smallpox in the Virginia countryside a few months before the siege of Yorktown

"DON'T LIKE THE WOODS," RUTH SAID AS we walked under the first trees.

"We spent weeks in the woods when we left Riverbend," I reminded her.

"With Aberdeen," she said.

Mayhaps it had been a mistake to use his name as a tool to get her away from the laundry.

"He keeps me safe," she added.

The tone in her voice caused me to turn and study her face. She was clearly sweet on him, though not old enough to be courted. Even if she were sixteen, I would never allow a fellow of such questionable honesty to spend time with her. But that was a problem for another day. For now I'd say anything to keep her walking beside me.

"Aberdeen's in Yorktown," I said, hoping it might be true. "It's on the other side of those woods."

"Woods have ghosts. Don't like them."

"We'll look for animals as we walk," I gently suggested. "Squirrels. Foxes. Maybe we'll see a possum with babies on her back."

"Skunks?"

"Not in the daytime," I said. "Don't worry."

"Ghosts steal souls."

"I'll keep you safe," I promised.

It took at least an hour to go the first mile and another mile after that, until the distance muffled the army's rattling drums. The travel was tortuous slow on account of fallen trees and thick-growing bushes armed with thorns. The sharp smell of death, like blood spilled on a hot iron pan, made me wrinkle my nose from time to time. It likely came from dead possums or a wounded deer that had fled from the hunters to die in the forest.

I listened close, hoping to hear the trickle of a stream, but the only sounds were the whine of bloodsucking insects and Ruth's careful footsteps behind me. She did not complain about her empty belly, though I knew she was as hungry as me.

The smell of death came again on the wind. It so distracted me that I walked face-first into an enormous, sticky spiderweb. I lashed out and cleared it off my face, then chuckled low. "Did you see that? I must have looked a right fool."

Ruth did not answer.

"Did you not see that?" I turned around.

She stood some ten paces behind me and a bit to the left, pointing at something under the ferns at her feet.

"Dead," she said.

"Dead?" I walked back, bracing myself for the sight of a rotting critter. "Come away from . . ."

I could not finish the sentence.

'Twas a hand poking out from the ferns. Its fingers curled gently toward the palm, as if beckoning us.

"Dear God," I murmured.

I crouched for a closer look, flinching as a thick wave of angry flies rose in the air. The hand belonged to the body of an ill-dressed black man, old enough to be my father. His face was a mask of agony, his skin covered with horrible smallpox pustules leaking their poison. His belly hadn't bloated up, nor was he showing signs of rot, though the air was hot enough to melt wax. I felt on his wrist but found no sign of his heartbeat. He had not been dead for long. He had woken up that morning, same as we had, but then he'd walked unto death.

Ruth crouched next to me.

"Smallpox," I murmured. "Don't fret. We had it when we were little."

Smallpox had been slow-burning its way through the country as long as I could remember. Some said it was a sign of God's anger, but they couldn't agree if God was angry at the Patriots for declaring independence or at the British for denying it.

I touched his fingertips. His hands were callused by a lifetime of work, and his feet were bare. He had freed himself, of that I was certain. Had he been on his way to find the wife he loved, or his children, or to see if his parents still lived? Whose name had been on his lips as he passed from this world to the next?

Ruth wiped the tears from my face.

"We can't leave him like this," I said after a while.

Ruth didn't move.

"I think we should bury him," I said.

She took a deep breath, then nodded. "Aye."

It was much harder than I figgered. We tried to dig using our washing bats, but the thick woven roots of the forest floor made the task near impossible. I tried to chop through the roots with my hatchet but achieved little except dulling the blade. Digging with our hands would have taken days. In the end we covered him with branches and leaves, fashioned a cross from two sticks, and laid it on the ground above his head.

I said a prayer.

"Amen," Ruth whispered.

Despite our walking farther and farther from the nameless man's grave, the oppressive stink of death grew stronger. I was so mired in melancholy, I did not pause to consider the oddity of that. There had been no talk of smallpox in Williamsburg, at least not that I'd heard mention of. The Continental troops were all required to have the variolation, then endure the disease in quarantine to prevent its spread. Had that man been infected where he lived, or had it cut him down as he ran?

We stooped under branches, backtracked when the brush grew too dense, then turned again in the direction of the river. Aberdeen had not mentioned how difficult the journey through these woods would be, which made me worry that we were lost. And the smell of death was growing stronger.

When we entered a clearing filled with golden light from the setting sun, the horrible truth revealed itself. The shock of the sight stopped us cold, rooting us both to the ground like saplings. Ruth gasped and clapped her hands over her mouth. A sob rose from my chest.

"Dear God!"

Five people lay on the ground, each covered with a thin shroud of fallen leaves. Two men, two boys, one woman. All dead. All of them so thin, they were more bone than muscle. The boys lay with their arms around each other. One of them reached for the woman, who had died curled up in a ball. One man lay facedown near the three of them. The other was a few paces away, alone.

Nature had started to consume them, a sign that they had lain here in death for days.

Ashes to ashes, dust to dust.

These were children of Africa, like me. Like my sister, and our mother, and our father. Like Curzon, Aberdeen, Serafina, Walter, the woman in the green skirt at the market, like the countless souls, some in their natural state of freedom, many, many, many more kidnapped, stolen, and forced into the unnatural state of slavery.

I wished that I knew their names. I would speak them out loud in quiet moments, in beautiful places, and in so doing, keep a part of them alive. Your true name was one of the few things they could not take away from you, hard though they tried.

"Halt!"

The barrel of a musket stuck out at us from behind a tree. A British soldier, no older than me, stepped forth. His uniform was filthy and torn, his sunburnt cheeks thin. He had no hat. Most of his ginger-colored hair had escaped its queue.

"Where are the Continentals?" he asked in a wavering voice.

I put my arm in front of Ruth and tried to push her behind me. She stood fast, immovable, but she took my hand in hers.

"How far?" the lad asked.

"They're on the road to Yorktown," I said.

"Everybody knows that. How far is that road from here?"

I scanned the woods behind him but could see no other men. Was he a scout? If so, he was terrible at the task.

"We've walked for hours," I said. "The thick brush slows you down."

He gestured with the musket. The barrel shook a bit, as if his arms did not have the strength to hold it for long. "You making for Yorktown?"

There was no point in lying. I nodded. "Hoping to work there. And . . . borrow some shovels. To care for them." I pointed at the sorrowful forms half hidden by leaves and shadows. "How close are we?"

He didn't hear my question. As he realized why we needed shovels, his face drained of the little color it had. The lad slumped against the tree, cursing quiet-like. His legs weakened and he slid until he was sitting on the ground. The musket fell beside him.

"Too many to bury," he said in a voice just above a whisper.

"It needs to be done," I said.

"It's not just them," he said. "We took in thousands of fugitives. Then smallpox hit, and we was running out of food. Couldn't feed 'em, wouldn't care for 'em. We got orders to force them out. Only the strongest men allowed to stay."

He wiped his eyes on the grimy sleeve of his jacket.

"You . . . that is, the British, they threw these folks out?" I asked, horrified.

"Some of them had worked with us for months," he said dully. "Officers ordered us to threaten them with bayonets. Thousands." His ragged voice sounded ancient and cursed with sorrow. "Promised 'em freedom and safety. Robbed 'em of both."

Thunder rumbled. I glanced up at the sky.

"Cannons," the soldier said. "It's beginning. Last place you want to go is Yorktown. If you do, you'll end up dead in these woods."

He picked up his musket.

"Where are you going?" I asked.

"Deserting. I mean to hand meself to the Continentals, tell 'em all I know. Beg for mercy." He wiped his eyes on his sleeve again. "My father will never forgive me."

He fled into the growing dark.

CHAPTER XXIX

Friday, September 28, 1781

WE DROVE BACK TO THE ENEMY ALL OF OUR BLACK FRIENDS, WHOM WE HAD TAKEN ALONG TO DESPOIL THE COUNTRYSIDE. WE HAD USED THEM TO GOOD ADVANTAGE AND SET THEM FREE, AND NOW, WITH FEAR AND TREMBLING, THEY HAD TO FACE THE REWARD OF THEIR CRUEL MASTERS.
—DIARY OF HESSIAN CAPTAIN JOHANN EWALD AT YORKTOWN

RUTH HELPED ME PILE MORE LEAVES over the dead. The light was fast disappearing. Instead of taking the time to fashion crosses for them, we drew crosses in the dirt and prayed for the five souls as we walked away.

We moved slow and careful through the woods until at last we reached a patch of ground that was mostly dry and smelled only of living forest.

"This is a good spot," I said. "Away from the trouble. We'll sleep here."

"No." Ruth shook her head, unhappy with my decision. "Ghosts."

I sighed. "Soldiers are more dangerous than ghosts. And besides, not all ghosts are bad and scary, no matter what Serafina told you."

"Can't sleep here," Ruth said. "Where's Deen?"

"I don't know," I said wearily.

"But you said."

"He might be in Yorktown, but I don't know for sure," I said. "That redcoat said we'll die if we go there."

"I want Aberdeen." Her loud voice filled the air.

"We're not going to find him, poppet. Not tonight."

"He keeps away the ghosts!"

"Shhh!" I hissed.

"You said we was to find him!" she shouted at me. "You lied!"

"We had to run!"

"Aberdeen!" She shook her head so violently, she stumbled, hollering his name over and over. "Aberdeen! Aberdeeeeen!"

"Hush!" I grabbed her wrists. "Stop screaming–there could be other soldiers about!"

She tried to pull away from me, but I held tighter. Ruth kicked at my legs, hard, and kept hollering.

"Stop!" I winced. "That hurts! Stop kicking me!" I twisted to get away from her heavy boots.

She pulled her wrists free. "You lied! You gonna give me to the ghosts!"

"No!" I shouted, trying to grab her wrists to settle her. "Calm down and listen. Don't kick me again! Curse it all, Ruth, why must you be so stupid?"

"You stupid!" she roared.

And then she slapped my face.

I acted without thought and slapped her back.

She jumped at me, eyes filled with tears and fury, but before she could land any more blows. I stepped back, then tripped. The two of us fell to the ground in a heap.

The shock of the fall stilled us both. For a moment all was silent, except for the whirring of insects and the hob-nobbing of frogs.

I sat up first, worried that her outburst heralded a fit

of her falling sickness. She sat up slower, scowling at me.

"Ruth . . ." I reached for her. "Are you hurt?"

She slapped at my hand and shifted a few paces away from me.

I was overcome with sorrow and confusion. I had searched for her for years and finally had her by my side, which I had wanted more than anything in the world. Yet I'd hurt her feelings, and worse, I'd hit her, though it was the last thing I'd ever wanted to do. The events of the day had woven a delicate thread of trust between us, and I had destroyed it. I was the most wretched sister who ever walked. I had the temper of a demon, the patience of a rabbit, and the cussed mouth of a sailor. I wished the ground would swallow me alive. It was growing dark; we were lost and surrounded by enemies. We had no food, no water, and little hope. And Ruth hated me.

She wrapped her arms around herself.

"I shouldn't have done that," I said. "I'm sorry."

As soon as I spoke, she started rocking back and forth.

I tried to keep my voice low and calming. "I said Aberdeen was in Yorktown because we needed to get away from the bad men. We can't look for him tonight. We need to hide here, in the woods, to be safe."

She shook her head and squeezed herself tighter and kept rocking.

"Will you please listen to me?"

Cannon fire echoed in the distance.

"Ghosts," she whispered. "Can't stay here."

"We can leave at dawn."

She lifted her head and looked at me. "You stay. I can't."

"You would leave me? You would wander on your own?"

She lowered her head again and rocked harder.

I was dizzy with fear. I couldn't make her stay but couldn't allow her to leave. The way north to Maryland was overrun with danger in the dark. To walk south or west in Virginia meant certain capture. To the east lay the ocean. The British at Yorktown would not welcome us. The French could not speak to us. The Patriots had already betrayed us.

Worst of all, I had betrayed Ruth.

The cannons boomed again. If I didn't do something, then our fate would be in the hands of others.

"I was wrong." I took a deep breath. "You were right. These woods have ghosts, so we won't stay here. We leave now, this very moment."

Ruth paused.

"'Way from ghosts?" she finally asked.

"Away from the ghosts, I swear. Take my hand, please."

We walked directly toward the sound of battle until the trees thinned into brush and scraggly bushes. In the distance to our left, where Yorktown lay, came red flashes of the cannons. In the silence between the blasts we could hear faint voices far to our right when the wind blew from that direction. I couldn't tell if they spoke French or English. Were we to continue straight ahead, I reckoned that we'd wind up right in the middle of the field of battle.

"Is this far enough?" I asked.

Ruth walked in a slow circle, looking low and high, pausing a few times to close her eyes for reasons I did not understand. She walked to a place ten paces to the front of me and dropped her haversack. She untied her blanket, spread it on the ground, and sat, her back to me.

She looked at me over her shoulder and said, "No ghosts."

The wind danced in the trees and brought the smells of

cook fires with it. The smell of smoke brought to mind the gigantical fire that had burned through New York after Ruth was stolen. The flames had blown like the Devil's hurricane, hungry to destroy everything. Hundreds of houses burned that night, too many bodies to count. Ashes blew through the streets for months. There had been plenty of ashes at Valley Forge, too, graying the snow and sticking to the horrid firecake that the lads had to eat. The ashes in the blacksmith's forge had glowed as the man fashioned the iron collar that was locked round my neck for months. I still woke from nightmares clutching my throat, feeling it choke me again.

Those terrible days had convinced me that I understood sadness. I had been wrong.

Above us the stars watched without comment. Trees rustled behind us. Ghosts stirred too. Ahead of me Ruth's shadow rocked back and forth, her thumb in her mouth.

The state of my own soul flashed before me as bright as lightning. I'd seen so much evil, endured so much cruelty, that my heart was indeed hardening. I'd been impatient with Ruth. I'd disregarded her feelings. Instead of seeking to understand how the tumult of these months had appeared to her, I'd fussed, complained, and been concerned more for my sentiments than hers.

Burnt dreams seemed to fill my mouth and smother my heart. The dreams of having Ruth by my side, of a future with Curzon in a world without war, they had all gone up in flames, leaving only the bitter taste of sorrow.

Missus Serafina's caution to keep my heart gentle and love-filled whispered to me.

I walked to Ruth's blanket. I knelt in front of her and bowed my head.

"I must apologize to you," I said. "I humbly beg your pardon for everything. I've been rough and mean and thoughtless." I tried to control the shaking of my voice. "I should not have yelled or called you a bad name or, God save me, hit you. I am truly, deeply sorry. I hope you can forgive me."

A cannon fired and we both flinched.

"You sending me back to Prentiss?" Ruth finally asked.

"What?"

Ruth looked down at her hands, folded in her lap. "You gonna send me 'way again?"

"Beg pardon?" I leaned closer, until I could see her face in the starlight. "I don't understand."

She looked in the direction of the cannons.

"You sent me to Riverbend on account of my stupid. When I was little. Stupid makes you angry, it does."

She could have been speaking in Dutch or Latin, for her words made no sense at all. How could she think that I had sent her to Riverbend? How could she think that I could have done such a horrible thing? It was unfathomable. But worse—she thought I'd done it on account of the way she was, her different manner of seeing things and understanding the world.

Ruth wasn't stupid or slow; she was just our Ruth, and I'd never thought otherwise. But she did not know that. She didn't know because I hadn't told her. All this time she had thought that I'd sent her away. All these months she'd been waiting for it to happen again. It explained everything.

"No!" I clutched her hands. "That witch Madam Lockton, she sent you away. Remember her? She took us to New York on a big ship. She kidnapped you, stole you from me!"

"She sent me to Missus Serafina and Mister Walter."

"That was God's work, not Lockton's. Those kind people

loved you and cared for you like one of their own. But I didn't want you to go, not ever. I wasn't angry. I could never be angry like that with you! Ruth, sweet girl, I fought to get you back. I broke all the rules, I made new rules for myself. I did everything—everything—I could to find you, to take care of you. I love you. I love you more than life. You're my sister. . . ."

The words stopped. Tears started and my world fell away.

And then Ruth leaned forward. She cupped her hands around my face. "Not angry at my stupid?"

I swallowed hard. "No, poppet. Never. You're perfect."

She traced my scar with her thumb. "Curzon said she burned your face."

"She did," I said. "But that didn't stop me."

A quiet moment passed. Owls called to one another in the woods.

"Curzon said you walked and walked and walked to find me."

"I walked and walked and walked to find you."

"You and Curzon."

"Indeed, me and Curzon."

Another long pause. Two cannon shots boomed, one after the other. When the last echoes died away, the owls hooted again. Bats swooped overhead.

She sat back, wrapped her arms around herself, and rocked back and forth, faster than before.

"What's the matter?" I asked.

She shook her head.

"Are you crying?" I asked, my own voice breaking. "Please! Did I say something wrong again? I'm so sorry, Ruth, I'll never run out of sorry."

She stilled herself, bit her lip. Finally she took a deep

breath and asked in a small, uncertain voice, "You gonna leave me again?"

It seemed as if a bolt of lightning had illuminated the truth. Ruth thought that I'd sent her away all those years ago, and she thought that I'd taken her away from Serafina and Walter and that I could abandon her at any moment. She had been carrying more fear in her heart than I could even imagine. So much fear that it threatened to drown me.

"Oh, no!" I cried. "Never, never, never! I will never stop loving you, I will never stop being your sister! We will never, ever be parted again, I swear to you!"

And then my arms went around her, and her arms held me so close that the beat of her heart fell into rhythm with mine, and we cried until we ran out of tears.

Later, after I'd fetched my blanket to cover us and we'd curled around each other like two spoons, the way we used to, she asked me to tell her the stories.

"What stories?"

"Stories you told when my foot was sick. 'Bout Momma and the garden."

"You were listening?"

"You my sister, Isabel." She patted my hand. "I always listen to you."

CHAPTER XXX

Saturday, September 29, 1781

THIS SIEGE WILL BE A VERY ANXIOUS BUSINESS.
—MAJOR JAMES MCHENRY WRITING TO MARYLAND GOVERNOR THOMAS SIM LEE FROM THE YORKTOWN ENCAMPMENT, OCTOBER 6, 1781

MOMMA USED TO SAY THAT ALL things were possible in the new of the morning. Never had I understood that sentiment so well. I awoke when the birds started singing, and lay content snuggled next to Ruth. By the time her eyes fluttered open, I had developed a plan. We had an old friend in this camp, and I was certain he would try his best to help us. But first I had to listen to Ruth's dream, which was filled with butterflies that drank cinnamon nectar from flowers as big as butter casks.

We moved south at first light, walking just inside the tree line until we found a stream that was sheltered enough to offer us privacy. We drank until our teeth chattered with cold and our bellies swelled round with water, then we washed off the stink of death and sweat. Once dried, we changed into the shifts that I had liberated from the laundry, part of our recompense for the weeks of work without pay.

Ruth sighed with contentment as she pulled on the fresh-washed linen over her head and arms.

"Clean clothes are a wonder," I said.

Her grin made my spirit sing. The heart-mending we'd done in the night seemed to be just as strong in the light of day.

I explained to her that we had to find work and food and a better place to sleep than an open field. Once all of that had been accomplished, we'd figure out where Aberdeen was hiding himself. She nodded gravely. In truth, we had little hope of finding him. He was either dead, captive, or running, but I couldn't tell her that until our circumstances were more secure.

We made our way south, toward the sound of men chopping trees. The voices of French soldiers cheered in high excitement with each falling giant, and the air was rich with the smell of wood chips and pine sap. Before we approached close enough to be seen, we filled our arms with kindling wood. This was to be our disguise; we'd pose as camp followers tasked with collecting wood for the fires, an ordinary chore done by ordinary lasses. I prayed that this shield of deception would protect us long enough.

Few men noticed us as we skirted the edges of the tree-felling. We followed the ruts carved in the dirt by the horse teams dragging the tree trunks. These led directly to the edge of the encampment where the trunks were stacked, waiting for the sawyers to plank, chop, carve, and whittle the wood into whatever things the army needed.

Ruth paused to greet a team of horses. After she'd conversated with them a bit, we went back to walking.

"Walk with purpose," I reminded her. "Chin up. Purpose and confidence."

"What's purpose?" she asked.

That required a moment of pondering. "To walk with purpose means that you know what your aim is, and you mean to follow after it."

"What's our aim?"

Before I could answer, a small French soldier doffed his hat and called, "*Bonjour*, Mademoiselle Ruth!" as he scurried past us, a large sack over his shoulder.

"Bow-zhoor!" Ruth shouted after him.

The sound of Frenchified speech in my sister's mouth shocked me. The fellow nodded with delight, plopped his hat back on his head, and hurried on.

"What did you just say?" I asked.

"Bow-zhoor," Ruth repeated. "They say it all the day long."

"But that fellow, he knew your name."

"He took the shirts."

"When you delivered the laundry?"

She nodded, looking rather pleased with herself. "Aberdeen, he talked with everyone. We gonna see him soon?"

I hesitated, then found a way to answer without lying. "I truly hope we will see him soon."

"'Tis a purpose," Ruth said. "Seeing Aberdeen."

"A good purpose," I said quietly.

There were women working among the French, but none sought out my eyes to offer silent advice or warning. We could not take a chance on the French, no matter how courtly they might act to my pretty sister. With us not speaking their language, they could openly discuss doing us harm and we would be none the wiser.

British cannons continued to fire as we trekked through the growing tent city. I caught sight of Yorktown when we topped a hill: a collection of houses that lay a scant mile distant, its back to a wide river. The placement of this rebel camp seemed mostly beyond cannon range, but we watched horror-struck as a screaming soldier—one leg ending in a blood-spurting mess at the place where his foot ought be—was rushed by, carried by anxious-looking companions.

Ruth turned to me, her eyes wide.

"'Tis also our purpose to avoid cannonballs," I assured her.

The encampment was much vaster than I had imagined, mayhaps two or three times winter camp at Valley Forge. Supply wagons were still arriving on the Williamsburg road. We walked on, staying at the edges of the stream of soldiery that created its own currents of movement across the boot-trampled greenery. After passing rows and rows of French soldiers busy raising tents and digging privy trenches, I turned us south again, angling eastward toward the rear of the encampment.

My notion of walking with confidence and purpose faltered as the day grew hotter. We hadn't eaten a bite in a day and a half. The kindling grew heavier and heavier. Sweat was rolling down my neck by the time we reached a noisome, broad plain where the tents the size of small houses were being raised.

The work there was under the direction of well-dressed, well-fed officers who—to my relief—barked orders in English. Those were likely the tents of the headquarters, where the general and his men would sleep, eat, scheme, and direct the maneuvers of the armies. Drums rattled as fresh-cut, sap-streaked flagpoles were raised paces away from the large tents. Camp tables were covered with papers being studied by Continental officers, who squinted through the glasses perched on the ends of their noses.

Farther on, a round-bellied man shouted at a group of lean soldiers marching with muskets on their shoulders. Donkeys brayed. Axes split logs. Men laughed, cursed, called in overloud voices. A piper played. Cartwheels rolled. Blacksmith hammers sang against their anvils.

"Make way!" shouted a voice. Others took up the call. "Make way! Make way!"

A quick-running group of riflemen dressed in the fringed hunting shirts of the mountains rushed by, their faces set in grim determination, guns in their hands. They ran south and west in the direction of the no-man's-land between the French encampment and Yorktown.

"Virginians," someone said. The most accurate riflemen of all.

A tall, strong-built white woman, her sleeves rolled up high, waved us over and pointed to a collection of kindling wood some paces from a cook fire. "You lasses can set that here."

"Yes, ma'am." I dumped the wood and motioned for Ruth to do the same.

The cook fire was laid in a rectangle-shaped pit dug as deep as a forearm into the ground. Iron rods had been sunk into the dirt at the long ends of the pit, and a long rod rested across them both. Fire burned high at one end, where a steaming kettle bigger than any at the Gray Boar hung. The woman shoveled hot coals from the burning end of the fire to the cool end, where covered pans rested in the dirt. She buried the pans with the coals, then swatted the sparks that had leapt to her skirt.

"Hungry?" she asked.

We gratefully accepted her offer of thick slices of bread before walking away. I dared not stay long enough for questions that I could not answer.

Ruth matched my stride as we walked to where the American troops were setting up camp.

"We're looking for an ally," I said. "A friend who can help us find our way in this camp."

"Aberdeen is our friend."

"I was thinking of someone else."

Before I could speak the name aloud, Ruth dug her boots into the dirt. She studied the regimental standard planted in front of a row of Continental tents. She waited as the weak breeze lifted the flag, then dropped it.

"Green tree on blue," Ruth muttered. "Driscoll's company."

I stopped. "Beg pardon?"

"Everybody has a flag. So they can find their tents."

"You know these flags?"

"Is it bad?" she asked, her eyes anxious.

"Not at all," I said quickly. "These flags identify the different companies and regiments. But how is it that you know them?"

"They needed their breeches, Isabel, after you washed them, 'member? I drove the breeches in the cart. Remembered the flags so I wouldn't get lost."

"Aberdeen showed you the learning of this when you made deliveries?"

She pushed back her shoulders and lifted her chin in evident pride. "Learned myself. He was busy some days."

"You found your way to deliver laundry by learning the regimental standards?"

She smiled and nodded, then broke into giggles as an escaped pig dashed down the lane, followed by a pack of shouting soldiers.

"Do you know the First Massachusetts Regiment?"

"First Massachusetts is a lion," she answered.

The surprises within my sister seemed endless that day. "How do you know what a lion looks like?"

"Yellow panther with a furry head. Wears a big collar of fur, too."

I laughed and kissed her cheek. "I've been struck by a new purpose."

"A new aim?" Ruth asked.

"My purpose is to find you some gingerbread as soon as possible!"

CHAPTER XXXI

Saturday, September 29, 1781

VERY SOON AFTER OUR WHOLE ARMY ARRIVING, WE PREPARED TO MOVE DOWN AND PAY OUR OLD ACQUAINTANCE, THE BRITISH AT YORKTOWN, A VISIT. I DOUBT NOT BUT THEIR WISH WAS NOT TO HAVE SO MANY OF US COME AT ONCE, AS THEIR ACCOMMODATIONS WERE RATHER SCANTY. THEY THOUGHT, "THE FEWER THE BETTER CHEER." WE THOUGHT, "THE MORE THE MERRIER."
–JOURNAL OF SERGEANT JOSEPH PLUMB MARTIN, CORPS OF SAPPERS AND MINERS

"YOU DAFT GOLLUMPUSES!" SERGEANT Ebenezer Woodruff roared at the two nervous soldiers in front of him. "You mutton-headed louts! Axes are for the chopping of wood! Pickaxes are for digging in the ground! You cannot use one for the task of the other. I'd flog you myself if there were time."

The objects of his wrath winced and sank their heads lower.

"Bah!" Ebenezer swatted a horsefly out of the air with his hat. "Take the axes to be sharpened, and tell the fellow at the grindstone to sharpen your wits while he's at it."

One of the soldiers looked up, fear in his eyes. "Sir?"

Eben closed his eyes, shook his head, and drew a long, slow breath. "Deliver the axes. Then join the lads in the swamp hauling water."

"Yes, sir," the soldiers answered in shaky voices.

"Now!" hollered Eben.

The two fellows leapt as if kicked by a horse, grabbed the dull axes that had caused this furor, and ran. Eben looked at the rest of the men standing around him. "What are you lot gawping at? Report to the latrine trenches. And dig deep; we're going to be here a spell."

I waited for the soldiers to hurry away and tried to find some courage. I'd never seen Eben in a temper. His uniform and boots were coated in dust, his hat looked like it had been trampled in the ox corral, and his face was flushed angry red.

Before I could figger what to say, Ruth stepped forward. "Good day, there!" she called.

Eben spun around, his face a frightful scowl. "What the devil!"

"I'm no devil," Ruth said.

Eben looked first to Ruth, then to me, then back to Ruth.

"Hullo, Eben." I tried to flavor my greeting with cheer. "Might we walk a bit? I, uh, we've need of your counsel." My talking to him had gathered the attention of a few lads setting up tents. "Sir," I quickly added with a short curtsy, which Ruth imitated.

He placed his hat on his head. "Pick up them small kettles and follow me."

Sergeant Ebenezer Woodruff walked with such long strides that we had to hurry to keep up with him. He led us past rows of half-raised tents, up to a rise where soldiers were unloading barrels with uncommon care.

"Gunpowder," Eben muttered. "They mean to set up the artillery park here. Keep stride, we're nearly there."

He led us to the rear of the encampment, close to where

we'd enjoyed our bread earlier. There were enough women and children of the army that we did not spark unusual interest here. I breathed easier.

Eben relaxed as well. "Now then," he said. "We can speak openly here. What has happened? Is he ill? Injured?"

It took a moment before I could read his meaning.

"Curzon? No, he is fine." I shook my head. "That is to say, I don't know." I hid my hands in the folds of my skirt and crossed my fingers for luck. "Our companionship . . . well, that is to say, our friendship has run its course. The last time I saw him was the night I saw you, when your regiment arrived to town."

"How dare he abandon you thus!" Ebenezer said. "In the middle of a war! Surrounded by danger! I shall punch his nose when next I see him. With your permission, of course."

"You may not, for you have grabbed the matter at the wrong end," I said. "'Twas not him, 'twas me, but then he agreed . . . we agreed that our companionship had reached its natural conclusion. He is determined to live his own life. As am I."

I did not enjoy the sensation that arose in me when I had to discuss Curzon. I gave my head a shake, then shared our tale with Eben—everything about the tavern, the laundry, the woods. I neglected to mention that we'd been in the woods on our way to the British lines. As I spoke, Ruth picked a handful of wildflowers and braided them into a chain.

"Can you help us?" I finally asked.

He looked at me in sorrow. "It pains me to say this, but I've no money, Isabel. The army paid us for the first time in years a while back. Had to buy boots, for my feet were almost naked. Took all my pay. I'm sorry to say I've nothing to give you."

"Oh, no!" I exclaimed. "I seek only work, nothing more. Even a few days would be welcome. Honest work in exchange for food."

Ruth set the braided chain of flowers upon her neck, as proud as if they were the jewels of a queen.

"He should never have left you in such a perilous position," Eben fumed. "Even if the bonds of friendship had frayed. He told me that his enlistment did not sit well with you."

"That is a gentle way to describe my strong disagreement. But that's no longer my concern."

"You've not seen him here in camp, then?"

"He made it very clear to me that our friendship was over. I agreed with him." I pulled my courage up to the surface and grabbed at it. "Could we work for your company or elsewhere in the regiment? You know we're accustomed to hardship."

"I figger you can do 'bout anything." He ran his hand over his face. "But the army has rules about how many women a regiment can take on. And my captain, he's a right dragon when it comes to the rules. That's why I had to holler so at my men back there. They're good lads, of course, but the captain insists on things being just so. He won't allow me to hire you on. That's the hard truth of the matter."

The surprise of his refusal left me speechless. I'd made the mistake of having only one plan. I should have known better.

"Of course," I murmured.

"Blast it all." Eben thrashed his leg with his hat, which did much to explain its ragged appearance. He seemed to hold a confab with his own self. "You cannot amble around the countryside, that's clear. It's just that . . . times being what they are . . . in ordinary circumstances . . . blast his eyes, there is no other remedy for this!"

He again beat his hat on his leg and then plopped it on his head.

"Follow me!" he commanded.

Eben strode back down the lane of tents at twice the pace he'd moved before. Ruth and I were forced to pick up our skirts and run to stay with him. He led us deep into the Continental forces; surrounded by so many soldiers, I dared not ask a single question of him. That unnerved me. Had I made a mistake putting our trust in him?

He finally stopped in front of an officer's tent that had a regimental standard with an anchor upon it. A large cook fire had been set in a properly dug pit, with a goodly amount of wood split down to the proper size to make burning easy. A hunk of salted beef sat upon a rough-hewn board set across two barrels, but there was no meal under preparation. Packs and haversacks were heaped on the ground, and a dozen muskets stood around an upturned log, properly grounded, so that the bit made for the shoulder rested in the dirt, and the muzzles pointed skyward.

Ebenezer looked at the soldiers going about the work of building the encampment. Tents stretched down a long slope, bringing to mind rows of whitecaps breaking on the shore.

"Wait here," he said. "I'll be right back."

"What company is this?" I whispered to Ruth as he vanished around the tent.

Ruth studied the flag and shrugged. "Don't know that one."

A black man dressed in knee breeches the color of dried tobacco and a linen shirt with the sleeves rolled up came around the side of the tent with a load of wood for the fire. He smiled at us, stacked the wood neatly, then brushed off his hands and bowed to us.

"May I be of service, miss?" he asked.

More soldiers came near, their arms heavy with logs to be split. Most of them were black men, all of them were sweat soaked but in high spirits.

"I'm awaiting the sergeant," I said to the first fellow. "Sergeant Woodruff."

The fellow tilted his head to the side and squinted at me. He stepped closer, staring at my face, at the mark on my cheek.

"Might you be the good wife of our Private Smith?"

I was so confounded by his question that I could not answer.

"Curzon's wife is here?" asked another fellow, grinning.

Wife?

"Is Curzon here?" Ruth asked cheerfully.

The fellow pointed at me. "If you are Missus Smith, then this"—he pointed to my flower-bedecked sister—"this must be Miss Ruth. Our angels have arrived!" he exclaimed. "They've come to save us!"

The delighted reaction of the new arrivals confuddled me even more. The soldiers hurried over, bowing, shouting huzzahs, babbling about my illness and Ruth's poor health, and how pleased the sergeant would be, and "of course, your husband."

Husband?

CHAPTER XXXII

Saturday, September 29, 1781

IT IS VOTED AND RESOLVED, THAT EVERY ABLE-BODIED NEGRO, MULATTO OR INDIAN MAN SLAVE IN THIS STATE, MAY ENLIST INTO EITHER OF THE SAID TWO BATTALIONS TO SERVE DURING . . . THE PRESENT WAR WITH GREAT BRITAIN; THAT EVERY SLAVE SO ENLISTING SHALL BE ENTITLED TO AND RECEIVE ALL THE BOUNTIES, WAGES, AND ENCOURAGEMENTS ALLOWED BY THE CONTINENTAL CONGRESS TO ANY SOLDIER ENLISTING IN THEIR SERVICE. . . .
EVERY SLAVE SO ENLISTING SHALL . . . BE IMMEDIATELY DISCHARGED FROM THE SERVICE OF HIS MASTER OR MISTRESS, AND BE ABSOLUTELY FREE, AS THOUGH HE HAD NEVER BEEN INCUMBERED WITH ANY KIND OF SERVITUDE OR SLAVERY.
–ACT OF THE RHODE ISLAND LEGISLATURE, FEBRUARY 1778

I OPENED MY MOUTH TO EXPLAIN that a mistake had been made, but before I could say anything, the first fellow ran off, waving his hat and shouting, "Sir! They're here! Missus Smith and her sister!"

Mayhaps I didn't hear him proper. I was certain that I would know it if I were a wife . . . or if I had a husband, which was largely the same thing. Mayhaps I was coming down with a fever that had stopped my ears from working. I felt my brow. Warm, it was, but not fevered.

Then Curzon arrived.

He wore the same dusty Continental breeches as the other lads and his old shirt with the ragged, too-short sleeves.

Sweat trickled down his face and along the thin scar on the left side of his chin. His gaze traveled to Ruth, to his companions, up to the heavens, and down to the dirt. He looked at every blessed thing, every person, but me.

Ruth bounced on her toes, as happy as I'd seen her since we left Riverbend. "We come to help you fight the redcoats, Curzon!"

The other fellows laughed heartily.

"Have ye been struck dumb and blind by the beauty of yer missus?" called one of the fellows.

"Give her a kiss!" called another.

He finally looked in my eyes. His haunted gaze was filled with misery and made me feel the worst sort of wretch, though I could not figger why. We seemed to be players in a game, but no one had explained the rules to me, and the stakes seemed dangerously high. What would a wife, a proper wife, do in a situation such as this?

"Good day," I said formally, bending my knees in a brief curtsy, keeping my back straight and tall.

"Good day," he answered. "Dear wife."

"We have much to discuss," I said.

"In more private circumstances," he said.

"Go on, you lout!" a soldier called. "Show her that you missed her!"

Curzon grimaced, as if the words had been a punch in his belly. He lifted his hat and performed a dramatic bow, like a highborn gentleman or a fop on a stage. It recalled to me the first time I saw him, at the end of a wharf in New York. He stood again and replaced his hat with an air of weariness. I knew now what made him seem so strange. He was not smiling. He looked as if he'd forgotten how.

"'Twas not my intention—" I started.

"Are you feeling well enough, wife?" Curzon asked in a hollow voice. "The intermittent fever had taken such a strong hold of you and Ruth."

"We are both well," I said. "Husband."

That word had never come forth from my mouth that way. It near choked me.

"I told the lads about your delicious way with pies." He sounded as joyful as a thief on his way to the gallows. This could have been because he had eaten my pies, or rather, tried to eat them. I'd not developed the kitchen skills of most lasses on account of our wanderings. I could cook the most basic of foods, but pies were beyond my reach.

One of his mates draped an arm around Curzon's shoulders. "I'd give my arm for one of my Phoebe's peach pies. She uses butter and peaches, but I don't know what else. Might be an incantation involved too. She's a magical lass, my Phoebe." He gave Curzon a hearty slap on the back. "Aren't you a lucky rogue!"

Ebenezer appeared between the tents, speaking with quiet intent to an officer of his same complexion and build. Curzon stiffened at the sight of the new man. The other fellows quickly turned back to the task of stacking the logs they'd brought.

"Missus Smith," the new officer said as he approached. It took Ebenezer clearing his throat uncommonly loud to remind me that the new officer truly thought that was my name.

The shock of it caused me to curtsy much lower than I needed to. Ruth imitated me and had the sense to mind her tongue in the presence of a white stranger.

"Sergeant Armstrong," he introduced himself. "We did not meet when your husband enlisted. A bit out of the ordinary, but Sergeant Woodruff is a man I trust. He assured me that he knew you both at Valley Forge and commended your skills and reputation. Have you fully recovered from your illnesses, you and your sister?"

I fought to make sense of this suddenly strange and swirling world. "Yes, sir," I answered. "Thank you, sir. We are quite well."

"I am relieved to have you restored to health and ready for service, ma'am. We sorely need your aid." He peered over my shoulder at my haversack. "Is that a washing bat I spy?"

"Indeed, sir. My sister has one as well, and we've a small crock of soap."

He chuckled. "That is most welcome. The stink of my men has become the talk of the brigade. Mayhaps you could turn your hand to washing their togs tomorrow. Some of the women of the army have established tents and brush huts at the back of the encampment. Would you care to sort out your sleeping arrangements now?"

"If I may sir," I said. "I'd rather prepare supper for the lads. They'll be hungry."

"Soldiers are always hungry." Sergeant Armstrong smiled. "A stew that didn't taste like rotted fish would be a welcome change. Two moments with your lady, Private Smith, then back to work." He touched his fingertips to the brim of his hat. "A pleasure to have you with us."

"Thank you, Sergeant, sir." I curtsied again. "And thank you, Sergeant Woodruff."

I gave Ruth a little kick. She bobbed and did not say a word, for which I said a short prayer of thanks.

Sergeant Armstrong turned and walked away, followed by his men and Ebenezer, who winked at us before he left. I watched them stride away until they were swallowed up in the hubbub of the growing camp.

Curzon still had not moved.

"Where is the best water found?" I asked him. "That beef wants to be boiled."

"No good water close by." He frowned. "You have to wade deep into a frog pond to get some that doesn't stink of sulfur. I'll fetch it for you."

I stepped closer. "It was not my intention for any of this. Ebenezer, this was his doing."

He ignored my words, pointing at a short stack of crates near the woodpile. "You'll find dried peas in one of those. Meat needs cutting, but I don't know where you can find a knife. Everything is still a jumble."

"My hatchet is plenty sharp," I said.

He paused, then nodded in a melancholy way. "Always was."

Two cannons fired in Yorktown. Ruth and I flinched. This part of the American encampment was closer to the British fortifications, and the noise was disturbingly louder.

"Their shots cannot reach this far," Curzon said. "You are well out of danger here."

He hesitated. For a moment I thought he'd say something about this strange circumstance we found ourselves in. That he'd explain and then laugh, and then we'd sort out the mess and everything would go back to the way it had been when we were friends.

But all he said was, "I'll fetch that water now."

CHAPTER XXXIII

Sunday September 30–Saturday, October 6, 1781

A MILITIA MAN THIS DAY, POSSESSED OF MORE BRAVERY [THAN] PRUDENCE, STOOD CONSTANTLY ON THE PARAPET AND D[––]D HIS SOUL IF HE WOULD DODGE FOR THE BUGGERS. HE HAD ESCAPED LONGER THAN COULD HAVE BEEN EXPECTED, AND, GROWING FOOL-HARDY, BRANDISHED HIS SPADE AT EVERY [CANNON]BALL THAT WAS FIRED, TILL, UNFORTUNATELY, A BALL CAME AND PUT AN END TO HIS CAPERS.
—DIARY OF CAPTAIN JAMES DUNCAN, PENNSYLVANIA LINE, OCTOBER 3, 1781

RISE, DEAR." A WOMAN WITH A KIND voice and jolly face shook my shoulder. "The sun will awake soon."

I sat up reluctantly. "Thank you, Sibby."

She nodded and crawled backward out of the brush hut. Sibby and a one-eyed white woman called Cristena had helped us construct this brush hut the night before, using poles and hemlock branches.

"Wake up, sister." I shook Ruth's arm. "We're in the army, heaven help us."

After visiting the women's privy trench, it took us only a few moments of swift walking to travel from the back of the encampment to the cook fire of our company. The ghostly forms of other lasses moved through the mist with us, everyone slapping at the infernal midges, mosquitoes, fleas, and lice. More tents had been put up in the night. Most could hold six, some bigger, others smaller. A few soldiers slept sprawled on the ground, on account of the heat, mayhaps, or the stench of their tent mates. All of them snored.

To earn our food rations, Ruth and I had to care for a company of forty-five lads. Sibby had given me bushels of advice about how to keep the fellows fed, clean, and fit for duty. "Get the cook fire going first," she said. "Once you trust that it won't burn out, hurry to the frog pond for water. Boil that soon as you can, for hot water is always in short supply. Beans take longer than peas to cook, and peas take longer than porridge. Maggots don't hurt no one, long as they are boiled with the meat."

When we arrived at the company that first morning, our lads were still asleep. Their snores made me wonder if their tents were inhabited by fat oxen instead of young soldiers. Someone had been kind enough to fill two of the kettles with water. That was a trip saved. But all of the firewood that had been split the night before had burned down to coal and ash.

"Niff-naffy nincompoops," I muttered.

Ruth sat on an upturned log. "You cursed."

"Beg pardon," I said automatically. "But they could have set some wood aside for the breakfast cooking." I picked up one of the axes that leaned against the woodpile and tested the blade. Not as sharp as I'd like, but it would do the job.

"I can chop," Ruth said.

She was willing, but I doubted she had the knack of it. At the laundry I'd done all the splitting of logs whilst she was out on her delivery rounds.

"You're too slender to swing an axe," I said. "You'll topple over backward."

Ruth held out her hand. "Bigger than you."

Much as it pained me, there was no denying that. And starting the day off with an argument would help no one.

"You can try," I said. "But that wood's green. Gonna take strength that you don't have. Go slow and take care."

Ruth rolled up her sleeves, muscled a log onto the chopping block, then hefted the axe in her hands, finding its balance. She eyed the log, stepped back, and swung the axe with skill. The blade cut the log cleanly in two, like it was made of butter, not newly felled pine.

She turned to me, smiling with pride.

"Huzzah indeed," I said in surprise. "Well done, sister."

"I'm no nincompoop," Ruth said.

The rhythm of our days was driven by the drums. Uniformed drummers gathered at the artillery park, at headquarters, and at the brigade common places to act as clocks of sound for the vast encampment. They drummed at dawn, then later to assemble the men for inspection and orders. They drummed to send them off to their duties of the day—patrolling, doing work details, standing guard, and foraging—and again when it was time to return to camp.

We worked from the dark before dawn to the dark after sunset. Sometimes we worked in the cool of the night, when the constant sound of British cannons firing hundreds of shots provided a strange rhythm of its own. After those nights we hungered for sleep as if it were bread.

At first Ruth kept close by my side, but as she became acquainted with a few of the camp's women, she began to venture with them on errands and chores. She smiled easily and enjoyed teasing me, though from time to time I found her staring at the columns of soldiers as they tramped by our cook fire, looking each one in the face. When I asked whom she was seeking, she claimed she was watching for Thomas, the donkey we'd left behind at the laundry. She said this with eyes downcast and her hands twisting at her skirt, both signals that she was lying. We'd discussed Thomas Boon frequently, and she understood that in all likelihood we would not see him again. I was certain that she was keeping an eye out for Aberdeen, but I resolved not to question her about it. I did not want to rob her of her dreams.

The men worked as if their breeches were on fire. Patrols constantly roamed the edges of the encampment, keeping a sharp eye out for sneak attacks of the British. Men rotated duties; one day felling trees, building bridges, and keeping the camp in good order, and the next drilling with muskets and bayonets. The anticipation of the day when they'd finally clash with their enemy built like steam in a lidded pot.

The fellows in our company were high spirited and friendly. Listening to the manner of their Rhode Island–flavored speech gave me comfort. Near half of them had joined the army to earn their freedom, Rhode Island being the only state to offer that opportunity to enslaved men. Black or white, they accorded me the respect due a married woman and teased Ruth as if she were their own sister.

Only one fellow among them kept his distance: Curzon Smith. He'd greet me same as his mates, thank me for the stew, bread, or coffee, then take himself away to eat out of sight of the cook fire. No one mentioned this odd behavior, but everyone noticed it, I was sure. I'd discovered that though he had signed us up when he enlisted himself, it was clear that I ought not read any sort of sentiment, any feeling of his heart, within that gesture. Likely he had not wanted to suffer the discomfort of filthy clothes, or mayhaps he wanted to have me close by in case there was a need to battle snakes or gators.

I was content to care for my fellow statesmen, filling their bellies and tending to washing their shirts. Ruth and I were safe, for the time being, and we had decent work. I decided that this temporary circumstance suited me just fine.

A thin, gray-grizzled soldier in our company named Henry took it upon himself to teach me the army's intents and purposes. The coming encounter with the British was not to be a great battle, as had been fought in Brooklyn in 1776 or Monmouth in 1778. Nay, this was to be a siege, a long, drawn-out affair that could last weeks or months. We had two soldiers for every one of theirs, so we could afford to move slow and steady.

He used a long stick to draw a map in the dirt for me. The river looked like a snake. He carved the shape of a bread loaf pan to show Yorktown's position upon the riverbank. Then he drew a vast shape of half of a pie—the straighter edge of it being the river, and the rounded part extending far from Yorktown. At the far edges of the half pie was the entire allied encampment, he said. The French controlled the west portion, and the Patriots controlled the east, though from a goodly distance, on account of the British continuing to shoot cannonballs through the air. In between the encampment and Yorktown the land was in some places dry, in others quite marshy.

Henry drew a circle in the middle of that no-man's-land. "Lobsterbacks have a redoubt, a small fort filled with sharpshooters, here at Pigeon Hill. We need to take control of that first off, if you ask me. With that in hand, our cannons will determine everything, soon as they arrive."

"But how?" I asked. "We sit here"–I pointed to the rounded edge of the encampment–"where the cannons cannot harm us. Can our guns shoot farther than theirs?"

"Not at all," Henry said. "That's why we're so busy chopping down every tree in the woods. We're preparing to open a parallel."

I'd never heard of such a word, "parallel." Its true meaning was "trench," Henry said. The troops were going to dig a dreadful-wide and deep trench that zigged and zagged through the middle of the no-man's-land. Once it was dug, they'd drag the cannons through the trench, aim them at Yorktown, and start blasting. Our cannons would inflict greater damage on account of being much closer to Yorktown than the British cannons were to us, and the deepness of the trench would help protect the men.

I thought it would take months to dig a trench that large, but I kept that opinion to myself. I stirred the barley soup that bubbled over the fire and asked Henry why the lads were so busy flattening the forest when their true aim was to dig a trench and blow up the town.

He laughed at that, but it was a kind laugh, not intended to make me feel like an ignorant looby. "The wood serves many purposes to protect the diggers. It helps hold the walls of the trench in place. From its branches we fashion large baskets that will be filled with the dirt dug from the trench. These will then be set as a protective wall at the front edge of the parallel."

"When you're in the woods," I said, lowering my voice, "have you seen fugitives out there, our people? The British drove them from Yorktown without food or aid. I've heard many died of smallpox."

"Aye," Henry said somberly. "We bury the bodies that we find. The officers don't like us taking the time to do it, so we don't burden them with the information. I'm a preacher of sorts, did the lads tell you that? I pray over each grave. I hope that gives those poor souls some comfort."

Loud cries of "Huzzah!" spread through the camp one morning shortly after sunrise. Under the cover of night the British had abandoned the Pigeon Hill redoubt and retreated to Yorktown. Our lads had taken control of the little fort, and we all celebrated. The army now controlled the middle of the no-man's-land. Better still, we controlled the stream of clean water that ran along the bottom of the hill; water the camp desperately needed. Our soup and coffee no longer tasted of frog, rotted eggs, and copper. We used the pond water only for washing after that. This must have surely distressed the poor fish, for the clothes of soldiers are the nastiest imaginable.

Sibby took Ruth with her to fetch potatoes and corn from the provision wagons, then to the new bake ovens established by Mister Ludwig, the Baker-General. Fresh-baked bread cheered the entire camp, but our lads most of all. I'd tried to bake a loaf in a small kettle and produced a hard lump of coal for my troubles. Took me most of the night to chip out the burnt bits with my hatchet.

The complications of a siege seemed endless.

CHAPTER XXXIV

Saturday, October 6, 1781

IT IS JUSTIFIABLE THAT NEGROES SHOULD HAVE THEIR FREEDOM, AND NONE AMONGST US HELD AS SLAVES, AS FREEDOM AND LIBERTY IS THE GRAND CONTROVERSY THAT WE ARE CONTENDING FOR.
—MASSACHUSETTS LIEUTENANT THOMAS KENCH, WRITING TO THE MASSACHUSETTS LEGISLATURE, 1778

SATURDAY DAWNED RAINY AND COOL. I kept a rag tucked in my pocket for the momentous sneezes that exploded from my snout at the worst times. Ruth had a cough, but at least her nose did not resemble a dripping spring.

We executed our daily maneuvers: cooking breakfast, washing up after the cooking, fetching the rations for the next three meals, preparing the lunch and starting on the supper, more washing up. We had a brief respite between lunch and supper, as the sergeant explained that our fellows would be late returning from fatigue duty. To take advantage of this break in our action, Ruth went with Sibby and the other women to the stream. I'd been tasked with convincing the brigade armorer to repair our smallest cook kettle, which now leaked, thanks to my chipping efforts with the hatchet.

The poor fellow was so busy hammering, he scarce had time to listen to my request. "Nay, lass," he said, sparks flying in the air. "Only allowed to repair digging tools today." He jerked his head toward the mound of axe heads, shovel blades, and billhooks behind him. "Yer welcome to leave it, if ye please."

Kettles and pans tended to go missing from the blacksmith's, Sibby had told me.

"I'll bring it on the morrow, thank you, sir."

I worked my way through the crowd, wondering if burning porridge to the bottom of the kettle would fashion a patch that would stop up the leak, when someone called out to me.

"Isabel!"

I turned to see Curzon running. I could scarce believe my eyes. He'd barely spoken to me since our arrival. Oh, he'd been polite enough when I served him roasted meat or coffee, but he never lingered for conversating or joked with me like the other lads did. Once his tin mug and wooden bowl were filled, off he went, his face cloudy and unreadable.

"Do you need something?" I asked, puzzled by this sudden change in his habits. "Lose a button from your breeches?"

He cracked his knuckles. "Nay."

We stepped off the rough road as a bear-size man drove a wagonload of tools to the blacksmith.

"Feeling poorly?" I asked. "Your belly or your pate?"

"It's not that."

The blacksmith and the wagon driver started arguing, shaking their fists at each other.

"Can we . . . ," Curzon started. "I was told . . ."

The wagon driver shouted that he had orders from headquarters requiring that everything in his wagon must be repaired by nightfall. The blacksmith erupted with a fountain of foul language that set everyone to chortling.

"May we go elsewhere?" he asked. "To talk?"

"I have to start the supper."

"No, you don't." He cleared his throat. "Sergeant told me to take you for a walk. On account of . . . how busy I've been, and . . . anyway. I tried to tell him you were occupied with your tasks, but he insisted. Fact is, he ordered me."

"He ordered you to take me for a walk?" I looked over his shoulder. Isaac, Drury, and Tall Will, all tent mates of Curzon's, stood between us and the blacksmith. They waved at me with great vigor and amusement. "Are they to accompany us?"

He rolled his eyes and shook his head. "They're making sure I follow the order. Our predicament gives them great sport."

"What predicament?"

He turned and scowled at his mates, then answered my question with one of his own. "I pray you, Isabel, may we take that walk?"

"Long as we head back to the company."

"By an indirect path, if it's all the same to you."

It wasn't, but his mysterious manner caused me to agree. We walked a bit in an awkward silence, passing a sutler's, where strong drink was sold to soldiers with coin to pay for it, then a slaughter yard, where the stench of steaming piles of offal had attracted battalions of buzzing flies.

"Mayhaps we ought turn upwind," I suggested.

"Agreed, but give me that kettle," he said. "Else the lads will chide me for being uncourtly."

I handed over the wounded pot. It felt wondrous strange to walk along with nothing in my arms or on my back. Then I sneezed loud as a horse and fumbled for my snot rag.

"You're not well," Curzon said. "You ought rest a day or two."

"Ruth can't do all that work herself. I'm fine."

"But you allow her to go on errands alone."

"She's more capable than I gave her credit for when first we found her. She doesn't have the wit for everything, but she is a fair hand at remembering the location of places—how to reach the washing stream, commissary stores, and the camp kitchen. Regular compass in her brainpan."

"She's never gotten lost?"

"Not once. She dawdles to talk to the horses, of course, but that's no crime."

He shifted the kettle to his other arm. "Seems her manner to you has softened some."

I tucked my rag back in my pocket. "We've softened to each other."

He returned my smile. "She's lucky to have a sister like you."

"I am lucky to have her. And grateful . . ." I paused as heat rushed my face and head. "Grateful for your steadfast assistance in finding her. I could never have done that on my own."

He shrugged. "Least I could do. I lost track of the number of times you saved my neck."

An acorn bounced off the kettle, thrown by one of the lads following us. I turned to scold them, but they stopped and stared up at a tree, marveling loudly at a nest perched in its branches.

"Ignore them," Curzon advised. "I saw Eben yesterday. He explained what happened with your papers, with Hallahan. How it was you came to the camp."

"'Twas never my intention to seek you out," I said in a rush. "I didn't know that Ebenezer—"

"He explained that you didn't want to involve me. But he knew that I'd listed you as my wife."

The word seemed to explode like a cannon shot. We walked again in silence.

"Why didn't you tell me?" I asked quietly.

"I tried to that night in Williamsburg, but we lost our tempers and you called me . . ."

"I called you a muzzy-headed blatherskite."

He lifted his eyebrows. "And you said I had a bizarre attachment to a cause that didn't give a damn about me."

"I've not yet changed my mind about that."

"Now who's the blatherskite? You're working for a company filled with black soldiers. We're treated the same as our white compatriots—same food, same risk, same tents."

"I don't see any black generals giving the orders."

"You will. Someday."

I sneezed again, but before I could dig out my rag, Curzon produced a much cleaner sort from his own pocket and gave it to me.

"I apologize," he said. "Shouldn't have signed you up without your knowledge and leave. I only did it to ensure your safety."

"It is not natural for me to admit that I'm ever in the wrong," I said, wiping my nose. "But I apologize for being so horrid that night. I'm happy you found us a place here. Grateful, again."

I handed him his rag, but he shook his head.

"Sleeve's good enough for me. You hear that we're finally ready to start the digging and open the parallel tonight?"

"Hmm," I grumbled. "Barmy idea, if you ask me." The planned trench that Henry had described to me had been the only topic of conversating round the cook fire for days.

"Constructing parallels is an ancient part of the proper

conduct of a siege. There is a military philosophy behind it all."

"Barmy," I repeated. "That trench won't be ready until Christmas."

"We'll be digging all day and all night," he protested. "Thousands of strong men armed with shovels."

"Don't matter."

He burst out laughing. "You're hardly an expert on the construction of siege parallels, Country."

"No, but I'm an expert on getting fields ready for planting. Do you know how heavy the dirt will be with all this rain? It would take weeks even if you weren't being blown to bits by the lobsterbacks."

He set down the kettle and scooped dirt from the road. "Put out your hand, please."

I sighed but allowed him to take my hand in his. The warmth of his skin startled me. The three loobies, Isaac, Drury, and Tall Will, hooted with delight.

"Digging is hard work in the heavy mud of Rhode Island." He poured a slow stream of damp, sandy soil into my palm. "But here the dirt is mostly sand, light as air. We'll have to work hard, but we can do this, you'll see."

I let the sand fall between my fingers. "A fellow in Captain Bond's company was killed by a nine-pound cannonball yesterday."

"We're at war, Isabel. Death is an ever-present danger."

The rain suddenly fell harder, pattering on the leaves. We walked again, our pace quickened.

"Perfect weather," Curzon said. "Harder for the British to see us tonight in mist and rain. We're supposed to work in silence to avoid detection."

"Thousands of our soldiers—silent? Is that even possible?"

"You said 'our.'"

"Yes, I said 'our.' Have you walked through camp in the dark?" I asked. "Even asleep our soldiers sound like ten thousand monsters roaring."

"No one will be sleeping whilst digging the parallel. What are you shaking your head about?"

"You always see the best of any circumstance, don't you? It's pouring down buckets of rain on our heads, and still you find sunshine."

"Rain's going to fall, can't change that. The trick of it is to find the good in the rain, the aspect of positivity. Rains come and rains go, but the sun is always waiting to shine, waiting on the far side of the clouds."

"What ho, Private Smith!" called Drury. He and the others stood a dozen paces behind us.

"Blasted bumpkins," Curzon muttered.

"You are neglecting your sergeant's command in this matter," Isaac said.

"What is he prattling on about?" I asked.

Curzon puffed out his cheeks with air, then exhaled noisily. "I must pretend to kiss you now, or we shall never hear the end of it."

I wasn't sure I'd heard him correctly. "I beg your pardon?"

"They won't shut their gobs about my mistreatment of you, my lack of husbandly kindness. Sergeant agrees, God help us, which is why those cods are following us and leering like jack-o'-lanterns. I'm supposed to make up for my recent coldness to you. My apologies, Isabel. 'Tis not my intention to be disrespectful or offer you insult."

Between the rain, my stuffed nose, and the unusual circumstance, I was not sure I understood what he was saying. "You want to kiss me?"

"They want me to kiss you."

That clarified things somewhat. "But you don't want to kiss me?"

"Yes. No." He shook his head in confusion. "Most of all I don't want to make you mad. I am uncommonly skilled at it."

"Indeed," I agreed. We both seemed unsure of this matter. "We require a ruse, methinks." I wiped the rain from my face and took my shawl from my head. "Think of this as a shield for our privacy. Hold that corner of it."

He did as I asked, then followed my motion as I raised the scarf until it fluttered in the rain like a curtain. Isaac, Drury, and Tall Will could not see if I was smiling or wiping my nose. "Bring your face in close to me. But don't you dare kiss me, if you value your life."

He followed my orders.

"May I touch your shoulder?" I whispered. His face was so close to mine that my eyes crossed a bit, making it look as if he had three eyes, not two. "Seems a touch like that is the sort of thing a person might do whilst kissing."

His mouth gaped open, then shut, like a fish flopping on a riverbank. "I do believe that is true."

I reached out with my free hand. Heat from his skin warmed his damp shirt. The muscles in his shoulder were hard as iron. I had the strangest sensation in my belly, like toads were hopping inside it again. I told myself this was a sign that my illness was moving from my nose to my innards.

I cleared my throat. "How long should we stand like this?"

"Bit longer," he whispered.

"Make me a promise?"

"Anything," he answered without hesitation.

"Stay clear of the cannonballs when you're digging that infernal trench."

His easy smile reminded me of the boy he'd once been. "I promise."

"Thank you." I stepped back, jerked the shawl from his fingers, and spun it so that it again covered my head and shoulders. I walked away with my dignity, trying to ignore the applause from our rowdy audience and the sudden heat that rushed to my face.

CHAPTER XXXV

Saturday, October 6–Monday, October 8, 1781

[SARAH] TOOK HER STAND JUST BACK OF THE AMERICAN TENTS . . . AND BUSIED HERSELF WASHING, MENDING, AND COOKING FOR THE SOLDIERS, IN WHICH SHE WAS ASSISTED BY THE OTHER FEMALES.
—PENSION APPLICATION OF SARAH OSBORN, WHO WORKED FOR HER HUSBAND'S UNIT, THE THIRD NEW YORK REGIMENT, AT YORKTOWN

GENERAL WASHINGTON OPENED THE trench. That is to say, he sank the first pickaxe into the ground. Normally, such a thing would have been done with banners waving and drums beating, but that would have drawn unwanted lobsterback attention. Thus, the general sank his pickaxe into the ground, bowed to a gentle applause, and stepped out of the way so the men could proceed with their task.

We could not see this work, of course. We stayed at the company campfire to keep it blazing high. The lads would need something hot to drink and would want to warm themselves when their night's work was done. Besides, it rained hard enough that we couldn't have seen the digging if we'd stood ten paces away.

The captain's tent was close to the fire, but we would

have broken ten kinds of rules had we stayed dry and warm in there. I suppose no one would have raised a fuss if we'd stayed in the tent where Curzon slept, seeing as they all thought he and I were wed, but that was quite a distance from the fire, and we'd get twice as wet dashing back and forth to keep the flames alive.

Ruth and I erected a sad excuse for a hut in an attempt to provide ourselves with fireside shelter. We hammered long poles into the ground a pace in front of the woodpile, then draped a cast-off piece of canvas atop the pile and tied it to the poles so that it could behave as a roof for us. It was not much for behaving, letting in as much rain as it kept out.

"Fool notion," Ruth grumbled as we huddled under the dripping canvas. "Being moles."

"We're not moles," I said. "Ducks mayhaps."

"Not us. Them. Moles dig holes. Not soldiers."

"Indeed." I paused and waited for the echoes from two cannon blasts to die away. "Must be busy moles tonight. Safe moles, I hope."

There was another long rumble. Thunder, not cannon fire.

"Quack," Ruth muttered.

"Beg pardon?"

"We're ducks. Quack. Quack."

It was a joke of sorts, but Ruth's smile was brief. She'd been troubled since we heard of the tales told by the latest British deserters. Conditions in Yorktown were dire, they said. Hundreds of the redcoats' horses had been shot because there was no food for them. Their bodies had been thrown into the river, in the hopes they'd be washed out to sea. The tide brought back the rotting corpses and deposited them on the riverbanks, where they remained. The soldiers were hungry too and limited to restricted rations. And now bilious fever had broken out.

She was heartbroken about the horses, of course, but her true concern was still for Aberdeen. I had hoped that her fondness for him would fade as she struck up new friendships in the camp, but it had not. He had been her friend for as long as she could remember. His absence weighed heavy on her heart, and I knew not how to ease her sorrow.

By the time the lads returned at dawn, filthy and soaked from hair to boots, we had the fire roaring despite the rain and served them fresh coffee and hot stew. Their voices fell over one another, teasing, boasting, hooting with laughter, as joyful as a group of boys who'd been chasing pigs for fun. To hear them tell it, the entire night had been one long game, each company trying to outdo the others in how much trench they could dig before dawn. The gloom and rain had indeed protected them from discovery. The false French attack on the western redoubts had helped too.

I finished serving out the stew but still had several bowlfuls in the kettle. I peered through the rain. I counted the men and came up short. Curzon and several others were missing.

And then he came running up the road, Isaac at one side of him, Henry on the other, all of them laughing. I sneezed again and shook my head in frustration. Staying awake all night in the rain was having a woeful effect on my health.

"All hail Lord Shellhawk!" crowed Drury.

"To Shellhawk!" The others lifted their cups in a toast directed at Curzon.

He grinned, abashed. "Enough of that. Let me eat."

I ladled out his stew. "What did they call you?"

"Yer man earned himself a nickname last night," Henry explained. "A shell flew in so quick upon the heels of a previous shot, no one could move fast enough, except for Lord Shellhawk there. He dove at the three lads in harm's way."

"Crushing our tender bones into the earth!" exclaimed a fellow by the woodpile.

"Saved them from harm."

"I need not have done it," Curzon said sheepishly. "Blasted thing landed far enough away."

"That's not the point," Henry said. "You sought to protect them from mortal danger."

"But how could a shell cause such harm?" I asked.

The men stared at me with astonished mortification.

"Beg pardon?" Henry said. "Do you not know what a shell is, missus?"

"I've held them in my hands, of course," I said. "The sea casts up all manner of shells; they can be fashioned into buttons–"

The fellows exploded into such loud laughter, it fair made the ground shake beneath. Indeed, a few laughed so hard that tears came to their eyes.

"Armies cast up much deadlier shells, Country," Curzon explained gently. "Mortar shells. Hollow iron balls packed with gunpowder and fired from cannons. A cannonball will kill a lad by taking off his leg or head. But the explosion of a shell can injure many, even kill them."

"Ready, lads?" called Isaac. "On yer feet for a new drill."

They all stood.

"Prepare for the Lord Shellhawk maneuver!"

They crouched, grinning like children.

"Shell!"

They launched at one another, tumbling and rolling in the

mud, laughing so hard, I thought they'd wet their breeches, which I'd then have to wash. But they'd earned their fun.

Curzon caught my eye. "I lived up to my promise, Country. Avoided all cannonballs and even the exploding shells."

"You must continue to do so," I said. "A true promise lasts forever."

The fever excitement of the encampment burned high as work continued on the trench, along with preparations for the cannons, which were due to arrive at any moment.

Ruth's mood, however, turned vexatious. She was not sour with me in particular, not like those dreadful months after we found her. She'd gotten out of sorts with the entire world, absentminded and secretive, unwilling to respond to the friendly teasing of Curzon and the others. I questioned her about this in a gentle manner, but she drew inside herself and would give me no answers.

The morning the long-anticipated cannons finally arrived, Sibby asked if I could spare Ruth to help her with the washing at the frog pond. I was grateful for the offer. With Ruth in trusted hands, I took the small kettle I'd injured with my hatchet to the blacksmith, who had finally agreed to repair it.

As I returned from the forge, I was startled to see Ruth walking ahead of me on the road. She should have been at the frog pond till midday. Something about her manner was odd. She walked slowly, her haversack over her shoulder, occasionally peering into the high thornbushes that grew on the right side of the road. Had a goat or pig escaped into the undergrowth? A chicken?

When we reached the crossroads, she turned left to make her way to the cook fire. I followed but said nothing to her about what I had seen. She was more vexatious as the day went on, forgetting to turn the pork and thus burning it, and neglecting to return the knives to their box. Come suppertime she claimed she was not hungry, wrapping her bread and meat in a rag and stowing it in her haversack. I felt her forehead for fever and made her remove her boot to prove that the old wound on her foot had not again filled with pus.

She called me a looby and stuck the foot in my face so I could fully appreciate the everyday stink of it. The old wound had not reopened, and my relief was such that I did not scold her.

Our fellows had the duty of guarding the trench diggers that night. They marched off as soon as they'd devoured their meal. While I washed up, Ruth split enough firewood to keep the fire going and make sure that our breakfast tasks would be easier. She swung the axe with anger, it seemed, but only shook her head when I asked if anything troubled her. Once she'd split and stacked enough wood, she said she was tired and wanted to go to our hut and sleep, even though it was long before we normally turned in.

"I'll walk with you," I said, thinking to ask Sibby and Cristena if they'd heard the rumors that the British prince, William Henry, was to be kidnapped from New York.

"No!" Ruth exclaimed. "You stay here!"

"Are you sure you feel well? There is camp fever in the Pennsylvania regiment, all manner of bowel disorders, they say."

"You stay here," she repeated.

She would not meet my eye, which signaled to me that she was definitely up to mischief.

"Go on, then," I said. "Sleep tight."

I followed her.

Her mind was not devious enough to check behind her

or try to disguise her path. She was not headed to our hut. I thought she might be planning to visit her friends in the horse corrals. That would explain why her supper was carefully wrapped in her haversack; she was bringing a treat for the pregnant mare owned by a French officer with an unpronounceable name. Critters made her feel better when people didn't.

Dark comes early in October, bringing pumpkin-bright sunsets and showers of falling leaves. A few drifted down upon Ruth, but she didn't look up, didn't marvel at their beauty. She strode forward until she reached the hedgerow of thornbushes where I'd spotted her earlier.

She paused then and for the first time looked about her. Her face brought to mind a child stealing a forbidden slice of cake. I slid behind a sutler's booth and watched, amazed, as the thorn hedge was mysteriously parted by unseen hands. Ruth removed her haversack and handed it through the opening. A moment later the sack reappeared, looking limp and empty. Ruth grabbed it, said something to the bushes that I could not hear, then hurried away in the direction of the women's huts.

She was crying.

I was torn between wanting to talk to her and needing to know who was hiding behind the hedge. I waited until she was out of sight, picked up a stout stick, and walked up to the hedge. The thornbushes parted.

Aberdeen's face appeared in the shadows.

"Please, Isabel!" he called hoarsely.

CHAPTER XXXVI

Monday, October 8, 1781

PERSUADED OF THE JUST RIGHT WHICH ALL MANKIND HAVE TO FREEDOM, NOTWITHSTANDING HIS OWN STATE OF BONDAGE, WITH AN HONEST DESIRE TO SERVE THIS COUNTRY . . . DID, DURING THE RAVAGES OF LORD CORNWALLIS THRO' THIS STATE . . . ENTER INTO THE SERVICE OF THE MARQUIS LAFAYETTE. . . . HE OFTEN AT PERIL OF HIS OWN LIFE FOUND MEANS TO FREQUENT THE BRITISH CAMP.
—SECOND PETITION OF JAMES ARMISTEAD TO THE VIRGINIA GENERAL ASSEMBLY FOR HIS FREEDOM BASED ON HIS SERVICE AS A SPY FOR THE PATRIOTS

WE MET AT THE FAR END OF THE hedgerow, away from passersby and prying eyes. He resembled more the boy I'd met at Riverbend than the confident lad who had tried to convince me to join the British. His filthy, ragged clothes looked like he'd been chased through acres of thorn hedges, and he gobbled Ruth's bread fast as a starving pig. But his appearance and manner did not move my heart.

"What in the name of heaven is wrong with you?" I demanded. "What did you do to Ruth to make her cry? And why are you hiding in the woods like a rogue?"

"Shhh," he warned. His desperate eyes darted, searching the shadows. "I did nothing to harm her; I never would! Walk with me. I'll tell you all, I swear."

"I cannot tarry."

"Please," he said. "I can talk quick."

I took in the sounds of the camp around us, measured which direction would offer a bit of privacy without danger. "Follow me," I said at last.

His story came out between bites of food and sips from the canteen slung over his neck. He had not been driven out of Yorktown like the dead we saw in the woods. Indeed, he was still acting the spy, reporting on conditions in the encampment to the British.

"When they treat you like this?" I asked, aghast.

"Like what?" He chewed a grisly bit of beef. "Everyone in Yorktown is hungry. But that will change any day. Redcoat army's coming from New York." He held up one hand. "Half will arrive in ships." He held up the other hand. "Half will arrive overland." He softly slapped his hands together. "Patriots and French gonna be trapped, smashed to bits between the two."

"What if you're wrong?"

"I'm not." He tried to smile, but it looked uncertain. "That's why I've come for Ruth. I mean to marry her."

"You're barmy." I snorted at the absurdity. "She's only twelve years old, and younger still in the way she sees the world."

"You ran off with Curzon at the same age."

"We escaped," I pointed out. "We journeyed as friends, as companions, nothing more. Ruth is not going anywhere with you." I picked up my skirts to leave him. "Farewell to you."

He grabbed my elbow. "Come with us."

I stopped as if he'd hit me in the face with a board.

"The noose is tightening, Isabel," he said. "This is my last trip. If you both come with me now, I can keep you safe.

You can wait upon the table of Lord Cornwallis himself!"

"He told you that, did he?"

"Nay," he admitted. "But we'll figger something."

"We're safe here," I said. "We have work and food and at least a few folks we can trust. The British deserters say that everyone in Yorktown is in despair, that people there are living in caves by the river."

His laugh startled me. "Never trust folks who betray their country."

"Like you?"

He lifted his chin. "Patriots ain't fighting for us, Isabel."

I thought about the men in our company, even the white ones, who were all committed to the same kind of freedom. However, there were more white people like Lockton, Hallahan, and Bellingham who looked at me and mine and saw not people, but tools that would earn them money. They did not see us for the people that we were, people just the same as them.

But Curzon's habit of remembering the sunshine that waited beyond the clouds had begun to infect me. "Some of them are fighting for us," I said. "And I mean to help them win."

"Then you'll lose everything," Aberdeen said bitterly. "Come with me, and bring Ruth."

A loud burst of laughter from a group of fellows on the road caused us both to freeze in the shadows. We waited until the boisterous voices had faded away.

"If you try to steal my sister," I warned, "I'll hand you over to General Washington myself."

"Don't fret." He sighed and sipped more water. "She won't leave without you."

"What?"

"Tried three times to get her to join me. She's a stubborn cuss, worse than that old donkey was."

His words made my heart sing, but his downcast face made it clear that his view of Ruth's choice was much different from mine.

"Mebbe my dreaming is overlarge," he admitted. "But with the three of us working for the King's army, we could get to New York for certain, or mebbe some other place."

"Like sugar plantations in Jamaica?" I asked. "Barbados? Oh, indeed, the British have plenty of work for people like us."

A shower of leaves fell between us.

"You used to say that both sides were wrong," he finally said.

"Mostly they are," I admitted. "But there might be enough good-hearted souls fighting for the Patriot cause to make a difference."

"Might?" he echoed. "What if you're wrong?"

"What if you're wrong about the British reinforcements?"

He shrugged. "King George rules the world, they say. They'll come."

"Your place is here. Stay with us," I urged. "We'll find you work with the French, if you can't stomach the Continentals. Think of how happy Ruth would be."

I surprised myself by bringing up Ruth like that. I'd been jealous of her affection for Aberdeen from the first moment I realized the depth of their friendship. Now I was encouraging him to join with us because it would cheer her and be the safest course for him.

He brushed the crumbs from his hands. "When the troops come from New York and destroy your army, I'll try to find you both."

The words were harsh, but his voice cracked as he said

them. He was caught between boyhood and manhood. It pained my heart to see him trying to be braver than he was.

He walked a few paces closer to the thorn hedge and peered through it before returning to me and asking in a low voice, "When will the rebel cannons get here?"

The question startled me. "Beg pardon?"

"They're digging the trench to blast cannonballs at us. So how many days until the cannons arrive? I need to know, so tell me."

"Your mission here is to spy on us?" I asked coldly. "You can go to the Devil. Get out of my sight before I scream and turn you in myself."

"The redcoats already know the cannons are here," he said, eyes sad. "I just wanted to know which side has truly claimed your heart."

CHAPTER XXXVII

Tuesday, October 9, 1781

How chequered is human life! How precarious is happiness! How easily do we often part with it for a shadow! These are the reflections that frequently intrude themselves upon me, with a painful application. I am going to do my duty.
—Letter from Colonel Alexander Hamilton to his wife, Elizabeth

I DID NOT SLEEP WELL AND ROSE LONG before dawn. That day's rations included a heavy bag of rice. I cooked it up with a lump of butter and added it to pork that had been stewing. It didn't taste of much, but it would fill the lads' bellies, and that was all that mattered.

They had been digging the trench all through the night. As the sun climbed into the sky, they returned to camp, tired and filthy, but in high spirits. I heated more water for washing. In those days of digging no man was ever clean in the proper sense of the word. The best I could do was to keep lice and other varmints from infesting their clothes, and insist that they dried their feet after working, so mushrooms wouldn't grow between their toes.

After eating, most of the fellows went to their tents to sleep while they could. Ruth sat by the fire holding the wooden cup and ball that Aberdeen had bought for her the day he first told me he was spying for the British. She stared into the flames, her face downcast, and did not play with the toy. She'd not spoken a word all morning.

Three men remained close to the campfire: Isaac and Tall Will, who cleaned their muskets whilst nattering about the best way to defeat the lobsterbacks, and Curzon, who was sharpening the axes. I washed the cook kettles, then washed them again, waiting for the moment when Curzon and I might be alone enough for a quiet confab, but it did not appear on its own.

Finally I cleared my throat.

"Curzon, might I trouble you to walk with me to fetch some water?"

He looked up in surprise as Isaac and Tall Will grinned. The lads of our company were as fond of romantical notions as any hero in a storybook.

"Aye," said the husband whom I had never married. "But I can fetch it on my own, if you'd rather stay here with Ruth."

My sister didn't even look up at the sound of her name.

"She's a bit poorly," I said. "And my legs are hungry for walking."

Isaac and Tall Will chuckled, but both Curzon and I ignored them. He glanced at the keen edge of the axe, then leaned it against the woodpile, picked up the two empty kettles, and joined me.

"Lead the way," he said.

I did not lead, nor did he follow. We walked side by side, occasionally so close to each other, when the path was crowded, that my skirts brushed against his legs and our elbows bumped. 'Twas a comfort to be walking in his company again, for it recalled the simpler days of our friendship. But we both held ourselves stiffly, recoiling from the elbow bumping as if burned by unseen sparks. He made a few observations about the dreary weather. I mentioned my irritation with the lack of variety in the meals I prepared for the company. Otherwise we walked in silence all the way to the spring and most of the way back.

Finally I stopped.

"You and Ruth are leaving?" he guessed.

"Beg pardon?"

"I know you're not happy here," he said, his eyes firmly fixed on the road ahead. "I figgered you've been busy finding a way out. The army will let you both leave, if you want. You're not bound to it the way an enlisted fellow is."

"We're not leaving," I said.

"You're not?" he quickly asked.

"That is, uh, I've not planned on it," I stammered. "It's hard enough keeping up with the work that every hour brings."

"You lasses work every bit as hard as we do," he said.

The words filled me with an unaccustomed sense of pride.

"Thank you," I said with great feeling. "'Tis kind of you to notice."

He kicked at the ground with his boot. "Have to be blind not to notice such a thing." He put his hands on his hips, then he crossed his arms over his chest, as if he was not certain how he should stand. "If you're not leaving, then why did you want me to walk with you? Was there something else on your mind?"

"Indeed." I glanced about to make sure that we could not be overheard. "I saw Aberdeen yesterday." I quickly told him all about my encounter. He listened close, frowning through much of it.

"Is there a way to tell the captain of the spying, without telling him the particulars of the spy?" I asked. "It's just . . ."

"You don't want Aberdeen in trouble, do you?"

I sighed. We'd met many folks on our journeying who had family or friends who supported the British. For the first time I truly understood how hard that was for them. "He chose the side he thought was right. He doesn't deserve to be punished for that."

"Don't trouble yourself," Curzon said gently. "What he told you is commonly known throughout the camp. We have spies too, more skilled than Aberdeen, I daresay. It's why we've been digging all night, every night. We must position the cannons closer to Yorktown before the British ships arrive from New York if we've any hope to win."

I was relieved that the Continentals were already aware of the threat, but I was still worried. "Is it possible to alert the officers to Aberdeen, mayhaps to describe him, so that if he is spotted–"

"Spying is a deadly business, Country. It matters not that Aberdeen is a friendly lad or that he's sweet on Ruth. It would go worse on him if I were to tell everyone what he looks like. It could guarantee his death."

"Best to keep quiet, then," I said.

He nodded. "If you see him again, come find me. Mayhaps I can talk sense into his thick head." An enormous yawn overtook the rest of his words.

"You must rest," I said. "A few more hours and they'll hand you a shovel again."

"I dare not lie down," he answered. "Captain ordered Isaac, Tall Will, and me to attend him at Colonel Hamilton's tent when the drums sound. . . ." He broke off speaking as the call of the drums echoed forth from the center of the encampment.

"What business would three privates from Rhode Island

have with a colonel?" I asked with concern. "Are you in trouble?"

"Doubtful," he said with another yawn. "Might be the fellow needs the lines of his tent tightened or some such. Officers are strange creatures. Does no good to try to understand orders; we just have to follow them."

CHAPTER XXXVIII

Tuesday, October 9–Saturday, October 13, 1781

I CONFESS I FELT A SECRET PRIDE SWELL MY HEART WHEN I SAW THE "STAR-SPANGLED BANNER" WAVING MAJESTICALLY IN THE VERY FACES OF OUR IMPLACABLE ADVERSARIES; IT APPEARED LIKE AN OMEN OF SUCCESS TO OUR ENTERPRISE.
–JOURNAL OF SERGEANT JOSEPH PLUMB MARTIN,
CORPS OF SAPPERS AND MINERS

LATE THAT AFTERNOON THE CONTINENTAL army's fife players and drummers gathered by the tall flagpole at the artillery park, playing loud and proud, stirring every spirit to hope. To the west a similar band played at the flagpole of the French, behind a row of French cannons. They raised their flag up its pole and cheered. Then the starred and striped flag of the United States of America was hauled up its own pole, to even louder cheering, drumming, and the shrill of pipes that sounded like eagles on the wind.

Both flags snapped to attention, mocking the British.

"I think that's General Washington," said a black-haired lass with a spray of freckles across her nose.

"Nay," said an older woman called Annie. "Too short. General's that giant of a man chatting to the round fellow. He's the German, Stooben."

"Von Steuben," I corrected.

"That's the one. Quite a mouth on him, curses like the Devil in three languages." Annie laughed heartily. "Mebbe four, how can you tell the difference?"

We were a regular flock, the women, girls, and boys of the army, gathered at the rear of the artillery park to view the ceremonial first firing of the cannons. No officers had come out and prohibited us from watching the grand ceremony. We all figgered that we owned a part of it too, seeing as those lads who had done the work of trenching, bridge building, and cannon dragging had been able to do their tasks on account of how well we took care of them.

General Washington had given the French the honor of the first shot. A dozen huge cannons at the Grand French Battery fired at once. Everyone huzzahed and laughed, and the small children squealed and covered their ears.

Our drums played louder. General Washington took the long-handled linstock from the matross and set its burning fuse to the cannon's touchhole. A breath later the first American cannon sent the general's most explosive regards to the British in Yorktown. Straightaway the general of the artillery shouted an order, and sixty more cannons and mortars roared into service, shaking the ground and causing the remaining trees to shed their leaves in fright.

To watch so many cannons fired creates within you an inestimable amount of awe. It also makes your ears ring as if church bells are clanging inside your brainpan. We burst into loud cheers, though we could scarce hear them. To my surprise, my eyes filled with tears, and an unexpected lump rose in my throat.

Sibby wiped at her eyes, then laughed at me doing the same.

"I'm filled with a patriotical sentiment," I admitted.

"Is that so strange?" she asked. "We all feel that."

"'Tis a new sensation for me."

"Some days that sensation is the only thing that makes me get up in the morning. That and the blasted fleas."

Ruth's tears fell too, but she wasn't smiling.

"People gonna get hurt." Her eyes were pinned on the small puffs of smoke rising from Yorktown. "From the cannons."

She was talking about Aberdeen, of course. Was it better to craft a story about his escape or be honest, as I had promised her?

"This is a war, sister," I said gently. "We are seeking to drive the King's men away from our country. They want to stay and rule us. So we fight them."

"If we don't fight, nobody gets hurt."

"If we don't fight, we cannot be free."

"The King could make us free."

"He doesn't want to. The only way to achieve freedom is to fight for it."

"Makes me sad," she said.

I had no answer but to fold my arms around her and hold her tight.

Our cannons fired day and night, hurling thousands of shells and cannonballs through the air. One night we fired hot shot: iron balls heated red hot before being carefully loaded into the muzzles of the cannons. They set four British ships in the river afire and rendered them useless. With the big guns firing every hour of the day and the night, the time had come to dig a second trench, again cutting the distance between our soldiers and Yorktown in half. Work proceeded more quickly than before, as our fellows were now seasoned to the task. It became more dangerous, too, as they were soon within musket range of the British.

Ruth and I were becoming accustomed to our tasks too. Though downcast about Aberdeen, she soldiered on with the business of fetching our rations and bread, and helping with the laundering of breeches and shirts. I spent the whole of one night caring for a lad who had contracted the worst sort of bloody flux. 'Twas a hideous business with a stench indescribable. At dawn they put him in the wagon bound for the hospital in Williamsburg. Ruth arrived then, yawning and sleep-stumbly. Without a word of complaint, she burned the straw bedding that had been befouled and served the breakfast so I could wash the filth of the night's work off of me.

Her worries about Aberdeen had increased now that thousands of American shells and cannonballs were being flung at his hiding place. She no longer took time to visit with the horses or blow bubbles from the clay pipe given to her by Henry. In our rare moments of rest she took to sitting close to me, sometimes leaning her head on my shoulder. I would kiss her brow then and rub circles of comfort on her back.

The hours our lads had to work on duty and in the trenches increased. It got so that some of the women of the camp decided that if the lads could not come to the cook fire for their meals, we would take the food to them. With the permission of our officers, I followed the lead of Sibby, Cristena, and Sarah, the white lass married to Aaron, the armorer. We fashioned yokes for ourselves, sturdy poles that had notches cut into each end and a blanket wrapped round the middle. From each end we hung a kettle, one with cooked meat, the other with coffee. Bread went into the haversacks we wore on our backs.

We carried the yokes across our shoulders, the way you carry buckets of milk in from a barn. The first trick of the thing was to walk slow and steady, else half the coffee would spill afore your reached the trench. The second was to await a lull in the cannonading.

The other lasses had much discussed the fear we'd face as we approached the parallels. By that point we had seen death and maiming caused by bullets, cannonballs, and exploding shells. Sibby had given me an odd look whilst the others talked but had had no chance to explain herself.

The sound of cannons grew louder as I approached the trench, as did the sound of thousands of working men, their shovels and picks biting into the dirt, and the shouts of officers, and the nervous whinnies of horses. I noticed it all and kept my eyes moving for cannonballs hurtling my way. I exchanged friendly nods with a black woman who was helping a limping soldier make his way back to camp. I'd never seen her before; there were hundreds of camp followers I hadn't met. But greeting her helped me understand what it was that I'd seen in Sibby's face: the understanding that we already knew what it was to walk in perilous circumstances. We had learned how to face fear and keep walking.

To my surprise, I was in high spirits despite the danger, for it was a danger shared by all of us. I'd grown tired of the drudgesome tasks of cooking and washing, and found myself whistling like a fifer as I approached the trench. The wind blew from the river and carried with it the mocking sound of the British musicians playing "Yankee Doodle Dandy." I changed my tune to match it. That song had become a point of pride with our army.

The officer of the watch bid me good day and directed me to the section of the trench where our company was working. The first six pairs of our lads were overjoyed to see me. Well, more likely, they were overjoyed to see the food. But I carried it, so I came in for some enthusiastic and welcome praise as well, which improved my mood even more.

Then Curzon stood up and caught sight of me. He was not pleased.

"What the devil are you doing here?" he demanded.

"Following orders, same as you." I bent down till the kettles sat on the ground. "Sergeant told me to feed you. Hello, Isaac," I said to the fellow working alongside Curzon. "Hungry?"

"Indeed, thanks, missus," he said.

"It's not safe!" Curzon exclaimed.

"Of course it's not." I handed some bread to Isaac, ducked under the yoke, and stood again. "Do you want your supper?"

Isaac snorted at the thunderstorm gathering on Curzon's face. I continued walking to the next pair of men, the cousins from Newport, Short Will and Bram.

"Look at us, being served by the prettiest lass in the army," Short Will called.

"Didn't dare bring stew," I said. "But the beef is fresh and the coffee will wake your senses."

"You've no call to be here," Curzon protested.

"I have a duty," I said, handing out the bread. "Same as you. Same as everyone."

"Much obliged, Missus Isabel," they said.

A distant shell exploded. I tried my best not to react to the noise, but he saw me jump.

"'Tis no game out here, Country!" he exclaimed. "Leave the kettles, I'll feed the lads and bring them back tonight."

"All the lasses are helping thus."

"If all the lasses decided to swim to France, would you join them?"

"Odsbodikins!" I laughed. "Such twaddle!"

Curzon followed, fuming in silence while I parceled out the food to the remaining lads, then began to walk back to the trench's entrance.

"Promise you won't ever do this again," he said.

"I'll do what the officers want, same as you. They gave us leave to make this delivery; indeed, they applauded our valor. Sergeant Armstrong did make a strange request, though. He's a great one for kissing, isn't he?"

"He kissed you?" Curzon shouted.

"Of course not!"

"He tried to kiss you and you knocked him to the ground?"

I chuckled. "He told me I should kiss you and wish you good luck."

"Did he tell you why?"

A sentry shouted, "Shell!"

Before I knew what was happening, the earth shook and I was thrown against the front wall of the trench. Dirt rained from heaven, and for a moment it seemed I'd gone deaf. Then the sound rushed back.

Curzon's face loomed over me. "Are you hurt? Can you hear me?"

I sat up, brushing the sand off my head and face.

"No harm done . . ." I peered into the kettles. "Except for the mud that's in the coffee. And bells are ringing in my ears."

He let out a shaky breath and sat next to me. The men around us were getting to their feet, laughing at themselves and cheerfully cursing Cornwallis and the King's army.

"Did it rattle your wits?" I asked.

"Possibly." He shook his collar so that the dirt fell out the bottom of his shirt. "I have to tell you something. Please allow me to say it straight through, without interruption."

I opened my mouth, but he held up his hands to stop me.

"Please!" he said. "I pray you, not a single word! If you want to listen, nod your head."

The explosion had most definitely rattled his wits. I nodded once. He was going to need a mustard poultice for his head when he returned to the cook fire.

"I won't be coming back to camp tonight," he said, as if he could hear my thoughts. "I have an assignment with another unit, along with Tall Will and Isaac."

"How long?"

His mouth moved, but the sound did not reach me.

"Beg pardon?" I shook my head. "Couldn't hear that. My ears are still ringing."

"You promised to listen," he said loudly. "It's just . . . close your eyes."

"What? Why?"

"I can't say this with you looking at me. Please."

"Make haste." I sighed and closed my eyes. He'd need a mustard plaster and maybe some leeches to drain off his imbalance of humors. "I need to get back to Ruth."

He cleared his throat. "We spent a lot of time looking for her," he said. "Ruth, I mean. I want you to know . . . I need to say . . . I didn't mind it, the looking for her. And–"

"Back to work, Private Smith!" called a gruff voice.

When Curzon spoke again, his mouth was quite near to my ear. "And I do love you, Isabel Gardener."

"Beg pardon?"

Did he just say that? I wasn't sure I'd heard him right. The shadow of his presence vanished. The air filled with the sounds of pickaxes, shovels, booming cannons, grunting men working hard.

"Curzon, what did you just say?"

I opened my eyes. He was gone.

CHAPTER XXXIX

Sunday, October 14, 1781

THE PETITION OF THE SUBSCRIBERS, NATIVES OF AFRICA, NOW FORCIBLY DETAINED IN SLAVERY . . . MOST HUMBLY [SHOWETH] THAT THE GOD OF NATURE GAVE THEM LIFE AND FREEDOM UPON THE TERMS OF THE MOST PERFECT EQUALITY WITH OTHER MEN. . . .
THEREFORE, YOUR HUMBLE SLAVES MOST DEVOUTLY PRAY FOR THE SAKE OF INJURED LIBERTY, FOR THE SAKE OF JUSTICE, HUMANITY, AND THE RIGHTS OF MANKIND . . . THAT THE NAME OF SLAVE MAY NOT MORE BE HEARD IN A LAND GLORIOUSLY CONTENDING FOR THE SWEETS OF FREEDOM.
—PETITION OF NINETEEN NEW HAMPSHIRE SLAVES THAT WAS SENT TO THEIR STATE'S HOUSE OF REPRESENTATIVES DURING THE REVOLUTION AND WAS DENIED

BY THE NEXT DAY I'D CONVINCED myself that he had not said what I thought he'd said. The shell explosion had rattled both our brainpans, in addition to filling my ears with dirt. Hearing him say, or rather not-hearing him say, or possibly not-hearing him not-say, that thing, that word, it set my mind to spinning like a weather vane in a windstorm.

He'd already departed the camp, which, in truth, was a relief.

I hung an armload of sweaty blankets on a line that I'd strung between tent poles.

Soldiers were often taken from various companies and

melded together in special details so as not to deplete any one brigade. These details were assigned to temporary tasks like guarding wagonloads of ammunition, requisitioning hay, or escorting Philadelphia politicians who wanted to observe the siege. But he could be carrying messages to General Greene in Carolina, or up to Jersey. Mayhaps as far as Boston, which would mean it could be weeks before he returned. Assuming he didn't end up captured, or shot, or dying alone in the wilderness after falling from a horse . . .

I gave myself a hard pinch. There was nothing to be gained by wallowing in dark thoughts. Half of these blankets needed to be beaten to get rid of the lice. I had duties. Curzon had duties, and he was more skilled than most at staying alive.

But he'd said that he didn't regret the years we looked for Ruth. As to the other thing he might have not-said . . .

I pinched myself harder, but it did nothing to calm the toads jumping in my belly.

Hours later, whilst feeding the fellows an early supper, I asked them about the rumors I'd heard at the bake ovens, that our officers were planning an attack on the heavily fortified and guarded outer redoubts.

"Why would the generals consider such an attack?" I asked. "The entire reason for digging the second parallel was to bring our cannons so close to Yorktown that the lobsterbacks would have to surrender or swim. You still have trench duty, right?"

The lads fell curiously silent. Most studied their stew with profound interest. Drury's knees bounced furiously, like he wanted to run, though he sat on an upturned log.

Henry stood up. "I'm telling her."

"No," said Short Will fiercely. "We promised."

"You made that promise on my behalf," Henry corrected. "Had he come to me direct, I'd have set him straight. You marry a lass, you owe her the truth."

"What truth?" I asked. "What is the meaning of all this?"

"Where did Curzon tell you he was headed?" Henry asked me.

"Didn't. Just said he had a temporary assignment."

He set down his bowl, looked direct at me, and spoke slow. "Curzon, Isaac, Tall Will, and four hundred other fellows will attack redoubt ten tonight. A similar group of Frenchmen will attack redoubt nine at the same time."

"I don't believe you," I declared. "There are no cannons positioned to offer them cover. Won't be for days. You yourself told me the purpose of digging that bloody second trench was to bring cannons closer to the enemy!"

"The ground there is too marshy to support the weight of cannons," Henry said. "The redoubts must be taken by storm."

Fire crackled in the silence. The conversating around other cook fires was similarly muted, but as ever the firing of cannons and mortars supplied a constant, low thudding, like the footsteps of an army of giants drawing ever closer.

I still could not believe what he was saying.

"This makes no sense," I told him. "They can't order men to simply attack the redoubts. They might as well tell them to waltz into Yorktown, don't mind the cannons and muskets, lads, just go thee hence. How can they hope to load and fire muskets whilst climbing into the thing? Lambs to the slaughter, is that what they're to be?"

"They're to use bayonets and hatchets only."

"They'll be fighting hand to hand?"

"Curzon has a quick mind, fast legs, and a brave heart," Henry said. "He was at Brooklyn and Saratoga, he survived Valley Forge. He's the perfect sort of soldier for this."

I barely heard him. I was seeing the redoubt in my mind. Its base was fortified by tree trunks with ends sharpened like spear points, woven into tangles like a monstrous porcupine, so that penetrating close meant injury. From on top the British defenders had a deadly angle. They could fire at will upon their attackers and serve up death with ease.

"When will this happen?" I asked in a small voice.

"They've already assembled, but the attack is not due for hours."

"Could he change his mind, tell them—"

"He wanted to go, Isabel. He volunteered, along with the others."

The fire gave a loud *pop*, causing me to jump.

"We know," Drury said from the other side of the fire. "We know everything. Curzon told us the real story of how you two, you three, came to be here. The circumstances of your past."

"Don't worry," Henry quickly added. "The officers don't know, nor shall they. In this war for freedom the people who are able to liberate themselves and the ones they love deserve the praise and support of all of us."

"Why would he tell you our secrets?"

"That's what friends do," Henry said gently. "They lift each other up, help carry burdens. He told us so that we could be the best sort of friends to you, to be your brothers, in the event you should ever need us."

Curzon trusted them. I'd normally be frightened or angry, because trusting others had caused so many problems for us in the past. But these fellows were different. They understood our sentiments, our fears, our thirst for true liberty. The kindness and concern in their faces near overwhelmed me. They were indeed our brothers of the heart.

"You've no need to worry," Henry said. "He's with men just as smart, fast, and strong as he is. Though likely not as brave."

Somehow I had moved from my position standing by the fire to sitting on a log. A damp cloth rested across my neck, and Ruth was handing me a mug of water. It was not clear how much she understood, but her face was solemn.

"Drink," Henry urged. "This has been a bit of a shock, this news."

I did so, trying to hold at bay the vision of all the terrible fates that could befall Curzon. He could be captured and held again as a prisoner of war, which usually proved fatal. He could be injured in countless ways that would mean a slow and painful death. When I considered all the suffering he might be forced to endure, it seemed a quick death would be the kindest mercy. But the thought of his death threatened to send me headlong into despair. I had to fight against that. I didn't know how, but I would have to find a way.

Drums rattled through the camp. A few curses were muttered as the fellows rose, throwing back the rest of their coffee.

"We're needed in the trenches tonight," Drury explained. "Digging continues."

"Would you like some of us to stay?" Henry asked. "We can report sick."

My thoughts were still stuck fast in the frustrating mud of Curzon's decision. Ever since I met him, he'd chosen fighting for the new United States of America time and time and time again. And now he had volunteered for a perilous mission, put himself at risk of death for a country not yet fully formed, that could promise us nothing.

"Why are you here?" I asked Henry.

The unexpected question puzzled him. "Beg pardon?"

"You're a very clever man," I said. "I know you enlisted for your freedom, but surely you've had countless opportunities since then to liberate yourself from the army and make your own way in the world, on your own terms."

"Indeed I have."

"So why have you stayed? That is the thing I cannot understand. Why do any of you stay and fight this bloody war for a confounded army that doesn't care about us?"

The other men stopped their leave-taking preparations to listen.

"We're earning our freedom," Henry said quietly.

"Only because by Fortune's strange luck you were born a slave in Rhode Island. Had you been born here in Virginia, you'd have been given as a prize, an enlistment bonus to a white man who didn't have the stomach or honor to join the army without the suitable temptation of slaves and a guarantee of land."

"The entire enterprise of this war seems to be by the grace of Fortune's strange luck." Henry looked at his mates. "Remember that preacher we heard outside Philadelphia, the young man who drove a salt wagon?"

Many heads nodded and quiet agreement was murmured.

"That fellow was like all of us: descended from good people who were stolen from their families and country, sailed over the sea, and forced into slavery. 'We don't let them steal our dignity,' that preacher said. Richard, his name was. He said they cannot steal our honor, our strength, or our love."

"True words," I said.

"Do you know what he said about this America?" Henry asked.

I shook my head.

"Remember, lads?" Henry asked his mates. "Join with me. He said, 'This land . . .'"

A half dozen voices spoke with Henry, strong black men sharing the preacher's words like a hymn or a prayer. "'Which we have watered with our tears and our blood, is now our mother country.'"

The words drifted up to the stars with the sparks from the fire.

"We go to war, Missus Isabel," Henry added, "in order to make our mother country, this land, free for everyone."

CHAPTER XL

Sunday, October 14–Monday, October 15, 1781

IT GIVES ME MORE PLEASURE THAN I CAN EXPRESS TO LEARN THAT YOU SUSTAIN WITH SO MUCH FORTITUDE, THE SHOCKS AND TERRORS OF THE TIMES. YOU ARE REALLY BRAVE MY DEAR, YOU ARE A HEROINE. AND YOU HAVE REASON TO BE.
—LETTER FROM JOHN ADAMS TO HIS WIFE, ABIGAIL

RUTH AND I WASHED UP AFTER THE supper, filled the kettles with water, and set them over a low fire. By the time we'd finished, the sun had set.

The emptiness of the camp unnerved me.

"Come, sister," I said.

Ruth took my hand.

We walked fast, our strides long and silent but for the swish of our skirts, ruffling like feathers in the night breeze. I had no destination in mind at first. Moving my legs was the only way to calm my agitated spirit. We walked up and down the rows of tents, past the New Jersey regiments, Pennsylvania, Virginia, Maryland. Past the hospitals, one French, one American, and the loud artillery parks, where the cannons and mortars fired, fired, fired at the enemy.

General Washington's giant marquee tent was lit up by candles and lanterns. The shadows of the men inside moved like puppets, bending over tables, gesturing with their arms, flipping back their coattails before sitting on a stool. The flaps of the tent stood open to the night air. A steady flow of aides-de-camp moved in and out, papers in hand. Tall Life Guards stood at the ready, charged with protecting His Excellency, General Washington, against any attack.

Ruth yawned and complained about being tired, but I wasn't ready to go back to the cook fire yet. We retired to a spot on a hill above the large marquee. She leaned against my shoulder, her thumb in her mouth, that childhood habit that appeared when she felt deep melancholy.

From our vantage the tent looked like a lantern itself, the shadows within it fluttering moths. The cannons continued their attack, mortar shells drawing comet trails of fire across the sky before dropping onto Yorktown. The distance created a sense that I was watching a play acted out upon a vast stage. If only that were true and we could applaud gently as the players bowed at the end of the performance.

The war for independence had been playing out in this, my mother country, for one third of my years. I'd never felt honor-bound to either side of the conflict, for both sides looked at me and mine with evil intent. Their distorted vision saw only property, not humanity.

Since Ruth was stolen away, I had only ever sought to find her and free us both. And, in truth, Curzon. Our friendship had been peppered by frequent battles as foolish and unresolved as the clashes between Patriots and the British. The biggest source of our unending conflict had been his affection for this army. Or rather, that was how I perceived it.

The conviction in Henry's voice still rang in my ears, louder even than the booming cannons. He knew his purpose, same as the other fellows in the company. Same as

Curzon. They believed that they were fighting for a country that would offer liberty to all of us. I did not share their certainty, but for the first time I found myself wanting to believe that it might be possible. Freedom would not be handed to us like a gift. Freedom had to be fought for and taken.

I was finally beginning to understand what had driven Curzon for as long as I'd known him. He favored the larger stage, the grand scale at which folks sought to improve the world. I had chosen to focus on the smaller stage, concerning myself only with my sister's circumstances. Now, from atop that hill, I recognized that there was a middle way, a purpose one could strive for that allowed personal concerns—those you love—to be on the one side, whilst the concerns of an entire people, of a country, to be on the other. I realized that Curzon did not care more for his army than me, or even feel that there was a choice to be made. His heart was so large, it could love multitudes. And it did.

My own heart was a curious organ, one that I'd tried to ignore for a very long time. But as the sparks flew heavenward and the officer moths danced round the lantern light of the marquee, I faced the true sentiments hidden within it. America was my mother country too. If this country could produce lasses like me, Ruth, Sibby, Serafina, and Becky Berry, and men such as Curzon, Walter, the lads of the Rhode Island regiment, Ebenezer Woodruff, and all the others willing to fight for the freedom and happiness of all, then our mother country was worth fighting for. My heart was large enough to love multitudes as well.

And I loved Curzon.

I'd been so afraid to admit love, terrified that my affection would be scorned. To love someone leaves you vulnerable.

To admit love opens the door to the possibility of pain and sorrow. However, to ignore love, to pretend that it does not exist, though you feel it every waking moment, guarantees not only pain and sorrow, but a withering of your very capacity to love, blaspheming the holy purpose of our days on this earth.

I must tell him. No matter what comes of the confession, I must tell him.

Most of the toads in my belly leapt with joy. A few quivered with fear.

Ruth's voice startled me. I thought she'd fallen asleep.

"They gonna die?"

Her question fell like a burning shell and shattered my reverie.

"Who?" I asked.

"Nancy Chicken. Thomas Boon, our donkey. Aberdeen." She wiped her eyes on the shoulder of my shift. "Curzon."

"They are survivors." I stood up and offered her my hand. "Like us."

We stopped first at the American hospital tent. It was not so much a hospital as it was a place to treat the worst of an injury. If the patient survived, he was shipped up to Williamsburg in the bottom of a jolting wagon. If he still lived by the end of that journey, he had a decent chance, for Bess was good at keeping lads alive, they said.

Worried about the injuries that Curzon, Isaac, and Tall Will might suffer in the attack, I requested bandages and fine thread from a hospital attendant.

"Can't give you none," the self-important looby said, his eyes bulging. "Need all the supplies here for the wounded."

"You must, good sir," I replied firmly. "We've got a fellow

just put a pickaxe through his foot. His uncle works for the Congress in Philadelphia. The captain himself sent me, said we should care for him at camp, leave the hospital free to treat those injured in fighting."

The looby's eyes widened and he complied. I curtsied, grateful that the confusions of war would make certain he never discovered my falsehood.

As we stood in line at the commissary, I overheard that the traitor Benedict Arnold had slaughtered militiamen in Connecticut. Any mob that ever laid its hands on that scoundrel would tear him limb from limb. When it was at last our turn, Ruth and I acquired a small cask of vinegar, flour, sacks of apples and turnips, and a fist-size ball of butter.

Back at our cook fire I boiled a bit of the vinegar, then covered it. I used all of the company's pans and pots but one to make apple and turnip pies, having questioned many women of the camp about the proper way to do such a thing. Ruth split wood till she couldn't hold the axe any longer. She fetched the blankets from our brush hut, spread them by the fire, and was soon asleep. I cooked my pies in the red-hot coals, then lay next to my sister, watching the planets of Jupiter and Venus descend through the western sky, and pouring out my heart in prayer for Curzon's safe return.

Next I looked, Jupiter and Venus were long gone. The pale of morning had crept into the east. I'd fallen asleep.

Shouts. I could hear shouting. Lots of voices, all hollering loud as possible, all of it coming from the direction of the trenches. Ruth awoke confuddled and anxious.

I stood up.

The noise grew louder with each heartbeat. It seemed to be rising with the same speed as the sun. Every moment the air brightened, the thunder of boots and the chorus of soldier voices strengthened by the same measure. And then a wave of soldiery invaded the camp, all bedecked in Patriot mud, shouting laughter and good cheer. They danced reels between the rows of tents, kicking high, crowing "Huzzah!" to the morning sun like an army of ten thousand roosters.

I grabbed a lad by his sleeve. "What news?"

"We took both redoubts! Dug all the night long until the new parallel was finished! We've got 'em trapped like rabbits in a bag!"

"Did anyone—" I started, but he ran off.

Every face I saw was alight with joy, but I could find not one fellow from our company in the throng. Were they in the trenches still? Had the men in the redoubt attack been taken straight to the hospital tent, or were they charged with staying in the redoubt to guard it?

"Isabel," Ruth said, joining me.

"Stand still." I hopped onto an upended log, my hand on her shoulder for balance, so I could better study the crowd coming up from the trenches. All I could see spread out before me were groups of tired, bedraggled, triumphant soldiers, slapping one another on the back, bowing, cheering, and drinking from mugs that I doubted contained coffee.

Ruth tugged on my skirt. "Isabel!"

I stepped down, planning how to discover the news I was so desperate for. I'd keep Ruth here minding the pies and porridge, whilst I ventured down to the trench in search of an officer.

"Isabel!" This time Ruth shouted. "Turn around, ninny—there he is!"

Curzon.

CHAPTER XLI

Monday, October 15, 1781

TWO NIGHTS AGO, MY ELIZA, MY DUTY AND MY HONOR OBLIGED ME TO TAKE A STEP IN WHICH YOUR HAPPINESS WAS TOO MUCH RISKED. I COMMANDED AN ATTACK UPON ONE OF THE ENEMY'S REDOUBTS; WE CARRIED IT IN AN INSTANT, AND WITH LITTLE LOSS. YOU WILL SEE THE PARTICULARS IN THE PHILADELPHIA PAPERS.

—LETTER FROM COLONEL ALEXANDER HAMILTON TO HIS WIFE, ELIZABETH

HE LAY MOTIONLESS ON A BLANKET carried by his friends, his face swollen and blood covered. His eyes were closed; his mouth hung slack. One arm and hand were wrapped in blood-soaked rags.

Curzon.

The world stopped spinning. The sounds of celebration and cannon fire silenced.

Curzon.

Hands lowered the blanket, moving slow, as if everyone were trapped in honey. I ran, unable to make sense of this horrid madness. The distance could not have been more than twenty paces, but it seemed to take years to reach him, as if I were running across the bottom of the sea.

I fell to my knees.

"Curzon, no!" His cold skin smelled coppery, like the slaughter yard. My heart stopped. I cradled his face in my hands. The ragged voice did not sound like it belonged to me. "You can't be dead," I cried. "Please don't be dead."

I leaned closer, hoping to feel the warmth of his breath on my cheek. My tears splashed on his face. My fingers slid to the spot on his throat where the beat of a heart might be felt.

"Don't leave me," I whispered.

My fingertips felt the low, steady thud-thud of his heartbeat.

He blinked, peered up, and lifted his unbandaged hand to my face.

"Hello, Country," he croaked.

Sunlight filled my heart.

"Hush." I took his hand in mine. "Did they shoot you? What hurts?"

"Poor lad," said Isaac. "First ye tell him to hush, then you fire your questions at him. He's encountered a bayonet with his arm, took a few punches to his nose."

"Gave more than I took," Curzon muttered.

"Twisted his knee fierce, but it ain't broke," Drury continued the accounting of injuries. "The ground in the redoubt was pockmarked with holes big enough to hold an ox. All kinds of twisted ankles and complaining knees."

"Did the fighting go on all night?" I asked, studying Curzon from head to toe. His eyes were again closed, as if he'd decided to take a nap in the midst of this commotion.

"Only minutes!" came the chorus of response.

Isaac limped over, his arm around the shoulder of Tall Will. "Colonel Hamilton led the charge, with all of us screaming like the night was on fire. The fighting was fierce, but we conquered them right quick. We was ordered to stay the night there, in case the lobsterbacks sought a counterattack. They didn't dare." He grinned, then winced, for he'd taken a blow to the mouth that left it swollen and raw.

I looked at Tall Will. "Why didn't you take them to the hospital tent?"

"We tried," Tall Will explained, "but Curzon caterwauled fierce and said we had to come here first. He sooner trusts you to sew him up."

"There are men with worse injuries needing the doctors," Henry added.

"Carry him to the fire, then," I said, grateful that I'd thought to secure the vinegar while I could. "I'll clean him up, take a look at the bayonet wound. If it's not too deep, I can sew it."

I went to stand, but Curzon's hand, which had relaxed its grip on mine, tightened again and would not release me. "Isabel."

"We're just going to move you a wee bit," I said.

"I have a surprise for you." His eyes opened again, and I leaned closer to hear his words. "I think we won."

"I have a surprise too." I put my mouth to his ear. "I love you, Curzon Smith."

"God's grace, Country." He sighed. "Then we have indeed finally won."

CHAPTER XLII

Monday, October 15–Wednesday, October 17, 1781

OUR WATCHWORD WAS "ROCHAMBEAU," THE COMMANDER OF THE FRENCH FORCES' NAME, A GOOD WATCHWORD, FOR BEING PRONOUNCED RO-SHAM-BOW, IT SOUNDED, WHEN PRONOUNCED QUICK, LIKE RUSH-ON-BOYS.
–JOURNAL OF SERGEANT JOSEPH PLUMB MARTIN, CORPS OF SAPPERS AND MINERS

THE BLOOD, CURZON TRIED TO ASSURE me, was mostly from the redcoats. In this, as in so many things, he was boastful. The bayonet had gone through his sleeve into the meat of his arm between the elbow and the shoulder, but not all the way to the bone. I set the vinegar over the fire to heat up again and had a quiet word with Henry, who then went off in search of rum.

As I studied the swollen messes of his knee and Isaac's ankle, the other fellows dug into my pies, which, they declared, were the best pies that had ever been created in all of the history of pies. I told them the secret spice I used was called "hunger." This set them to roaring with laughter again. The day itself had been seasoned with victory and relief, and served with a bowl of fatigue, so they were in the greatest cheer imaginable.

Isaac preferred to clean his own cuts and bumps, possibly

on account of the rather severe look given to him by Curzon. That freed me to clean the cuts on Curzon's brow, his knuckles, and his split lip. As I washed the dirt from his wounds, and he grunted and tried not to complain, the lads told and told again the stories of the night before, whilst Ruth served a second round of my apple and turnip pies, which Bram dubbed "Isabel's Irresistible Victuals."

Our men had attacked redoubt 10, and a French company of a similar size had attacked redoubt 9 at the same time. I could tell he was softening the description of the action, thinking to spare me the worst of the details. Of the eight hundred attackers, twenty-four were killed and more than one hundred were wounded—broken ribs, bones shattered by musketballs, and limbs and bellies torn open by bayonets.

As soon as the redoubts were in our possession, thousands of men attacked the second parallel with shovels and pickaxes, digging like an army of moles through the night. The dawn shone down on the second parallel completed from the west end to the east, where it led direct to our newly captured redoubts. Before the sun had even warmed the ground, men were dragging cannons to the redoubts. They were pointed at Yorktown.

The captain of our company, older than most and wealthy enough to own three changes of uniform, visited our cook fire for the very first time to check on Curzon and Isaac. He brought rum, at Henry's suggestion, to ease the painful work of the cleaning and sewing of the bayonet wound.

"I buttered him like a parsnip, I did," Henry whispered to me as the captain shared a few words with the heroes of the redoubt. "Filled him with tales of the lads' glory. He's sending along enough for the entire company this eve."

Ruth and I fetched the morning bread whilst the captain

and lads exchanged tales of the night's work. By the time we returned, Henry had gotten Curzon well muddy in drink. As I approached him, armed with needle, thread, and steaming-hot bandages, he gave me a lopsided smile and slurred, "Did I tell you we won, darling Isabel?"

The things he shouted during my assault on his wound do not bear repeating. I made the stitches deep, necessary close together, and tight as could be. When the sewing was done, I asked the lads to hold him fast as I poured the rest of the still-warm vinegar on the needlework I'd stitched into his wound. 'Tis thought that the sharp tang of hot vinegar balances the humors within a wound and so helps with the healing.

"I thought you wanted me alive!" he roared.

I winked at him. "Seems I got my wish."

Everything happened right quick after that.

Henry explained the facts mathematical to me. The cannons positioned at the first parallel had needed to fire six hundred yards to hit the enemy, he said. From the second parallel the distance was less than half of that. The guns on the second parallel fired a constant cannonade against Yorktown, an attack so violent, all wondered how any living thing could survive it.

By midday Monday Curzon's knee had swollen to the size of a sheep's head and was as hard and unmovable as a stone. I sent Drury in search of one-eyed Cristena, for she knew where leeches could be found in the marsh. He brought back a half dozen of the tiny, writhing creatures, which happily attached themselves to Curzon's knee. The sight of it made him puke up his breakfast. By the time darkness fell, the leeches had gorged themselves and dropped to the dirt. Thanks to the leeches, the swelling of the knee was so much reduced that I no longer feared it would split open. I stayed with him through the night, putting on fresh poultices and forcing him to drink willow bark tea. Come morning, his knee was soft as a boiled apple, tender but not fatal.

Between the knee and the arm Curzon was greatly pained, tho' he thought he was actor enough to hide it from us. He tried to stand as the other fellows went off to patrol for foolish British soldiers.

The entire company ordered him to fasten his backside to the ground.

Tuesday was gray and unsettled.

Wednesday dawned cold and wet, but the air quickly filled with laughter that spread from tent to tent, cook fire to cook fire, until the camp was roaring with delight at the news: Lord Cornwallis had tried to escape in the night . . . and failed.

His plan had been to row his entire army across the river. It was not a frightful distance, but as the evacuation began, the most extraordinary storm of pelting rain and violent wind boiled up and prevented the boats from crossing. It called to mind the night of the Battle of Brooklyn years earlier, when a thick fog rolled in that allowed the Patriot forces to escape capture by the British. God always seemed to provide favorable weather for the Americans, folks said. That was the sign that He supported General Washington and our fight for liberty.

Later that day, as I was sewing the tear in Curzon's sleeve made by the British bayonet, the world fell silent. Seemed as if a gigantical velvet cloak had somehow been thrown over all the things that made noise: cannons, drums, wagon wheels, hammers, saws, calling voices, shouts, and laughter.

"Run to the regiment headquarters and ask what news," Curzon said.

I picked my skirts up and took a few steps, but he called after me, "Stop! Come back!"

"You cannot have it both ways," I said.

He motioned to Ruth to help him stand. "I must go with you."

"You can barely stand," I said.

"I could lean on you."

He put his good arm over my shoulders, gritted his teeth, and took a step. Before he could take a second, Drury and Bram appeared, running, waving their hats and hollering.

"The British have surrendered!"

CHAPTER XLIII

Friday, October 19, 1781

Oh, God! It is all over!
—Reaction of British prime minister Lord North
to the news of Cornwallis's defeat at Yorktown

THE BRITISH DID NOT HAVE THE COURtesy to be on time for their own ceremony of surrender. The waiting allied forces lined the Hampton Road for a full mile, French soldiers on the left side and Americans on the right. The French uniforms were crisp and colorful, while our boys seemed a bit drab and ragged in contrast, but everyone was in the highest of spirits, convinced that their sacrifices and dangerous work had struck a death blow to the war.

Seeing all of the men together at once filled my heart with pride. At the beginning of the war black men had not been allowed to enlist, but they had continued in their efforts to do so until General Washington, the Congress, and the states changed their laws. At Valley Forge one fellow out of ten had been a black man, Curzon among them. Our proportion was much higher now—one in four, as far as I could see—with a scattering of fellows from various Indian nations. Our mother country had sons of all sorts who joined together to defend her honor.

Our company proudly took its place with the rest of the Rhode Island regiment. In fact, our fellows were some of the earliest arrivals. They'd left camp right after breakfast to make sure that they had enough time to get there, given Curzon's slow pace. His knee and arm would heal, of that I was confident, but he wouldn't fire a musket or chase an enemy patrol for a good while.

In the days leading up to the official surrender, my sentiments had been as changeable as the wind; one moment I'd felt content around him, and the next, confuddled. I'd sat next to him when the chores of the day were done. It was the most natural thing in the world for us, sitting thus, to lean our shoulders against each other, sharing warmth and strength. But neither of us spoke of anything more than the weather, the pain of his wounds, and how hard it was to chew the tough meat. The strong words we had shared after the redoubt attack seemed too dangerous or awkward to discuss. I did not regret telling him the sentiments of my heart, of that I was almost certain. But we'd landed ourselves in an unknown country, and neither of us knew how to navigate in it.

Ruth and I took up our observation positions with the other women of the army, in the midst of countless spectators who had crowded in, eager to watch the humiliation of the enemy, who had despoiled the countryside for months. We worked our way with Cristena and Sibby until we stood with Annie, the older woman we'd met the day our cannons began firing. She served several of the officers who worked with General Washington and thus was better informed than most.

Annie surveyed the carriages of newcomers who had dressed in finery as if this were a fancy ball instead an army encampment. "Prognosticators and campfire politicians, they are," she said scornfully. "All cozying up to the generals in hopes of favor and profit. Them folks"—she pointed at the group of Oneida men who had been invited to observe the siege by General Washington—"they're the only ones who have a right to be here. They've been fighting on our side from the beginning."

Cristena passed out gingercakes that had been prepared by the Baker-General and apples that had newly arrived. We were seated on the ground by then, as were many of the men still waiting on the road. The British had not yet appeared. Annie speculated that Cornwallis was having his wig powdered for the occasion. The lasses around me nattered about the baby just born to a woman who worked for the Maryland regiment, and the rumored romance between an officer and a married dame in Williamsburg.

I was not concerned with star-crossed lovers whom I'd never met. I kept watch on Curzon, laughing with his friends on the road, and Ruth, who sat uncommon still and quiet by my side. Knowing that they both were safe and well eased my mind more than I thought possible.

I tipped my face back and enjoyed the contrary sensations of the sun's heat and the cool autumn breeze. The colors of the leaves were as varied and bright as the uniform coats of the soldiers. This was harvesting weather, the time to pick corn and thresh wheat, to store potatoes and squash in a deep-dug root cellar. We'd spent so many years waging our own wars for freedom, I'd rarely thought about the simple luxuries of an ordinary life lived without fear. Would the end of the country's war open the door for a life such as that?

Finally the drums rattled and the most anticipated event of our war for independence began.

"About bloody time," huffed Annie as we all stood and

shook out our skirts. "This delay is just another way of insulting us, mark my words."

As the line of British wound its way toward us, a muttering grumble rose through the crowd like a low roll of thunder. In the gravest insult of all Lord Cornwallis did not lead his troops to their honorable surrender. In fact, Cornwallis was nowhere to be found. He had sent his number two fellow so as not to expose himself to the shame of defeat.

Annie spat on the ground. "General Washington ought ride into Yorktown hisself and drag that coward Cornwallis out by the ear!"

The fellow who substituted for Cornwallis offered his sword to General Washington, a ceremonial gesture that signified to all that the British had been fully humbled and beaten. Washington shook his head and indicated that the sword of surrender ought be given to the number two man on our side, Major General Lincoln. This caused a tremendous roar of approval, with many shouts and hoots from the allied troops and spectators.

After rows of officers marched by, there came near eight thousand defeated soldiers. The British were first, clad mostly in red, along with a regiment of Scotsmen dressed in their strange plaid skirts called kilts, and then the Hessians, who mostly dressed in blue. They did not march in an orderly fashion, and their regimental musicians played so poorly, we all thought they were muddy in drink. The final insult was the direction of their gaze: As they passed between the rows of their conquerors, the British all turned their eyes to the French side of the road, showing our fellows the backs of their heads.

"Arrogant clodpates," Annie declared.

"Where's Aberdeen?" Ruth asked me.

"He's not a British soldier, poppet," I said. She'd been asking about him regular as a clock since the siege ended.

"But he was in Yorktown." She pointed at the column of soldiers caterpillaring down the road. "They're from Yorktown."

"Mebbe he has already sailed away," I said, trying hard to find a way to offer comfort to her. "He wanted to go to Scotland, remember?"

She frowned but did not answer.

At the end of the march the British threw down their muskets, swords, and cartridge boxes onto a large circle of ground. They then had to walk back between the French and American troops. As they did, they continued to insult our men by not looking at them. Some Continental soldiers were angered by the disrespect and commenced to shouting and waving their fists.

"Looks to me like another battle is about to break out," said Sibby.

But our officers barked commands and our soldiers regained their dignity.

As the prisoners (for that was their new title, "prisoners of war") headed back to Yorktown, where they would be kept under guard, we gathered up our baskets and canteens.

"Look there," Sibby said, pointing at the road.

At the tail of the British forces, walking without weapons or uniforms, came their women and children, near one hundred by my count. Many of our soldiers had left the road as soon as the last of the defeated enemy's forces had passed by, so the women and children attached to the British forces were accorded little notice.

Our band of lasses stood with respectful attention. We understood their sacrifice.

CHAPTER XLIV

Saturday, October 20–Saturday, November 3, 1781

TELL THEM THAT IF I AM BLACK, I AM FREE BORN AMERICAN AND A REVOLUTIONARY SOLDIER AND THEREFORE OUGHT NOT TO BE THROWN ENTIRELY OUT OF THE SCALE OF NOTICE.
–LETTER OF JOHN CHAVIS, FIFTH VIRGINIA REGIMENT, WHO FOUNDED AN INTEGRATED SCHOOL IN NORTH CAROLINA THAT WAS FORCED TO CLOSE AFTER NAT TURNER'S REBELLION IN 1831

ALONG WITH EIGHT THOUSAND PRISoners and thousands of muskets, empty cartridge boxes, and heavily used cannons, the victory provided us with countless bolts of heavy woolen cloth. This was a treasure indeed, for winter was fast approaching and many of our lads lacked enough clothes to keep warm. A military sewing circle was established around the campfires in the women's section of the camp, and near half the lasses were detailed to sit there and sew all the day long. Ruth was among them, working silently next to Sibby, who'd promised to keep an eye on her.

I struggled on my own but somehow managed the cooking, washing, mending, and nursing of the lads in our company. The frantic pace of the work was a welcome distraction from the unanswered questions about our future.

The surrender of Cornwallis was a brilliant victory for the

Patriots, but we were still at war. Scouts kept an eye on the river in case the British fleet arrived to surprise us. All our cannons had to be pulled back out of the trenches, repaired, and readied for the next battle. Near half of the camp—the regiments from Pennsylvania, Maryland, and Virginia—marched south to meet up with the forces of General Greene and drive the British out of the Carolinas and Georgia. The rest of us would soon be headed north, to spend the winter near New York, the city that overflowed with British soldiers and Loyalist refugees. General Washington wanted to keep a close eye on his enemies while he waited for the return of the battle season.

Curzon was detailed to help the armorers. He couldn't walk far and his injured arm was still sling-bound, but with his good arm and some clever positioning of the required tools, he could clean muskets and sharpen bayonets. He told me it was best for him to take his meals and to sleep with the other forge workers, in order to spare his bad knee all the painful walking to and from our company's encampment.

I was not sure that I believed him. I offered to bring him his supper each night, or to come later, to sit and chat by the fire. He told me it would be better if I didn't, then he limped off with the help of Tall Will.

"Lad's got a lot on his mind," Henry said to me. "Give him a few days and he'll be back to his sunny ways."

I didn't know what to think.

When our troops entered what was left of Yorktown, they found horror there. Our cannonballs and explosive shells had reduced the buildings to rubble. Much worse was the sight of the arms and legs and other parts of bodies that had been torn asunder and left scattered. They had belonged to the black people, the white people, men, women, soldiers, laborers, and townsfolk. The men of our army buried them all. When that mournful job was done, they buried the rotting corpses of the horses, too.

Strangers started arriving in camp. Wellborn politicians with warm overcoats and hands that had never seen work lingered, asking questions and trying to cozy up to the generals. Wealthy plantation owners arrived with their overseers, looking for slaves who had liberated themselves. Sergeant Armstrong told everyone in our company that we should travel only in groups of twos and threes. 'Twas unlikely, he claimed, that anyone would be foolish enough to try to enslave a Continental soldier, but that didn't mean we should make the task easy for them. His orders were meant for me as well, which made any visit to check on Curzon near impossible.

That night Sibby motioned for me to join her by the fire after Ruth lay down in our brush hut to sleep. I nodded to the other lasses gathered there, and they smiled pleasant. We all wore our blankets around our shoulders for warmth and crowded the fire for heat. A few of the women squinted as they tried to sew in the dim light, their fingers stiff with the cold.

I took my place on the log next to Sibby.

"We both need sleep, so I'll come right to it," she said bluntly.

"Has Ruth done something wrong?" I asked.

She broke into hearty laughter that echoed in the dark. "Gracious, no! That child is a godsend! Never complains, and works as hard as any of us. That's why I started thinking upon my grand notion."

The other lasses watched us close. I suspected they already knew the notion she was talking about.

"It starts with a secret," she said, smiling impishly.

"Hardly a secret now!" called Annie from the other side of the fire.

"I'm with child." Sibby grinned.

"Huzzah!" I cried, embracing her. "What magnificent news! Scipio must be overjoyed!"

"You'd think he invented the condition," she said. "And now he thinks I've suddenly become much too fragile for army living."

That led to hoots and laughter around the fire.

"He doesn't want his child born in an army camp," she continued. "When we head north, I'll go to my mother's house, outside Kingston."

"'Tis a sound idea," I said.

"Care to join me?" Her face lit with glee. "You and Ruth both. My father died last year, and Mama could use the help. The two of you know farming, and the three of us get along fine."

"But . . ." I couldn't believe what she was saying, the generosity of her offer.

She rushed on. "I figger the babe will arrive near April. If the war is still going on by then, you can stay with us or return to the army afore they start their marching again. If not, Curzon will know where to find you–safe and secure–when he's discharged. He and Scipio can travel back together."

There was a third possibility, though Sibby did not know of it, of course. If Curzon and I were not destined for life together, then time working and living with Sibby's family would help Ruth and me get our feet under us.

"What do ye say, gal?" Annie asked. "She's offering you a life of luxury—a bed to sleep in and a roof over ye head!"

"I hardly know what to say." I forced a smile. "Other than to thank you for the fantastical offer." I surprised myself by laughing. "Truth be told, it's mighty tempting!"

"Talk over the matter with yer man," Annie suggested. "But you decide for you."

The next evening Ruth insisted that we join the small group of folks who watched as the captured British were marched out of Yorktown, under the guard of thousands of Virginia militiamen. 'Twas the beginning of their journey north to the prisoner-of-war camps awaiting them in Maryland and Pennsylvania. There were no officers among them, of course. Cornwallis and the other men of rank were allowed to stay in comfort on their ships in the river. They'd soon be sailing to New York, and from there, home to England in exchange for American prisoners being held by the British.

Ruth was certain that we'd see Aberdeen among the redcoat troops marching north. The truth of the matter was that he was likely dead, but I could not bring myself to tell her so.

Together we watched the bedraggled and defeated army trudge past. I filled my apron with acorns as my thoughts bounced from the fate of the prisoners to the questions of our own future. Ought we take up Sibby's kind offer and enjoy a secure winter in a home with kind people? What of Curzon? Had our declarations of romantical sentiments been the product of the closeness of death? Did he regret his words to me? I did not regret mine, but it stung terribly to think that we were no longer of the same mind. Was he avoiding me because he was ashamed to admit this?

I shook my head. For years I'd dreamed of the time when our lives would not be in constant peril, when I'd have the luxury of choosing the course to take. Turned out that having choices could be nearly as prickly and upsetting as having none.

Ruth stood fixed in place, silent and steady as a wooden dame carved upon the prow of a ship. She studied every single face until the last person crested the hill to the north and disappeared.

The drums rattled from the center of camp, calling for the evening's chores to begin.

"We need to go back for supper," I said quietly. "The lads will be hungry."

Ruth acted as if she'd not heard me. She tilted her head to watch the arrow-shaped flocks of geese flying above.

"Why they going south?" she asked.

"The geese?" The question surprised me almost as much as the fact that she'd spoken. She had been slipping back into her silent ways since the surrender. "Winter's on the way," I explained. "They fly south to keep warm."

"Geese fly north in spring. Walter told me."

"He's right," I agreed. "In the years when you and me were apart, I used to watch the geese go south, to where you lived. And then in the spring, when it got hot in Carolina, you'd watch the geese fly north."

"They flew north to you?"

"Indeed. We likely saw the same geese. Do you understand?"

"Aye. But we can't fly. 'Tain't safe. . . ." Her voice trailed off.

I watched her close, worried that any moment might bring an explosion of grief or rage. She picked up a stick, and to my surprise, she used it to draw two letters in the dirt, an *A* and a lopsided *R*.

"*A* is for 'Aberdeen,'" she explained. "He showed me how."

"That was a kindness," I said gently.

She pointed to the *R*. "That's my mark, next to his."

I nodded, unsure where this course of her pondering would take us.

She squatted down and studied the two letters long and hard. The north wind blew cold, but I waited, for the moment seemed a precious one for her.

"Aberdeen, he'll see our geese," Ruth said after a good long while. "No fretting."

I could not follow her thinking. "You won't worry about him?"

"No fretting." She rocked back and forth the tiniest bit. "Deen's safe. He'll watch Nancy Chicken and Thomas Boon and Serafina and Walter. They're all safe."

I opened my mouth to explain that she wasn't making sense, that the chicken was long dead, the donkey likely stolen, and Aberdeen . . .

I closed my gob just in time. Ruth was building a story that would let her keep loving all those critters and people. If she held tight to it, she might be able to survive their loss.

"That's very sensible, poppet," I said. "Sensible and true."

Ruth leaned forward and put one hand on the *A* and the other on the *R*.

"All safe in my heart," she whispered.

CHAPTER XLV

Sunday, November 4–Monday, November 5, 1781

WE FEEL THAT WE HAVE NOT FOUGHT IN VAIN. . . .
I KNOW NOW THAT I HAVE BEEN AN ACTOR IN EVENTS
WHICH THE WORLD AND HISTORY WILL NEVER FORGET.
—FRENCH SOLDIER GASTON DE LA BASTIE WRITING
TO HIS MOTHER AFTER THE YORKTOWN VICTORY

EVERY TIME I ACCUSTOMED MYSELF to the rhythms of a place or of a circumstance, it altered. Changeability was the only constant, and that distressed me deeply. I longed for a stretch of time, even a few months, during which I would live in the same place, tend to the same tasks, and endure only the ordinary difficulties of life, such as a cow that kicked the milk bucket or rows of bean plants that needed weeding.

I gave myself a pinch. Wishing was for loobies and fools. I had only a few hours left and days of work to accomplish in them.

I spread the ragged blanket on the ground next to the company cook fire so that the light shone upon it. The night was cold, but dry for a change, and that suited me fine. I had a dish of corn bread baking in the coals and pork roasting over the flames. The men of our company had all retired to their tents to sleep for a few hours. Ruth slept too, back at our brush hut. I could finally steal some time to sort through my seed collection, which I had put off doing overlong.

I dumped my haversack out onto the blanket and picked up the seeds one at a time, examining each for signs of mold or a doomed attempt at sprouting. Seeds kept dry will wait for years to be planted. Sadly, a goodly portion of mine had fallen damp. They needed to be removed lest they ruined the others.

My hands thus employed, my mind wandered, still frustrated at the latest turn of events. At first the officers had told us that we'd be leaving in three days' time. I had planned accordingly. The first day I would again walk past the armorer's camp and greet Curzon with a casual smile. Mayhaps engage the forge workers in a light confab about the weather. The second day I'd bake an apple pie for all of them and deliver it, but again would not tarry, pleading the number of tasks awaiting me. The third day, that was when I'd make my move. I'd beg leave of the armorer to speak in privacy with my "husband." I'd bake a second pie, if necessary.

I gave myself another pinch. Getting trapped in old dreams was as foolish as wishing.

The officers had changed their minds, of course. The army was to leave at first light, beginning our long march to the Hudson River in New York. The fellows had spent the day loading wagons, burying slaughter-yard offal, and filling in the foul privy trenches. They had worked in high spirits and good cheer. As soon as their bellies were full, they'd trooped off to snore like fat bears in their tents.

I sighed. The pile of seeds gone bad was already bigger than the good.

A shadow fell over me. Alarmed, I looked up.

"Hello, Country." Curzon leaned heavily on a crutch.

"Oh!" The frogs in my belly awoke with a start and commenced to flopping and leaping up my throat. "Why are you here? Are you to travel with the company tomorrow? Surely, you'll be allowed to ride in a wagon."

He limped to the far side of the fire and sat on a log, wincing. The crutch was nothing more than a shovel handle with a pad of rags fastened to the top end. His shirt was filthy and his coat had small burn holes in it, as well as a rip at the shoulder.

"That knee wants supporting." I rolled a log over and upended it. "Hand me your stick."

He did so without a word. I propped it so that it provided a bridge of sorts, then helped him move his leg until his foot rested on the log, and the weight of the limb rested on the crutch.

"That's better," he said with a sigh. "Thank you."

I gently felt the swollen knee through the fabric of his breeches. "Did you twist it again?"

"Been walking overmuch," he muttered.

I looked up at him. His face bore new injuries too: dried blood from a fresh cut on his lip, and a pouch of swelling like a small egg under his left eye. "Did you walk into a wall or someone's fist?"

His face went rigid with rage as he stared into the fire.

"Three fists," he finally muttered.

I waited, but he gave no more details. I could not tell his reason for coming, not by looking at him, but I was unsure how to proceed with conversating. I stood and resumed my cooking tasks, using the metal hooks to lift the pan of corn bread from the coals and set it on the dirt to cool.

"How's Ruth?" he asked at last.

"She suffers from melancholy," I said. "Mourning Aberdeen. We watched the prisoners march out, but he was not with them."

"I looked for him too." His shoulders drooped. "Went to the garrison to see if he was with the fugitives."

"What garrison?"

He coughed, then spat in the fire. "Have you not heard how the army's treating the fugitive sons and daughters of Africa?"

I'd never heard such bitterness in his voice. "What are you talking about?"

He stared into the fire. "They say that in Virginia tens of thousands freed themselves and ran to the British."

"Aye." I nodded. "Many died of smallpox. Others starved. But surely, thousands more have found safety and are living free."

"Not all of them. Hundreds were found in Yorktown. Others have been captured on their way north or west."

In his face I saw the hopeful boy he'd once been and the righteous man he was trying to be, both clouded by the deepest sorrow I'd ever seen. He turned away, glared at the flames, and started to explain.

The self-liberated people captured by the American army—*our* army—had been locked away under guard in the garrison. Curzon and others of our regiment had complained most vigorously to the officers, asking that the captured fugitives be considered as Loyalists, for they'd chosen the British side. Thus, they ought be sent to the prisoner-of-war camps with the rest of the British forces. But the officers did not listen. General Washington himself signed the order that created the garrison. 'Twas rumored that Washington had found some of his own slaves among the fugitives, and some belonging to Thomas Jefferson as well. Newspapers were advertising for plantation owners to come and reclaim their runaways. Anyone who was not claimed would become the property of the state of Virginia and sent to work in the lead mines.

Our army that was fighting for freedom was delivering people into slavery.

Curzon had gone to the garrison himself to see the conditions there and look for Aberdeen. He got into a fight with the guards, who then attempted to lock him up, and would have succeeded had not Ebenezer accompanied Curzon. He was grateful to have a friend at his side, but angrier still that the guards paid heed to Eben on account of his complexion matching theirs. And there was no sign of Aberdeen.

He talked at length about the injustice of the circumstances, the horrible hypocrisy of it all. As he spoke, I made more corn bread and roasted the mutton. I offered him a cup of water, which he drank, and meat and bread, which he did not eat.

At the end of his tale he stood and leaned on the crutch. "I had faith in them, Isabel. Even when they handed me back to Bellingham, I convinced myself that things would change; they just needed to see our dedication, how smart and hardworking and patriotic we were."

"You've always believed in the Revolution," I said carefully. "You had a mountain of faith in it."

"I was wrong." He spat in the fire again. "I should have listened to you and Aberdeen. We could have fled to Spanish Florida or the mountains to the west." He took a deep breath. "Or even joined the British."

I added wood to the fire. "So we could be imprisoned in the garrison right now, headed to a life in the lead mines? No, thank you."

"Five weeks of camp life and suddenly you're a Patriot?" he asked. "You've been arguing against the war for years. You always said the Patriots talk a good game of freedom, but the proof is in their actions, not their words. What was that Scripture you quoted till I wanted to scream?"

"Ye shall know them by their fruits," I murmured.

"That's the one," he said. "Well, the fruits of this revolution will be given only to white hands."

He limped a few steps, turned, and limped back. His crutch snagged on something in the dirt, and he pitched forward, off balance. I grabbed at him and he held on to my arms. We swayed for a moment.

"You should sit yourself down," I said.

He nodded and let me help him hop back to the log by the fire. Once he was seated, I sat by his side. It was a comfort to be so close to him again.

"What's that mess you've made on the blanket over there?" he asked.

"Sorting my seeds. They're all ajumble, and I've lost three quarters of them."

"Why bother? You won't know what you're planting."

"Not until they sprout, I won't," I admitted. "But I've got to start with something. Once they grow and bloom, I'll know what to call them, and eventually the garden will be orderly."

"A fool-headed way to farm," he grumbled.

"'Tis a fool-headed way to grow a country, too, but that's what we're doing."

"Now you've gone barmy, Isabel," he said sourly.

I walked over to the blanket, gathered the small handful of the good seeds, and sat back down next to him.

"Seems to me this is the seed time for America." I took

his hand and poured the seeds into it, as he had poured dirt into mine weeks earlier. "War's nearly over. Now we've got to grow a proper nation. That will require stouthearted folks who understand the true meaning of freedom. People like us."

"They won't let us."

"They won't have a choice," I said firmly. "This is our mother country too. Ponder this–the Revolution won't end on account of Cornwallis being captured. The real revolution is the black and Indian men of the Rhode Island regiment. It's you and Isaac and Tall Will fighting alongside Hamilton and Lafayette in the redoubt. It's Ruth and Sibby and me and all the other black women of the army doing our share and being accorded the same respect and earning wages, just like Annie and Cristena. It's Ebenezer, who was ignorant when he met you, but who became your friend and opened his heart to people who didn't look like him and his."

"That's not enough." He turned his head away from me.

"Of course it's not, fool. It's not enough and it's not right and it's not fair. But it's what we have. Think on Serafina and Walter. They couldn't run, but they made sure a whole passel of people could. Think on the fellows in our company. Imagine if we all settled close to one another after the war. Imagine a town of veteran soldiers and their wives and children, all folks who understand the struggle and believe in the same kind of freedom."

"I try not to think about what happens after the war," he grumbled. "All I think about is freedom."

"Freedom never gets handed to anyone. You told me that, over and over." I reached out and gently turned his chin so that he faced me. "We have to fight for it, my friend, no matter how long it takes. We must claim it for ourselves and our brothers and sisters."

The fierce anger in his face softened a bit.

"You're dreaming, Country," he said quietly.

"I'm ready to dream," I admitted. "It's taken a long time, but I know my aim in life. I know my purpose."

I hesitated, suddenly nervous. The fire crackled and popped, and sparks shot into the air.

"Does your purpose include me?" he asked.

I leaned forward and cupped my hand along his jaw. In his eyes I found the home and comfort my heart had long been seeking. "Indeed it does, you muzzy-headed blatherskite."

"Does that mean . . ." His voice tightened, and he paused to clear his throat. "Are you saying . . ."

"I'm saying we should marry, aye." My heart was pounding louder than wild horses. "I want you for my husband. What say you, Private Smith?"

"I've been in love with you, Country, since the first moment I clapped eyes on you. I want to marry you—"

The rest of his words were lost in the most delightful kiss ever enjoyed by a campfire.

Ruth woke with a squeal when I whispered my secret into her ear. I stole a few moments to wash my face and tidy my hair, while she plunged into the brush behind the woodpile. She emerged from the shadows with her hands filled with autumn leaves arranged as if they were the most beautiful roses and larkspurs.

"Got to hold some pretty when you wed," she explained with a grin.

By the time we returned to the cook fire, Henry and Curzon were standing with the rest of our lads, some of them still yawning and rubbing the sleep from their eyes. The fire had been built up so that it blazed high and threw a warming light over all.

We married under the gaze of heaven and in a company of good people who cared about us. Henry preached a short sermon in which he talked about marriage being when two people come together as one to start their life anew. He said it made him think about thirteen colonies that were trying to become one nation. We laughed about that, but he had a point.

The stars wheeled to the west, and the first birds of morning began to call up the sun. As our friends huzzahed and bowed to me, and clapped my husband on the back, and celebrated our union with dreadful coffee and not-quite-dreadful corn bread, I watched the kind ghosts gathering in the mist at the edge of the woods.

Momma used to say that the best time to talk to ghosts was just before the sun came up. That's when they could hear us true. That's when they could answer us.

"We're free, Momma," I whispered. "We're free and we're strong."

Ruth smiled at me from the other side of the fire.

"And we're together," I said.

I held Momma and Poppa in my heart so they could see us both and know that we were well. Then I squared my shoulders and shook out my skirts. A new day was dawning and there was work to be done.

APPENDIX

1. Are Isabel, Ruth, and Curzon based on real people? How did you develop their characters?

Isabel, Ruth, and Curzon are fictional characters, as are all of the people they directly interact with in the book. The details of their lives were built on the lives of real people who freed themselves from slavery and later wrote down their experiences. Advertisements about runaway slaves gave a lot of information about how people escaped slavery and the kinds of things they carried with them when they fled. Some African American veterans of the American Revolution later applied for pensions, and those applications offered wonderful insight into their time in the military. Pension applications of white Revolutionary War soldiers and camp women occasionally mentioned African American soldiers too.

Read more:

Sylvia R. Frey, *Water from the Rock: Black Resistance in a Revolutionary Age*.

David Waldstreicher, "Reading the Runaways: Self-Fashioning, Print Culture, and Confidence in Slavery in the Eighteenth-Century Mid-Atlantic," *The William and Mary Quarterly*, April 1999.

Revolutionary War Pension and Bounty-Land-Warrant Application Files, National Archives microfilm, 1974.

2. Are there any real people or incidents in the story?

Many! Yorktown was a very exciting place to be in 1781,

though mayhaps not if you favored the cause of King George. General Washington was there, of course, and the Marquis de Lafayette, Alexander Hamilton, and a host of officers and aides-de-camp who went on to play significant roles in the early days of America.

These scenes from the book are all based on what really happened:

- The chaos in the South caused by the war
- The walk from South Carolina to Virginia
- The American and French armies in Williamsburg
- Baptist worship service led by enslaved preacher Gowan Pamphlet
- The Siege of Yorktown
- The men of the Rhode Island regiment and the large number of African American soldiers throughout the Continental Army
- The roles played by the women of the army
- The British surrender
- How the British treated the self-liberated people who had joined them
- The Continental Army's role in recapturing those self-liberated people and returning them to slavery

Read more:

Douglas R. Egerton, *Death or Liberty: African Americans and Revolutionary America*.

Jerome A. Greene, *The Guns of Independence: The Siege of Yorktown, 1781*.

Richard M. Ketchum, *Victory at Yorktown: The Campaign That Won the Revolution*.

Gary B. Nash, *The Unknown American Revolution: The Unruly Birth of Democracy and the Struggle to Create America*.

Benjamin Quarles, *The Negro in the American Revolution*, introduction by Gary Nash, foreword by Thad W. Tate.
Ray Raphael, *A People's History of the American Revolution: How Common People Shaped the Fight for Independence*.

3. What happened to the people held in slavery by Washington and Jefferson who escaped and ran to the British?

Twenty-three of Thomas Jefferson's slaves from three plantations fled to join the British. From Jefferson's Elk Hill plantation, Joe, Jenny, Nat, Judy, and Black Sal with her three small children all escaped. Hannibal; his wife, Patty, and their six children; an old woman named Lucy; and Sam and his wife, Nancy, left the Willis Creek plantation. Robin, Barnaby, Harry, and Will all ran from Monticello. We know the details of their names from the records that Jefferson kept.

After the fall of Yorktown, Jefferson sent a man to look for his fugitive slaves. The man found six of them: Robin, Barnaby, Will, Nat, Judy, and Isabel, who was the daughter of Hannibal and Patty. Isabel was given to Jefferson's sister in 1786, Barnaby died shortly after being returned to Jefferson, and the other four were sold. Historians believe that the rest of the escapees likely died of smallpox because Jefferson did not inoculate his slaves against the disease. But there is a chance they survived to live in freedom.

In April of 1781, fourteen men and three women who were held as slaves at George Washington's Mount Vernon plantation escaped and fled to the British. Two of them were found and enslaved again after Yorktown, as were those later found in Philadelphia. A few of Washington's slaves made it to New York and found safety with the British there. Washington worked hard to convince the British to return those people to him, but the British authorities refused. Instead, the self-liberated former slaves of George Washington traveled with other Loyalist refugees to Nova Scotia when the British left New York in 1783.

Read more:

Cassandra Pybus, "Jefferson's Faulty Math: The Question of Slave Defections in the American Revolution," *The William and Mary Quarterly*, April 2005.

Michael Kranish, *Flight from Monticello: Thomas Jefferson at War.*

Henry Wiencek, *An Imperfect God: George Washington, His Slaves, and the Creation of America.*

4. How could such important Founding Fathers as George Washington and Thomas Jefferson own slaves when they worked so hard to make America free of British rule? Doesn't that make them hypocrites?

The fact that the Founding Fathers could devote their lives to freeing America from British rule while holding people in slavery is an appalling hypocrisy. British newspapers and opinion makers enjoyed pointing this out, even though their own nation had been responsible for the kidnapping, transportation, and enslaving of millions of Africans.

Slave-owning leaders of the Revolution, like Thomas Jefferson, John Jay, Patrick Henry, George Mason, James Madison, and Henry Laurens wrote of the evils of slavery but spent their lives enjoying luxuries they could afford because of the unpaid labor of slaves. George Washington and Benjamin Franklin also bought, sold, and profited from the work of enslaved people, but they freed their slaves after their deaths. In Franklin's case, that meant that one man, Bob, went free, because all of Franklin's other slaves had already died. Washington's death in 1799 meant bittersweet freedom for the 123 people he freed, because many of them were related by blood or marriage to people still owned by Martha Washington. The newly freed people had to leave their loved ones behind or else risk re-enslavement.

Americans in earlier times preferred to think only about the positive contributions made by the Founding Fathers: the way they won the Revolution and set about laying the groundwork for the United States of America. Today we have a more nuanced view: we can appreciate the good and recognize the bad. It is possible to admire the Founding Fathers for their positive contributions while at the same time feeling enraged, sorrowful, or confused because of the damage they inflicted to generations of people who didn't look like them. If they had truly had the courage of their convictions, then the world-changing language of the Declaration of Independence—"We hold these truths to be self-evident, that all men are created equal, that they are endowed by their Creator with certain unalienable Rights, that among these are Life, Liberty, and the pursuit of Happiness"—would have guaranteed the equality, protection, and opportunities of all Americans since the day the nation liberated itself.

Read more:

Lucia Stanton, *"Those Who Labor for My Happiness": Slavery at Thomas Jefferson's Monticello.*

David Waldstreicher, *Runaway America: Benjamin Franklin, Slavery, and the American Revolution.*

Henry Wiencek, *An Imperfect God: George Washington, His Slaves, and the Creation of America.*

5. How many slaves freed themselves during the Revolution?

This wonderfully important question does not have a simple answer.

We can only speculate about the number of families who freed themselves and blended into the fabric of society, most often on the Western border, or with Native American nations, or in Northern communities that already had a significant number of free African Americans. Self-liberated people had to be private about their escape in order to protect their families.

We have better primary source evidence for the numbers of enslaved people who joined either the Patriot or the British army. The estimates come from British and American military records and from claims for losses that were later submitted by American slaveholders.

Historians estimate that at least five thousand black men fought for the Patriots. Most of them were free. Some were enslaved and fought as a "substitute," in place of a white person. The enslaved men who fought in the Rhode Island regiment were granted freedom by the state in exchange for their service. Some enslaved people who fought for the Patriots remained in slavery after the war.

Given that supporting the Patriots offered no guarantee of freedom, it makes perfect sense that many more people fled to the British when trying to free themselves. Estimates vary but it appears likely that tens of thousands escaped in this way. Author and historian Ray Raphael estimates that the number of people who were able to liberate themselves during the Revolution is comparable in scope to the number of people who escaped slavery through the legendary Underground Railroad before the Civil War.

Historian Gary B. Nash called the exodus to the freedom offered by the British, "the greatest slave rebellion in the history of Great Britain's New World colonies."

Read more:

Alan Gilbert, *Black Patriots and Loyalists: Fighting for Emancipation in the War for Independence.*

Gary B. Nash, *The Forgotten Fifth: African Americans in the Age of Revolution*.
Ray Raphael, *Founding Myths: Stories That Hide Our Patriotic Past*.

6. What happened to the fugitive slaves who joined the British and survived the war?

Those black Loyalists wound up all over the world.

Nearly ten thousand black Loyalists who had escaped slavery in British-held New York City fled the city before it was turned over to the Patriots, likely to start their lives in freedom in the North or West. An estimated 400–1000 black Loyalists emigrated to London. The African American soldiers who served under Hessian Baron von Riedesel emigrated with their company to Germany after the war. An untold number of black Loyalists were forced back into slavery, some given to white Loyalists to offset the financial losses they suffered during the war. Others were sent against their will to East Florida and the Caribbean.

The British government resettled roughly thirty thousand Loyalist refugees in Nova Scotia. Historian Alan Gilbert has calculated that approximately one third of them—ten thousand children, women, and men—were African American.

Conditions in Nova Scotia were desperately harsh. There was not enough land for all the refugees. What was available was generally rocky and unsuitable for farming. The black Loyalists faced violent, devastating racism. They were not given as much land as white Loyalists, and the land they were given was the worst in the settlement. Some were forced to work in order to get what white settlers were given for free.

Thomas Peters became a leader of the black refugees. Kidnapped from what is now known as Nigeria around 1760, when he was in his early twenties, Peters (his birth name is unknown, but he is believed to have been of the Egba group of the Yoruba people) was eventually taken to Wilmington, North Carolina. Peters and his family fled to the British. Peters rose to the rank of sergeant in the Black Pioneers, the most famous black Loyalist militia unit.

After the end of the war, Peters and his family joined the Loyalists who resettled in Canada. Angered by the unequal treatment that blacks received there, Peters tried negotiating with local officials but got nowhere with them. He traveled to London in 1790 to meet with British leaders. The British offered to resettle the black Loyalists again, this time in the African nation of Sierra Leone. Under Peters's dedicated leadership, twelve hundred black Loyalists who had spent eight dreadful years in Nova Scotia sailed to Freetown, Sierra Leone, in 1792.

Among those who sailed with Peters was a man named Henry Washington. Henry was born in West Africa, near the Gambia River. Sadly, there is no evidence of his birth name. He was kidnapped in his twenties and eventually sold to George Washington before the Revolution started. In Virginia, Henry dug canals in the Great Dismal Swamp and worked with horses at Mount Vernon. He escaped in 1771 but was recaptured and returned to the plantation. Five years later, Henry escaped again. This time, he made it to the British. When the British evacuated New York, Henry and his wife, Jenney, went with them and settled in Birchtown, Nova Scotia. The couple joined Thomas Peters in the journey to Freetown, Sierra Leone, where they lived out the rest of their days.

Read more:

Alan Gilbert, *Black Patriots and Loyalists: Fighting for Emancipation in the War for Independence.*

Cassandra Pybus, *Epic Journeys of Freedom: Runaway Slaves of the American Revolution and Their Global Quest for Liberty.*
Gary B. Nash, "Thomas Peters: Millwright and Deliverer," *The American Revolution*, website created by PBS, Humanities & Social Sciences Online, National Endowment for the Humanities, Michigan State University, and the Omohundro Institute of Early American History and Culture, http://revolution.h-net.msu.edu/essays/nash.html
Benjamin Quarles, *The Negro in the American Revolution*, introduction by Gary Nash, foreword by Thad W. Tate.
Ray Raphael, *A People's History of the American Revolution: How Common People Shaped the Fight for Independence.*
Gregory J. W. Urwin, "When Freedom Wore a Red Coat: How Cornwallis' 1781 Campaign Threatened the Revolution in Virginia," *Army History*, Summer 2008.
Simon Schama, *Rough Crossings: Britain, the Slaves and the American Revolution.*

7. Did the Revolution change the way anyone thought about slavery?

It changed the opinion of some white Americans. Revolutionary rhetoric—the language used to talk about the fight for independence—made them examine the morality of slavery and decide that was wrong.

This change in attitude led states in the North to pass laws that eventually outlawed slavery there. With the exception of Massachusetts, the Northern states banned slavery very slowly. Slave owners were given the chance to keep making money from their slaves for a generation, or to sell them out of state for a quick profit. A few slave owners manumitted their slaves, freeing them legally. Manumission was not legal in all areas.

In 1760, there were 350,000 black children, women, and men held in slavery in the American Colonies. By the beginning of the American Revolution in 1775, there were approximately 500,000 enslaved people, a full 20 percent of the country's population.

By 1790, there were almost 700,000 enslaved people in the United States. This was despite the fact that tens of thousands had liberated themselves during the Revolution, the state of Massachusetts had outlawed slavery, and manumissions were on the rise. This sharp rise in population was the result of a dramatic increase in the number of African people who were kidnapped, enslaved, and transported to the United States. The population of enslaved Americans continued to rise until 1865, when slavery was finally abolished, freeing nearly four million people. At that point there were 27 million white Americans and nearly 500,000 black African Americans who were already living in freedom.

Read more:

Gary B. Nash, *The Unknown American Revolution: The Unruly Birth of Democracy and the Struggle to Create America.*

Gary B. Nash, *The Forgotten Fifth: African Americans in the Age of Revolution.*

8. When were the people held in slavery in the original thirteen states freed?

Connecticut–At the beginning of the American Revolution, 6,464 people were held in slavery in Connecticut, more than any other state in New England. The state passed a gradual emancipation act in 1784 and amended it in 1797. Slavery was finally outlawed in 1848.

Massachusetts–In 1783, the Massachusetts state supreme court ruled that the state constitution, passed in 1780, prohibited slavery in the state because it declared that, "all men are born free and equal."

New Hampshire–The language of the 1783 state

constitution closely mirrored that of Massachusetts, but there was some confusion about if it applied to the people held in slavery the day the constitution was adopted or if it only applied to children born after that day. The 1790 census showed 158 enslaved people, and the number dwindled after that. In 1857 the state passed a law that fully prohibited slavery.

New Jersey–The gradual abolition law passed by New Jersey in 1804 contained plenty of loopholes. By 1830, more than half of the remaining slaves in the North lived in New Jersey. The last eighteen enslaved people in the state were freed in 1865, when the Thirteenth Amendment to the Constitution became law.

New York–The 1790 federal census showed twenty thousand enslaved people in New York State. There was tremendous tension between the state's abolitionists and those who supported slavery, but by 1799 the state passed a very gradual emancipation bill. In 1817 that was amended to free all enslaved people by July 4, 1827. The 1830 census showed seventy-five enslaved people in the state. The 1840 census showed none.

Pennsylvania–The state passed a gradual abolition act that freed children born to enslaved mothers after 1780, though those children were required to work as indentured servants until they were twenty-eight years old. Historians believe that there were no slaves in Pennsylvania after 1847.

Rhode Island–A gradual emancipation was passed by Rhode Island in 1784. All enslaved boys who were born after March 1 of that year were freed when they turned twenty-one years old. Girls would be freed when they turned eighteen years old.

Virginia–The state made it easier for enslaved people to

be manumitted in 1782, but slavery did not end until 1865, when the Thirteenth Amendment became law.

Vermont–Though technically not one of the original thirteen states, Vermont was created out of New York State in 1777. The state constitution written that year declared all slaves free without any payment to the people who owned them. This ruling only applied to women older than eighteen and men older than twenty-one. Loopholes in the law allowed the continued slavery of children, and the kidnapping of free black Vermonters so they could be sold out of state. Those loopholes were closed and penalties enforced for kidnapping blacks and holding people in slavery in 1806.

Delaware, Georgia, Maryland, and North and South Carolina–Slavery did not end until 1865, when the Thirteenth Amendment to the Constitution, which ended slavery throughout America, became law.

Read more:

Anne Farrow, Joel Lang, and Jenifer Frank, *Complicity: How the North Promoted, Prolonged, and Profited from Slavery.*

Harvey Amani Whitfield, *The Problem of Slavery in Early Vermont, 1777–1810.*

Website: *Slavery in the North*, http://slavenorth.com/

9. Was Florida controlled by Spain during the Revolution? Which side of the war did the Spanish King Carlos III support?

At the time of the American Revolution, the area we now call Florida and other parts of the Gulf Coast region were claimed by two European countries: Great Britain and Spain. Great Britain, Spain, and France had been battling for territory in the Americas and Caribbean for years, destroying the lives of countless Indigenous peoples and robbing them of their land.

During the Revolution, both France and Spain sided with

the young United States against Great Britain. France contributed money, guns, soldiers, and her navy to the American cause. Spain's contributions are not as well known, but were equally important.

Spain declared war against Great Britain in 1779, forcing the British to fight not only the United States, but the Spanish military in the Gulf Coast region, the Mississippi River Valley, and Central America. The British army had to divide its forces, which weakened it. In April 1781, Spanish forces, including Spain's Irish Hibernia Regiment as well as free Afro-Cubans, battled the British in Pensacola and won possession of West Florida. Then the wealthy families of Havana, Cuba, loaned an enormous amount of money to French Admiral de Grasse, which allowed the French navy to sail North to the Chesapeake region and assist Washington at the Siege of Yorktown.

Read more:

Thomas E. Chávez, *Spain and the Independence of the United States: An Intrinsic Gift*.

Kathleen DuVal, *Independence Lost: Lives on the Edge of the American Revolution*.

Allan J. Kuethe, *Cuba*, 1753–1815: Crown, Military, and Society.

10. Was there really a Baker General at the Yorktown encampment?

Indeed! Christopher Ludwig (or Ludwick) was born in Germany in 1720. After working as a soldier and a ship's baker, he immigrated to Philadelphia with fancy gingerbread molds and European baking recipes and skills. With his wife, he established a popular bakery that specialized in common gingerbread loaves, cookies, and elegant pastries. He was a founding member of the German Society of Pennsylvania, which offered English language classes to German-speaking immigrants. His business prospered.

At the beginning of the American Revolution, Ludwig collected, stored, and transported gunpowder for Washington's troops. In 1776, at age 56, he volunteered for the Continental Army, where he served as a spy and worked to convince captured Hessians (mercenary German soldiers who fought for the British) to change sides. Congress later appointed Ludwig the "director of baking" for the army. He and his company of seventy bakers worked at the Valley Forge winter encampment but struggled to find enough flour to feed the men. Ludwig, now affectionately known as the "Baker General," and his company of bakers also supplied bread (and perhaps gingerbread) to the troops at the Siege of Yorktown.

Read more:

"Christopher Ludwig (1720–1801)" on *Immigrant Entrepreneurship: German-American Business Biographies* (http://www.immigrantentrepreneurship.org/entry.php?rec=175)

William Ward Condit, "Christopher Ludwick, Patriotic Gingerbread Baker," *The Pennsylvania Magazine of History and Biography*, October 1957.

11. Why didn't the Patriots kidnap Prince William Henry in New York City?

They almost did.

Prince William Henry of Great Britain, third son of King George III, arrived in British-held New York in September 1781, just before the Patriot Army left Williamsburg and marched to Yorktown. The sixteen-year-old midshipman was the first member of the royal family to visit America. During the winter of 1781–82, Prince William spent time with high-ranking British officials but also made sure to enjoy himself. He liked sitting in a chair being pushed around a frozen lake, among other things.

In March of 1782, five months after the Yorktown victory, New Jersey Colonel Matthias Ogden developed plans to sneak into New York with forty men and capture the prince and British Admiral Robert Digby. It was a bold and dangerous plan. Washington approved it, but before Ogden could strike, the British greatly increased security around the prince and Digby Ogden's kidnapping plans were canceled. By August, news of peace negotiations between the Americans and the British became public.

Prince William Henry didn't become King of England until 1830, when he was sixty-four years old. When he died seven years later, he was succeeded by his niece, Victoria. In other words, Queen Victoria, who ruled Great Britain from 1837 to 1901, was the granddaughter of King George III, who saw his American colonies declare, fight for, and win their independence.

Read more:

Janice Hadlow, *A Royal Experiment: The Private Life of King George III.*

Judith L. Van Buskirk, *Generous Enemies: Patriots and Loyalists in Revolutionary New York.*

12. Did the Patriot victory at Yorktown end the American Revolution?

Both sides of the conflict recognized Washington's win at Yorktown as an important victory, but it did not end the war right away. The armies fought minor skirmishes as the politicians pondered what the end of the war should look like. In March 1782, the British people voted a new Parliament into office. In 1783, both countries signed the Treaty of Paris, which officially ended the war.

The Revolution was only the first step on the road to build a new country. America's leaders had to structure the government and stabilize the economy, so they got to work writing the Constitution, which laid out the foundation of the United States.

Slavery became a central topic of debate during the Constitutional Convention. Delegates from the Northern states, whose economies were not as dependent on slave labor, argued to end the institution of slavery and gradually free all people held in slavery. The Southern states disagreed. "South Carolina and Georgia cannot do without slaves," said South Carolina delegate, Charles Cotesworth Pinckney. There was talk of the two states seceding and rejoining Great Britain if the Constitution outlawed slavery.

The final draft of the Constitution was filled with compromises that ensured that millions of Americans would be held in slavery for the next seventy-eight years, until the Union's victory in the Civil War and the Thirteenth Amendment to the Constitution set all people free.

The struggle for total equality of rights and opportunity for all Americans has continued ever since.

Read more:

Thomas Fleming, *The Perils of Peace: America's Struggle for Survival After Yorktown.*

Joseph J. Ellis, *Founding Brothers: The Revolutionary Generation.*

Gary B. Nash, *The Forgotten Fifth: African Americans in the Age of Revolution.*

VOCABULARY WORDS

addlepated: foolish or silly
bairn: child
balderdash: nonsense
barmy: crazy
befuddled: confused
betwixt: between
blatherskite: person who talks on and on without making any sense
bloody flux: dysentery, a deadly infection that causes bloody diarrhea
breeches: Colonial-era pants that ended just below the knee, where they were fastened with a string, buttons, or buckles
buffoon: ridiculous person, clown
clodpate: blockhead, fool
confab: conversation
consarned: confounded, darned
caterwauled: complaining
frippery: frivolous thing
gob: mouth
gollumpus: big clumsy person, oaf
haint: ghost
hexed: magically enchanted
hullabaloo: commotion
lackwit: fool
lobsterback: British soldier
looby: awkward person who does dumb things

lout: mean person who is up to no good
muzzy-headed: confused
mutton-headed: foolish
niff-naffy nincompoop: lazy fool
odsbodikins: a mild curse word
pate: skull, head
pestilent: dangerous, harmful
poppet: affectionate nickname for a child
poultice: cloth soaked in medication, often heated, that is placed on the skin to reduce inflammation
pox on you: a mild curse that shows anger or disgust
rogue: dishonest person, scoundrel
queue: short ponytail worn by many boys and men during the Revolution
slubberdegullion: slobbering or worthless person
sluggard: a lazy person
sutler: someone who sells things to soldiers
totty-headed: confused, ridiculous
varlet: a dishonest person
vex, vexation: irritating, frustrating

ACKNOWLEDGMENTS

I've been working on the Seeds of America trilogy for nearly half of my career. It has been an incredible journey, both as a writer and as an American. You can find a bibliography of the sources I used for the trilogy on my website, but I'd like to thank the people who were particularly helpful in the creation of *Ashes* here.

Historian, professor, and researcher Ray Raphael, author of groundbreaking books about the American Revolution such as *A People's History of the American Revolution: How Common People Shaped the Fight for Independence* and *Founding Myths: Stories That Hide Our Patriotic Past*, and his wife, author Marie Raphael, generously read and commented on the book. They helped me sort through some confusing contradictions and verified important details. I used many of Ray's books in the research for the entire trilogy and am grateful beyond words for the help and enthusiastic encouragement of him and Marie.

Martha Katz-Hyman, curator of the Jamestown-Yorktown Foundation, specialist on African-American material culture of the eighteenth century, and co-editor (with Kym S. Rice) of *World of a Slave: Encyclopedia of the Material Life of Slaves in the United States*, kindly combed the manuscript for errors in my description of the lives led by the heroes of *Ashes*. Her attention is very much appreciated.

Three leaders in the field of education read *Ashes* with an eye toward the representation of the African American children in the book:

Dr. Marcelle Haddix, chair of Reading and Language Arts, dean's associate professor in the School of Education at Syracuse University, and author of *Cultivating Racial and Linguistic*

Diversity in Literacy Teacher Education: Teachers Like Me is an acclaimed scholar on the experiences of students of color in literacy, English teaching, and teacher education.

Dr. Detra Price-Dennis, assistant professor of Elementary and Inclusive Education at Teachers College at Columbia University, explores culturally relevant literacy pedagogy with her teaching, service, and scholarship that includes the examination of race, equity, and social justice, multicultural literature, and critical literacies in teacher education.

Dr. Ebony Elizabeth Thomas, assistant professor in the Reading/Writing/Literacy Division of the Graduate School of Education at the University of Pennsylvania, focuses her research and writing on the teaching of African-American literature, history, and culture in K–12 classrooms as well as the roles that race, class, and gender play in the classroom. She is the co-editor (with Shanesha R. F. Brooks-Tatum), of *Reading African American Experiences in the Obama Era: Theory, Advocacy, Activism.*

My cup overflows with gratitude for these scholars. In the midst of their very busy professional lives, they all made the time to review *Ashes* and question me about culture references that I might not have otherwise considered. Those of us who write for children have a special responsibility to hold ourselves to the highest standards of research and craft, especially when we are writing outside of our cultural experience. *Ashes* is a better book for the thoughtful assistance of these three women.

Many thanks also to Dr. Gregory J. W. Urwin, expert in military history and professor of history at Temple University, for sharing his thoughts about the number of enslaved Virginians who fled to the British army, how many of those people were captured at Yorktown after the surrender, and the treatment they then suffered at the hands of the Continental army. Katherine Ludwig, the wonderful librarian at the David Library of the American Revolution, kindly facilitated my correspondence with Dr. Urwin.

A tip of my researcher's hat to Dr. John Bezís-Selfa, Associate Professor of History and Chair of the History Department at Wheaton College. Reading his article "A Tale of Two Ironworks: Slavery, Free Labor, Work, and Resistance in the Early Republic," published in *The William and Mary Quarterly*, 3d Series, October 1999, opened my understanding of the aftermath of the Revolution for enslaved Americans, and led to other research critical for the writing of this book. A second tip of my tricorn to the good people at JSTOR (jstor.org), a digital archive of thousands of academic journals, books, and primary sources. A few years ago JSTOR began making much of their content available to individual subscribers instead of limiting access to researchers affiliated with institutions. The opportunity to use the journals on JSTOR made a significant difference to the quality of my work.

There are other treasure-filled digital resources that deserve a round of applause: The George Washington Papers at the Library of Congress (memory.loc.gov/ammem/gwhtml/gwhome.html), Letters of Delegates to Congress at the Library of Congress (memory.loc.gov/ammem/amlaw/lwdg.html), Adams Family Papers: An Electronic Archive at the Massachusetts Historical Society (masshist.org/digitaladams/archive), and The Gilder Lehrman Institute of American History (gilderlehrman.org). Thanks to the archivists, administration, donors, and taxpayers who support these institutions and make these Founding-Era documents available to everyone.

I also frequented plenty of brick-and-mortar institutions. My thanks to the Cornell University Library, the Bird Library of Syracuse University, Penfield Library of the State University of

New York at Oswego, and the wonderful lending capability of the New York North Country Library System, which I use in my hometown book heaven, the Mexico, NY Public Library. Special thanks go to Mary Jo Fairchild, Senior Archivist at the South Carolina Historical Society, Charleston, SC, and Katherine Ludwig of the David Library of the American Revolution, Washington, DC, for putting up with me requesting a ridiculous amount of material for days on end.

I was fortunate to have two young beta-readers who saw this book in manuscript form and gave me some much needed support: Elise Simon of Washington, DC, and Martha Laramore-Josey of Michigan. Thank you so much! A round of gingerbread for you both! Thanks also to my friend, Jason Reynolds, who read the story with a keen eye and kind heart and said exactly the right things. Thanks also to the members of my writer's group, TOG, for listening, laughing, crying, and cheering.

The incredible people at Simon & Schuster have been patient and steadfast while waiting for the completion of *Ashes*. Since I turned in the manuscript, they have had the fifes playing and drums beating as they prepare to share the entire trilogy with the world. A hearty huzzah of thanks must go to Jon Anderson, President of Simon & Schuster Children's Publishing; Justin Chanda, VP and Publisher of Simon & Schuster Books for Young Readers; Anne Zafian, VP and Deputy Publisher; Lucille Rettino, Director of Marketing; Michelle Leo, VP and Director of Education and Library Marketing; Candace Greene-McManus, Senior Marketing Manager; Chrissy Noh, Marketing Director; Andrea Cruise, Education and Library department; Katy Hershberger, my miracle-working publicist; Clare McGlade, copy editor (sorry for my comma issues, Clare); Debra Sfetsios-Conover, designer; Elizabeth Blake-Linn, production genius; and the entire heroic sales and marketing team.

Special thanks goes to the talented artist Christopher Silas Neal, who has illustrated every cover in the trilogy. I feel very lucky to have my stories graced by his art.

Caitlyn Dlouhy, VP and Editorial Director of Caitlyn Dlouhy Books, is so incredible that they named an imprint after her. She is the editor of my dreams. She has been patient and supportive as I navigated the family and health issues that led to several delays of this book, she read my drafts with compassion and integrity, and she set off celebratory fireworks when Isabel finally brought the story to its conclusion. More than being just an editor, she is a visionary American and I am proud to call her my friend. Thank you, Caitlyn. You and I are heart-kin.

All love and appreciation and gratitude to my wonderful agent Amy Berkower, along with her hard-working team at Writers House; to my best friend and sister-girl Deborah Heiligman, who has stood by my side through absolutely everything; and to my friend and former editor Kevin Lewis, who set me on the path of this trilogy by editing *Chains*, and who has remained a constant supporter of both it and me.

Our family has grown considerable in recent years, much to my delight. Thanks to our children, Stephanie, Jessica, Meredith, and Christian; and their partners, Trevor, Ryan, Steven, and Maria; and to our grandchildren, Logan, Owen, Nikolai, and Nolan for being patient as I turn holiday dinners into yet another episode of Why The American Revolution Was The Coolest Thing Ever, complete with footnotes. I love you all.

Finally, this book could not have been written without the unflagging support and good cheer of my Dearest Friend and beloved husband, Scot. Thank you, my love, for sheltering me from the storms, for the endless pots of coffee, and for a soft space in front of the crackling fire at the end of the day.

Reading Group Guide *for* ASHES

"TELL THEM THAT IF I AM BLACK, I AM FREE BORN AMERICAN AND A REVOLUTIONARY SOLDIER AND THEREFORE OUGHT NOT TO BE THROWN ENTIRELY OUT OF THE SCALE OF NOTICE."
—JOHN CHAVIS, FIFTH VIRGINIA REGIMENT

Discussion Questions

1. Explain what Isabel means when she says, "Time and hard travel had changed us both." Debate whether she is referring to her relationship with Curzon, or their individual goals.

2. Isabel says, "Everyone was fighting for freedom, but few could agree on the meaning of the word." Compare and contrast Isabel and Curzon's definition of freedom. Explain what she means when she says, "Neither side was talking about freedom for people who looked like us."

3. Why is Curzon indebted to Isabel? Discuss how Isabel needs him to help her find Ruth. How do they learn that Ruth is at Riverbend? Why is the Charleston region an especially unsafe place for Isabel and Curzon?

4. Isabel says, "It did no good to let desire and dream race ahead of common sense." What is her desire and dream? How do she and Curzon use "common sense" as they journey south in search of Ruth? How do their dreams look differently at the end of the novel?

5. Isabel and Curzon find Ruth under the loving care of Mister Walter and Missus Serafina, two slaves at Riverbend Plantation. How do they understand Ruth and know how to calm her "fits"? How does Ruth respond to them?

6. How does Missus Serafina describe Madam Lockton? Isabel learns that Madam Lockton has gone to England until the end of the war. How might Ruth's life have been harder had Madam Lockton been at Riverbend in Charleston?

7. Mister Walter and Missus Serafina know that Ruth should be with her sister. Explain Mister Walter's parting message to Ruth, "Keep home in your heart where no one can steal it away."

8. Missus Serafina offers Isabel the following advice in dealing with Ruth: "Don't forget how to be gentle. Don't let the hardness of the world steal the softness of your heart." How has the hardness of the world affected Isabel? At what point does she learn to be gentle with Ruth?

9. Describe Isabel's reunion with Ruth. How is it different than what she expected? Why won't Ruth make eye contact with Isabel? What advice does Missus Serafina give Isabel about dealing with Ruth? At what point does Isabel heed the advice?

10. Explain the close relationship between Ruth and Aberdeen. What do they have in common? How does Isabel depend on Aberdeen to help her understand Ruth? Why is Isabel so determined to "wean" Ruth from Aberdeen?

11. Curzon and Isabel agree that they need to find work, but they disagree about which city is the safest for them. Why does Curzon think that Williamsburg, Virginia, is safe? Does he have an ulterior motive in staying there? Why does Isabel doubt Curzon's honesty about "all his doings"?

12. What is the source of most arguments between Isabel and Curzon? How does their fighting affect Ruth?

13. Why is Widow Hallahan reluctant to hire Isabel? How does Isabel convince her that she and Ruth make a good team? Contrast the way Isabel and Ruth are forced to live and work to that of Kate and Elspeth, indentured servants at the laundry.

14. Discuss why Isabel and Ruth leave their work at the laundry. Explain what Isabel means when she says, "We had been forced back into war for our liberty."

15. Describe Isabel's emotions when she learns that Ruth thought she sent her away. How does this explain Ruth's response to Isabel?

16. How does Henry help Isabel understand the true meaning of friendship? Discuss how the harshness of the times causes Isabel to be suspicious of making friends. Who is her best friend in the novel?

17. Isabel says that Curzon prefers "the larger stage," and she the smaller. Explain the difference. Discuss how these differences ultimately help them bring out the best in each other? What makes Isabel realize that there is a "middle" ground?

18. Curzon admits that he was wrong about freedom and the war. Trace this long journey of discovery. How long does it take a person to admit that he or she is wrong? Why does Curzon say that only "people like us" understand the true meaning of freedom?

19. Discuss the title of the novel. How is it an appropriate title for the final book in the trilogy?

Discussing the Trilogy

1. How is The Seeds of America an appropriate title for the trilogy?

2. *Chains* is told in first person from Isabel's point of view. *Forge* is told in Curzon's voice. Why do you think the author wrote *Ashes* from Isabel's point of view?

3. How does Isabel give a different meaning to the *I* branded on her cheek in the three novels? Discuss how her explanation reveals her growth as an individual.

4. Fear is something that Isabel has lived with all of her life. Trace the way she deals with fear throughout the three novels. In *Ashes*, she says, "I want to live the rest of my days without fear." Debate whether that ever happens for Isabel.

5. The author divides *Chains* and *Forge* into three parts. What is the purpose of this organization? How does it contribute to the readers' understanding of the "order" of events? Why do you think *Ashes* isn't organized in the same way?

Looking for another great book?
Find it
IN THE MIDDLE.

Fun, fantastic books for kids
in the in-be**TWEEN** age.

IntheMiddleBooks.com

SIMON & SCHUSTER Children's Publishing

/SimonKids

@SimonKids

What does it mean to be brave?

At the beginning of summer, Genie thinks it's not being afraid of Grandpop's dumb ol' dog.

Or trying to fix something important that he's broken.

But is that it? Or is it just as important to own up to what you've done? Even if it's really, *really* bad?

atheneum

PRINT AND EBOOK EDITIONS AVAILABLE

A Caitlyn Dlouhy Book • SimonandSchuster.com/kids

More books that you can't put down

from #1 *New York Times* bestselling author

SHARON M. DRAPER

"Draper adeptly paints a convincing portrayal of how young people think, act, feel, and interact with one another."

—*School Library Journal* on **DOUBLE DUTCH**

★ "Unflinching and realistic . . . Rich in details of both the essential normalcy and the difficulties of a young person with cerebral palsy."

—*Kirkus Reviews* on **OUT OF MY MIND**, starred review

★ "This compelling story brims with courage, compassion, creativity, and resilience."

—*Publisher Weekly* on **STELLA BY STARLIGHT**, starred review

atheneum

PRINT AND EBOOK EDITIONS AVAILABLE
Caitlyn Dlouhy Books
simonandschuster.com/kids

SUMMER'S YEAR HAS BEEN FILLED WITH LOTS OF THINGS, but luck sure hasn't been one of them. So it's no surprise when things go from bad to worse. But if she can't find a way to swing her family's fortune around, they could lose everything—from their jobs as migrant workers to the very house they live in. Desperate to help, Summer takes action. After all, there's just no way things can get any *worse* . . . right?

CYNTHIA KADOHATA, the Newbery Medal-winning author of KIRA-KIRA

PRINT AND EBOOK EDITIONS AVAILABLE

atheneum

KIDS.SimonandSchuster.com